HOSTILE WITNESS

SANCTUARY, INC

NONNA HENRY

For Muffin, Winky, and Bud
I love you so

1

———

Tia O'Rourke swallowed the dry lump in her throat as she contemplated the precinct doors across the parking lot. It shouldn't be this hard. She was a thirtysomething woman with a little history here. So what? Her stomach cramped in disagreement. It had been eighteen months since she'd walked through that police station entrance and even longer since she'd done it with her head held high.

Girl . . . just nod at the fear and start walking. Grabbing her purse and the huge caramel macchiato she'd bought to fortify herself, Tia plodded through the sea of cars with dread settling around her feet like leaden boots. So much for self-talk.

None of this would be happening if she hadn't bid on the police ride along at her school's Valentine's Day silent auction. She'd promised her third-grade students she would win the auction experience that her uncle, the chief of police, had donated. Her extravagant proxy bid had secured the win, and she'd used a personal day for the ride along.

She would stick to the plan because she loved her students, and their curiosity about different professions had her introducing a new workplace every couple of weeks. And today, hopefully she'd ride alongside an older cop who'd enjoy conversation and a few doughnuts. Tia's stomach pitched at the thought of food, and she gripped the Louis Vuitton cross-body purse her best friend, Mo, had given her.

She stopped within feet of the entrance as the memories clawed at her psyche. The personal questions, the interrogation room, the acrid taste of stale coffee, and the humiliation tore through her in a sprint of panic. She squeezed her caramel macchiato cup so hard that liquid dribbled down the sides. Maybe she'd waited too long to face this place? The memories had won. Perhaps it was best to go home and use the personal day to organize her office or look for an older rescue dog. *Absolutely*. Those two projects had been on her to-do list for what . . . six months?

No and no. She'd gotten this far even though her heart pounded like a drummer on a rogue solo. Facing down the terror and proving she was stronger than the urge to run was crucial for her emotional health going forward. It had sounded like an easy fix in the therapy session, and the money she'd spent on the auction supported the PTA. More importantly, she'd promised the kids.

Omigod. She must look like an idiot. How long had she been standing here?

Someone rushed by her in a blur of blue and held the door open. It was an older policeman and one she didn't recognize. He was probably her ride. "You coming, miss?"

Tia forced her leaden legs to move. "Um, yes, thank you." The scents of sweat, antiseptic, and coffee slammed her as she approached the information desk. She signed in and sat down in a newish-looking blue-plaid chair. They'd redecorated since her last horrific visit.

"O'Rourke?" the young cadet behind the desk called out.

She raised her hand. "That's me," she croaked weakly. What

the heck was she doing? This wasn't school—hand raising not required.

He narrowed his eyes. "You're the ride along?"

She nodded but turned away when one of the cops she knew walked through the hallway.

The cadet motioned her to the desk and gave her forms to fill out. "Make sure you sign the informed release. You can initial the rest. The guy you're riding with says to be ready in five minutes."

Tia hurried through the forms while maintaining a death grip on her purse and ducked out of sight again when a familiar investigator strolled from one office into another. Face the precinct? Sure. But no way in hell was she ready to square off with the prick who'd interrogated her. In the past, she'd happily signed in and waited for an escort to her uncle's private office for impromptu visits that had brightened his day. But that was a long time ago.

She sipped her coffee and tried to act normal, ambling over to the picture window and inhaling several deep breaths. The new asphalt and parking-space lines looked great in the lot, and a couple of large planters with winter pansies strategically placed near the entrance were welcome additions. *I wonder if they finally replaced the broken refrigerator in the break room? And that nasty coffeepot they'd duct-taped together?*

Someone close by cleared their throat.

"You're deep in thought. Are you ready to go?"

Tia wheeled around and looked up. *Whoa.* This guy would never consider defiling his body with a doughnut. He was a six-foot-plus wall of intimidation, and bulging arm muscles rippled under his tight uniform jacket. Where was the fatherly cop she'd hoped for? Swallowing hard, she rasped, "I'm riding with you?"

He raised an eyebrow. "Appears so." He stuck out his hand. "Detective Ethan Kelley."

She regarded his massive paw with caution but slid her palm into his. "Tia O'Rourke." His warm hand was reassuring enough, but due to her recent past, this gorgeous man was off-limits. Although . . . there was something vaguely familiar about him. Where had she seen him before?

He jerked a thumb toward the doors. "Got your gear? Let's go."

Tia bolted after Detective Kelley in a state of numb disbelief. "I thought detectives didn't allow ride alongs at this precinct?"

He turned as he reached the cruiser. "You are correct. But we've been short-staffed ever since I arrived a year ago. There've been a lot of retirements and transfers, and the recruiting has slowed. We cover for each other if we're even remotely proficient at something. I had a lot of ride alongs when I was a beat cop in Baltimore. I'm filling in today because we're short on patrol. Thus the uniform."

Tia halted abruptly at the curb. "Maybe I should let you go alone and do whatever it is you're supposed to be doing."

He tossed his duffel bag into the trunk and slipped on a pair of sunglasses. "Why? You don't want to go now? Or you don't want to ride with me?"

She squeezed her purse tightly. *Both.* "I don't want to be an imposition." And she *had* achieved her goal of actually going into the precinct in spite of the memories.

Detective Kelley shrugged a bulky shoulder. "It's up to you, but Chief Carson assigned me personally. He wants you to have a positive educational experience—his words, not mine."

Oh yeah. Her uncle had taken the time to donate and arrange this ride. If she backed out now, she'd let him down. More importantly, she'd disappoint herself. *Again.*

He opened his car door and started issuing orders. "Hop in. You can ride in the front, but don't touch the computer or any of the equipment in the vehicle."

In a hurried rush, Tia slid into the seat and set her purse on the floor. The front passenger area wasn't as roomy as she'd imagined.

"Buckle up. You must remain in the cruiser at all times unless directed otherwise. Do not follow me into a building. Feel free to ask questions when a call or traffic stop has been completed. We'll break for lunch in the early afternoon."

His list of instructions and controlled tone mimicked a recitation of her Miranda rights. He left no doubt as to who was in charge. Tia fastened her seat belt and shrank back into the lumpy seat as a wave of relief washed over her. She'd not only gone into the police station but now sat in a police car. These were huge accomplishments.

Aside from the way-too-hot overbearing cop next to her, the rest of the day should be easy, right?

2

———

Tia crossed her legs and stifled a whimper.

An hour and a half ago, she'd finally chugged her twenty-ounce iced caramel macchiato like a sailor drinking whiskey on shore leave as they'd driven to their first call for a minor traffic accident.

Add to that the seventeen-ounce bottle of water she'd drunk after her morning workout and the usual cup of hot coffee. Her bladder threatened to detonate any second. It wouldn't be a problem, but she was in the driveway of a home on Glen Cove Road, in Detective Kelley's cruiser, with no access to—ahem—the facilities.

Tia groaned and pressed her thighs together. She should've used the restroom instead of waiting in the car when they'd stopped at the convenience store. And now, the detective's stern warning not to follow him into a building reverberated in her head.

Adjusting the angle of her hips to relieve the ungodly pressure, she frantically pondered her options. *C'mon.* This stop wasn't an armed robbery all-points bulletin. It was a routine call from a neighbor about a persistent barking dog.

Wincing in agony, she turned around to look for any signs of movement on the property. The calm air carried the sounds of early spring birds. Detective Kelley had been in the house for at least fifteen minutes.

Tires churned on the gravel to her right as a police K9 SUV dashed into the driveway. An officer jumped out, glanced her way, and gave a swift nod. Tia opened her door to let him know she needed a restroom, but his brisk half run had him at the front door in less than five seconds.

Her bladder pulsed in a relentless beat, reminding her every few seconds of imminent disaster. Tia checked her phone. She'd been sitting here almost twenty minutes now. Why hadn't she hopped out quicker to tell the second cop she needed a restroom?

The property had scattered trees, but they were thin pin oaks with no coverage to hide her bare butt. And who knew if the neighbor that had called 911 for a barking dog was now watching the yard from afar with binoculars? *Crap.* This was no time for a lengthy inner discussion over the lack of facilities. As much as she didn't look forward to the lecture she'd get from the detective, staying in the car was no longer an option. According to her throbbing bladder, she needed to act fast. Grabbing tissues from her purse, Tia swung out of the cruiser and gingerly made her way to the back of the house.

She spied a well-hidden spot between two huge bushes near the back door. *Perfect.* She hurried over and shimmied her pants down, braced one arm on the brick behind her, and lowered into a crouch while uttering a silent plea that she wouldn't pee all over her clothes. With a sudden crackling of leaves, several mice darted between her legs, scattering through the yard. Choking back a scream, she yanked her pants up.

Dear lord, the pee is gonna come out. But the dog wasn't barking anymore, which meant Kelley and company must have the situation under control. *Right?* She hobbled to the back steps and tried the door. It was unlocked.

Tia gave a quick knock. No answer.

She opened the glass door and slipped inside, but she kicked a small object and froze in fear. Had they heard the noise? With her heart thumping an erratic beat, she tiptoed through the kitchen, peering left and right. She really, *really* shouldn't be in here. This *had* to be what breaking and entering felt like.

Maybe she could pee and get back to the car without them knowing she'd been inside. But what if she found a bathroom and they cornered her in a compromised position with their service weapons drawn? Well, it wouldn't be the first time she'd been the punch line of a precinct joke.

Voices drifted from the hallway on her right. Sneaking in that direction, Tia quietly opened doors, hoping for a powder room, but discovered a coat closet and a pantry. She clenched her fists as a bladder spasm forced her to double over.

Once she'd recovered enough to stand up, she limped through a large archway into a great room with a vaulted ceiling. Rich wood panels warmed the decor, which included a black lacquered baby grand piano on her left and a massive stone fireplace at the far end.

The blood spatter on the white love seat was her first clue. The second was the broken glass and the objects strewn at odd intervals. Glancing down . . . her feet stopped short. She was standing in a puddle of scarlet. A woman's lifeless body lay on the ornate Oriental rug in front of a glass-top coffee table. Detective Kelley was talking into his radio by the fireplace, and the K9 cop knelt on the floor tending to a bloodied dog.

She took a step backward, mumbled her need for a bathroom, and gaped at the woman's body again. The poor soul was a mess. Tia's right hand flew to her mouth. Nausea churned, and her ears rang. Her eyes locked onto Kelley's as he leaped across an overturned ottoman and ran toward her in slow motion.

She opened her mouth to explain why she'd left the police car, but the words wheezed from her throat. Her hand slipped when she tried to steady herself on a nearby round mother-of-pearl door handle. Jerking her fingers away, she wiped crimson on her pants.

Detective Kelley tossed her over his shoulder. He should've been a linebacker. Total anarchy ensued as her stomach joined forces with her bladder. Gagging and dazed, she swiped at her breakfast on the back of Kelley's uniform, but the attempt at cleanup was futile.

He unceremoniously deposited her into the back seat of the police cruiser, then everything went black.

SIRENS WAILED, and voices spoke in varying degrees of urgency, demanding assistance and stating facts. *Murder. Crime scene. Brutal.* The words swirled around her like morning fog, but her attention focused when a male voice commented, "Poor dog barked himself hoarse, tore the fur and flesh off his neck trying to free himself from the grooming apparatus. We should all hope for a dog that devoted."

Tia squinted against the bright sunlight.

"Hey, how are you doing? You warm enough?" A female police officer stared down at her with a kind face and took her pulse

Tia tried to sit up, but the woman said, "Whoa, you've just had quite a shock. Let's wait for the gurney and the fellas." Feeling Tia's forehead, she smiled. "Do you remember where you are, honey?"

"Yeah. I was on a ride along with an officer, big guy." What the heck was his name? She honestly couldn't remember right now.

"Yes, Detective Kelley. Do you remember what happened?"

"There was so much blood. I needed to use the bathroom, and I think I hurled on the guy." She must've, because her mouth was sour. Heated embarrassment crept up her neck, scalding her cheeks.

"You walked in on an awful scene. Fact is, we haven't had a murder around here in five years. In this ocean-resort community, we usually deal with drunk vacationers, speeding violations, and a few domestics. My name's Odessa Wright. I'm a police officer, but I was a nurse first, so when anyone needs a band-aid, they call on me."

Odessa surveyed the busy yard, shook her head, and muttered, "Here comes Dr. Fletcher. Don't pay him any mind."

Tia listened intently to a man yelling about *someone* puking on his crime scene. She moaned and forced herself up to see the man in question waving his arms while shouting a colorful stream of accusatory words at Detective Kelley and the K9 cop.

Two paramedics arrived with a stretcher, and Odessa moved to give them room. "Miss O'Rourke, Chief Carson insists a physician check you out before you go home." Tia rolled her eyes at Odessa, who shook her head reassuringly and smiled.

"Just tell my uncle I'm fine. A little shook up is all. I don't need to go to the hospital." She anchored her feet on the driveway and stood, gripping the cruiser door for balance. The paramedics glanced at Odessa.

The older attendant spoke up. "Miss, we don't want to tell the chief you refused medical attention. He's already concerned that he sent you on a ride along to a tragic crime scene. It's a smart idea to get evaluated by a professional."

Tia waved them away. "I'm okay, see? Just let me stand here." If they'd only give her a little space, she'd be fine. Her body wobbled slightly to the left, and the younger paramedic stepped closer.

Odessa peered into Tia's eyes. "Here, honey, bend at the waist, and keep your head down. You'll feel more stable in a minute."

Tia rested her hands on her thighs and kept her head low to appease Odessa. Her pants were soaked almost to the knees. The realization set in that she had not only doused the officer with breakfast but peed herself to boot. The whole department would know she'd managed to contaminate a crime scene with bodily fluids, of all things. What a nightmare. This would make for epic-proportion gossip at the precinct.

On a startled gasp, she remembered where she'd seen Detective Kelley before. It was the beach bonfire the spring of her sophomore year in high school. Her cheeks flamed as she glanced his way. Yeah, that was him all right. He'd changed a lot in fifteen years. The boy she'd made out with under a blanket had grown a lot taller, bulked up, and become a man.

Officer Wright broke into her reverie. "It won't take that long to get evaluated since you'll be arriving in an ambulance, Tia."

Oh, what the hell . . . she needed a ride out of this place anyway. It wasn't like she was qualified to help, and the embarrassment of standing on the sidelines with wet pants was more than she could bear. One paramedic helped her onto the gurney, and the other fastened the safety straps.

In the short bumpy ride to the ambulance, Tia counted seven police and fire vehicles, including the one marked *Coroner* in bold black letters. That poor woman on the rug and that valiant bloodied dog. Who would do such a thing? What would become of the woman's dog?

3

Ethan spent hours working on the report for the homicide
on Glen Cove Road. It turned out the victim was Lieutenant Marjorie Plante, originally from the Bronx. Fifty-seven
years old at TOD. Retired twenty months ago with honors. She'd
started her career in patrol and worked her way up the ranks.
She had thirty-five years of outstanding service in New York and
had inherited the house on Glen Cove Road from her parents.

She'd been an only child and had decided to keep the house
and move to the eastern shore of Maryland because she loved golf,
the beach, and riding her ATVs. Married in 1986, then divorced in
1992. She'd never remarried. No kids. Her partner was a police dog
named Flynn. They'd worked together for five years in narcotics
until she'd pensioned out. *Hmm.* Flynn had taken a bullet to the
hip during a drug bust ten months before she'd retired. He was
effectively retired because of a lingering limp. They'd both worked
in the NYPD Cadet Corps for their final nine months on duty. He
whistled low and long while glancing over her financial state-
ments. She had amassed quite a retirement between her police
benefits, her IRAs, and the sale of the brownstone she'd owned in

New York. Was she dirty somewhere along the road to retirement? Or simply a smart, professional woman who'd managed her money well? After discovering six pages of awards and accolades she'd received, he concluded it was the latter.

This woman was a beloved legend in New York. He scanned the pages listing her volunteer work off the job and learned of several cancer centers, a Little League sponsorship in the name of her narcotics squad, a homeless shelter, and a battered women's residence. She'd cooked and served Thanksgiving dinner for twenty-eight years at the homeless shelter.

Ethan rubbed his face. How many enemies had Margie Plante acquired during thirty-five years of service on the right side of the law? Had anyone made threats against her? Hell, he'd already collected a dozen or more enemies in only ten years. How many threats would a woman of this caliber receive over several decades?

A smile tugged at his lips when he read that she'd landed only one Internal Affairs probe with her name on it. Allegedly, she'd tackled a drug suspect and smashed him with a ripe pineapple obtained from a street stand after he'd shot her K9, Flynn. And yes, the report included details of very colorful language used in the same assault. The investigation was completed and no charges filed. The lieutenant must've exercised tremendous self-control to hurl a pineapple at him instead of using her baton. She could have done some damage with the baton.

Perusing a copy of her will, he noted that her estate was slated for liquidation and all monies to be split between the homeless shelter and women's home where she'd volunteered in New York. The next page listed her funeral arrangement wishes. Burial would be at Magnolia Park cemetery next to her parents. The plot? Already paid for. She'd left a hefty stipend for the care of her K9. *Of course she had.* This woman dotted her i's and crossed the t's.

Considering the lieutenant's stellar reputation, the NYPD brass would drive to the Eastern Shore of Maryland for her funeral. Had she prewritten an obituary? He had to find out because New York was already nudging the department for funeral details.

Satisfied with the facts, Ethan leaned back in his chair, his thoughts drifting. Why had Tia O'Rourke hesitated to go on the ride along with him? Had she figured out who he was? Possibly. He'd recognized her when he'd stowed his gear in the cruiser trunk and the sun had shimmered a gold hue on her red hair like that day on the beach when they were teenagers. How long ago was that? Maybe the spring he'd graduated from high school?

If only the cops hadn't shown up and raided the bonfire that evening long ago. There had to have been fifty kids there, most of them underage, and the kegs had flowed like fountains for hours. He'd spun around to grab her hand so they could run together, but she'd already been gone. Every time he and Mac had hit the beach that summer, he'd secretly hoped to see her again but never had.

Nah, she hadn't recognized him yesterday. He'd keep his mouth shut and the memory to himself. She probably had someone special in her life now.

4

Tia shoved the test papers aside and rubbed the crick in her neck. Who was knocking on her front door? She'd fallen asleep on the couch.

A second knock echoed. What time was it? Scrambling off the couch, she grabbed her phone and slid into the bunny slippers her students had given her last year. It was seven forty-five a.m., Saturday. She tapped the doorbell app and saw—*oh no*—Detective Kelley. All crisp and clean, he could've been a cover model for a law-enforcement magazine.

Adrenaline zoomed through her chest. Why was he here? She didn't know anything about the murder yesterday, and under no circumstances would she agree to go to the precinct for questioning. Stunned, Tia glanced in the hallway mirror. She couldn't answer the door looking like this. Finger combing her hair, she enlarged the app picture on her phone. He was holding two coffees. Hmm . . . just like that day on the beach when he'd offered her his extra iced tea.

Well, he obviously wasn't here to tie a neat little bow on her ride along experience, because, hell, she hadn't even begun to process it.

But he did arrive bearing coffee, and that was a definite plus, considering her coffeepot had quit working last night.

The detective rang the bell again, took a step back, and waved at the camera.

All right, all right. If she didn't answer the door, he might alert her uncle and worry him. Right about now, Tia wished her uncle didn't hold such a special place in her heart. She'd been avoiding him for a year and a half because he'd become so overprotective she could hardly breathe in his presence.

She buttoned her cartoon pajamas all the way up to her neck and wrapped herself in a thick cardigan before opening the front door. With a sweeping gesture of her arm, she greeted her uninvited guest. "Good morning, Detective. What brings you by so early?"

"Hey." He gave her a slow downward perusal and stopped at the bunny slippers. One side of his mouth quirked up. "Glad to see you've got a doorbell camera."

She nodded. The camera was an easy setup. "What can I do for you?"

"May I come in?"

Tia opened the door wider. "If you must."

He held out one of the coffees. "Here. I got this for you. It's black. I have no idea what you like in it."

"Thank you. You must've been inspired. My coffeepot stopped working last night."

"I notice small details, and you brought a carafe size of caffeine with you yesterday." After taking a couple steps, he glanced into the little den area. "Your uncle asked me to stop by, make sure the place was secure. Do you mind if I check the windows and door locks on the main floor? Yesterday was a homicide. Whoever committed the crime is still at-large."

Oh, really? Her uncle had been hounding her for almost a year to install some kind of security system. Wouldn't he be surprised to know she'd scheduled the installation for next month?

Tia held her arms open wide. "Okay, take a look." She made a beeline for the creamer in her fridge.

"Nice place." He examined the living room windows. "This Cape Cod is one of the original homes in this neighborhood."

"Yes, it is, and thank you. I bought it with my college roommate a few years ago. We both like the ocean. It's a little piece of paradise during the warmer months."

"Does your roommate live here, too?"

None of your business, buddy. Tia sipped the coffee and leaned against the counter. It tasted like the nectar of the gods, so she decided to answer him anyway. "No, she lives in Baltimore now but stays here some in the summer."

He muscled a sash until it groaned and lifted. "You've got old windows."

"I know. The renovations happen one room at a time every summer."

"I understand all too well. Got a fixer-upper myself a few miles up the coast. You need a security system though."

"It's scheduled for next month. I had to get in line. Many of the owners down here are installing keyless entry systems for the summer rental crowds." See? She had her crap together and didn't need a guy around to hover and fix things. As a matter of fact, a few weeks ago she'd managed to install an elaborate closet system without help from anyone. Granted, it had taken her the whole weekend and a lot of choice words, but the end result was most satisfying.

His voice broke into her reverie. "If you decide you want more cameras installed, I've got a few extra lying around that I'm not using. I'd be happy to set them up for you."

Tia gave him a polite smile. "Thank you. I'll let you know."

And that was exactly how guys reeled you in. They offered to help, rescue, protect, and one thing led to another, and once you developed feelings for them, they disappointed you. Well, she was no damsel in distress, and she was quite capable of climbing the crab apple in the backyard and the big sugar maple in the front yard to attach the cameras herself. *No, thank you, Detective.*

He pointed at the Mylar balloons occupying the far corner by the sofa. "Recent celebration?"

"Um, no. Some people buy themselves flowers; I buy balloons. They're happy, you know?"

A quizzical expression crossed his face. "I guess so. They give new meaning to the *celebrate each day* line of thinking."

She rubbed a finger on the white quartz countertop. "I didn't get to apologize yesterday considering the circumstances, but I'm really sorry for contaminating you and the crime scene." Of course, the fact that she wasn't handling trauma very well these days played a major role in yesterday's outcome, but she wouldn't overshare that tidbit with him.

He tossed a glance over his shoulder as he tested the lock on her back door. "No worries, it happens sometimes. I'm kind of used to it. Walking in on a scene like that is a lot to take in. You ought to see the recruits during smelly-cadaver day at the police academy. It flattens some of the toughest people I've ever met."

Tia leaned against the counter, trying to depict an ease she didn't feel. "That's kind of you to give me a pass. I meant to ask yesterday: Do you guys still visit classrooms and talk to kids about jobs in law enforcement? Age-appropriate info for third to fifth grade?"

Ethan nodded with a smile. "Sure. We have plenty of swag for that kind of community-outreach event. I'll usually cover the basic Officer Friendly topics like stranger danger and bike safety. Just call the precinct, and they'll set it up."

Her hand holding the coffee cup froze midair. There was no way she'd be calling the station anytime soon. For goodness' sake, she'd barely gotten through going into the precinct yesterday. And anyway, she'd been thinking about asking Odessa Wright and not Detective Kelley. "Do you know what happened to the dog from Glen Cove Road?"

"Bayside Animal Hospital picked him up, and he's recovering from surgery. You may have seen on the news that the poor dog sustained a lot of injuries because somebody kicked and beat him. He's a K9 and desperately tried to help the victim. Bayside will take good care of him though, and he'll be placed in a new home once he recuperates."

"Was he the woman's service dog?"

"Yes. They were both retired. K9s deserve the gold-standard treatment. A lot of folks don't want to take them in as pets because they're not sure if the dog will blend well with their family. What if they're aggressive? Retired dogs are usually older, and the medical expenses increase as they age. But there are pictures all over that house of the lieutenant and the dog. She loved him. It's no wonder he hurt himself trying to protect her."

The detective's profile softened as he talked. He wasn't the impersonal prick she'd originally thought, even though the boy she'd made out with on a beach one clear spring night was long gone. He'd grown and toughened, and his muscles were impressive. He'd picked her up and carried her outside yesterday as if she weighed twenty pounds.

"Right now, they have him sedated," he continued. "The vet said whenever the dog woke up last night, he whined as though his heart were breaking. Bayside has been taking care of that dog's medical needs for a couple of years. But he doesn't like getting clipped, so the owner had attached him to a homemade grooming station she'd bolted into the floor to clip and brush him. If she would've unhooked him before answering the door, he'd have protected her with his life."

Omigod. "So she's dead and he's injured, all because he doesn't like to be groomed?" A cold knot formed in her stomach.

Kelley pierced her with eyes the green of an Irish meadow in summer and shrugged. "We've all got our vulnerable spots. His is grooming." Without taking his eyes off her, he grabbed his coffee and sipped.

Uncomfortable under his gaze, Tia looked away, rubbing the goose bumps from her arms.

He pointed toward the family room. "I see you've got a doggie door. Where's the dog?"

Ah, that. "The dog door was there when I bought the place. There's no puppy."

Running his hands over the frame, Ethan examined the wood like a doctor would a patient. "Probably just as well. It's the original door and has rotted over the decades." He glanced at her. "You need a new one. This is a security risk. I bet if I gave it a good shove from the outside, it would give way and take the dead bolt with it because the molding's soft. If you'd like, I know a guy over on Eighty-Seventh Street . . ."

There he went again, offering to help her out. The steel door she'd picked out had been on back order for months. Tia cleared her throat. "Thank you, Detective. I'll get to it as soon as I can."

Kelley gave a quick nod. "Suit yourself." He strode into the kitchen and began checking her windows.

Good lord, he was way too much man in her little kitchen.

"Would you consider letting me nail a few of these old windows shut to tighten up security?"

What? "And close off the ocean breeze? Absolutely not!" A tense silence enveloped the room.

Tia crossed her arms. "Thank you for checking on me and for the wake-me-up coffee. I am now in the proceed-with-caution portion of my day because of this." She held up her coffee. "Is there anything else you need, Detective?"

Placing both hands on his hips, he faced her with frustration rolling off him in waves. "I hope you've got a gun on the premises, because this place has the security of a sieve. If you do own a firearm, keep it loaded—safety on—and close by until we find the person who killed Margie Plante." He looked at her expectantly. "Tell me you at least own a gun."

The bloodstained white love seat flashed through her mind. *That poor woman.* Tia had a love-hate relationship with guns, loving the protection and hating the thought of hurting anyone. Her uncle had insisted on a gun-safety course and had taught her to shoot when she'd turned twenty-one. Target practice was scheduled every two months, just in case.

"I do own a firearm. I practice regularly and clean it after every use. I'm also proficient in Krav Maga, thanks to my uncle. Every now and then, the police academy will invite me to hone my skills on the recruits during training." She gave him an appraising look. "You look to be about six foot four, maybe two forty? Take off your shoes. I'll prove it to you now." She kicked her bunny slippers to the side and crooked a finger in his direction. "C'mon, attack me."

Amusement tugged at his lips. "No, I value my nuts."

She winced and laughed. "As you should, Detective."

"Then why did your uncle send me over here to check on you?"

"Because he remembers when I was six and he'd buy me cotton candy on the boardwalk and take me for rides on the Ferris wheel. He also fancies himself the head of our family since my father passed away eight years ago."

Ethan held his hands up. "I'm sorry. I'll tell the chief you're fine and have the situation under control."

Tia's inner badass fist-pumped. "Thanks again for the coffee. I appreciate it."

He headed for the front door. "You're welcome. I won't bother you again."

Right answer. She leaned against the front doorjamb as he strode down the walk. "In my former life, I also worked for the Secret Service."

He wheeled around, narrowing his eyes.

Tia laughed. "Only kidding. Thanks again." She shut the door. *Well, he's gone.* One of these days her uncle would stop sending men to her house to take care of her. She could only hope he'd give up and believe her when she said no more, never again, she was just fine on her own.

5

Vince admired his new flattop buzz cut. It had been worth the twelve-mile drive to the next-largest town to have it done. Surveying himself in the mirror from both sides, he grinned. That fat barber, Ralph, had done okay by him. He tucked the business card for the barbershop into the pocket of his blue uniform shirt. The things you could buy online these days were amazing. He'd spent seven hundred dollars and purchased himself a whole week's supply of work clothes. If he was going to work down here, blending in with the locals was paramount.

Leaning against the doorjamb, he slid the hotel-room closet open and reveled in the neat row of ironed police uniforms. What a score. Five shirts, three pairs of pants, two eight-point hats, a bulletproof vest, one bona fide duty belt, handcuffs, a stun gun and charger, and a pair of kick-ass police boots from the world's largest online marketplace. He looked every bit as good as the cops he'd observed in this two-bit county. The pace was way too slow down here. This was nothing like New York.

It was a definite bonus to have a relative who wore the shield. They resembled each other enough for it to pass the quick glance test. And it wasn't like civilians asked to see a policeman's badge often during routine traffic stops. In addition, he'd purchased a name tag with *R. Smith* engraved on it. It wouldn't have been right to take his cousin's name tag and risk getting him in trouble.

He was glad he'd stuck around and watched the commotion after Plante's demise through his high-powered binoculars. The redheaded lady cop had a great body but not an impressive IQ. Why hadn't she just gone inside and used the bathroom instead of squatting in the bushes?

He studied his uniform in the mirrored closet doors. There was no doubt he looked like a sworn officer. He had even purchased and installed a light bar for his car that had come with easy removal instructions. Tomorrow, he'd start pulling folks over.

Pointing the radar gun at his hotel television, he pretended to shoot. *Sweet.* Radar was an absolute must-have for traffic stops. He patted his hip and stroked the new leather on his holster. *Thank you, Margie Plante, for the Glock secured inside it.* He snickered.

You owed me anyway, bitch.

6

Tia dialed the number for Bayside Animal Hospital. She'd kept up with a classmate from high school on social media, and he'd mentioned working there. And yes, he answered.

"Hey, Mike, it's Tia O'Rourke. How are you?"

"Good, Tia, I'm good. What a nice surprise. Did you finally get a puppy?"

As much as she loved dogs, she didn't have the time to devote to train a puppy. "No, not yet. I'm actually calling because I heard you have a K9 there recuperating from surgery whose owner passed away. His name is Flynn. Is there any way I can stop by and visit him for a few minutes?"

"Sure. I've got to warn you though; he's in rough shape. I've been here since six this morning keeping an eye on the fella. He's sedated, but you're welcome to sit with him for a little bit."

That was exactly what she'd hoped he would say. "I'm in the empty parking lot across the street from you."

"Really? Well, come on in." A few seconds later, Mike opened the door and waved.

She bolted from her car and headed over. Wow. Mike had

changed. He wore a white doctor's coat and was at least half a foot taller than she remembered. What a weird week, seeing acquaintances from her high school days.

"Tia, you look great." He took her jacket and hung it up on one of the big racks in the foyer. "If you don't mind me asking, what interest do you have in Flynn?"

"I was on a ride along with the officer who found him yesterday, and I wanted to see how he was doing."

Mike nodded knowingly. "I operated on him last night. Big guy freaks out every time he wakes up. I decided to keep him slightly sedated for a couple of days so his stitches heal better. He's holding his own physically."

Tia was stunned. "Are you *the* new vet in town?"

"Sure am. I finished my residency a year ago and decided to move back and buy the practice from Doc Wagner." He grinned. "Do you remember Casey Thomas from Spanish our senior year? We bought this animal hospital together, and we've set our wedding date for June."

Awww. "Congratulations. I'm happy for you guys. And congrats on the veterinary practice, too. Thanks for letting me see Flynn on such short notice. I realize it's a bit unorthodox to stop by when you're closed, late on a Sunday afternoon."

"No problem. We're open for emergencies." He leaned in as if he were telling a secret. "I'm glad to have a break from sitting with him. He's back here in Room Two. Be careful if you touch him. He's covered in bruises. We had to shave him for surgery, and right now he resembles a mummy with all the gauze. Let him hear your voice before you touch him."

Tia's gut twisted when she saw Flynn. How could anybody batter an animal so brutally? "If he wakes up, will he be aggressive?"

"No, quite the opposite. He whimpers when he comes to. This one's a smart fella, and he remembers the attack. Until the police piece this case together, Flynn here is the only one who truly knows what happened."

"What's his prognosis?"

"We're optimistic and hoping for a full recovery but honestly won't know for a while." Mike hesitated. "I'll leave the door ajar. Call me if he wakes up, and feel free to stay as long as you like. Another vet will take over at six, but I'll be here until then." He left the room.

Tia hurt just looking at Flynn. He was a huge dog but so vulnerable. Fighting back tears, she sat in the chair Mike had provided. *Now what?* Ever so gently, Tia spoke in soft murmurs and stroked the fur on his face from his snout to his ears.

"You're a brave boy, Flynn. I saw you yesterday at your house, and I'm so sorry this happened. I never would've seen you, but I needed a bathroom. Well, the moral of that story is: Don't drink your whole water bowl before a long car ride." She chuckled to herself. "Actually, buddy, it was worse than that. I ended up peeing myself and dousing the detective who found you. I'm sure it wasn't his finest day, either."

She soothed Flynn's unbandaged paws with gentle petting. "You know, my third-grade students would be very interested in meeting you if you feel like it when you get better. Which reminds me, I still need to turn in my lesson plans for the coming week. The weekend is so short, you know?"

Tia relaxed into the chair and closed her eyes. She hadn't been this still in a long time. Life was so busy. There was something quietly profound about touching an injured dog in a tender way. She felt a little bit like she, too, was mending on the inside. "I know all about recovery, Flynn. Got the big scars just like you. It's a good thing your fur will grow back and cover them. I wish I had fur to cover mine." She startled when a tongue licked her pinkie finger. The dog stared straight at her.

Oh. "I'm so sorry you lost your person, Flynn. Hang in there. I had a special person once..."

Mike strolled into the room. "You've got the touch with animals, Tia. He's so relaxed with you. Are you sure you don't want to give up your teaching job and be my vet assistant?" He laughed, checking Flynn's monitors and fluid levels. "I'm putting a mild sedative in his drip so he nods off again. We want to keep him quiet until tomorrow morning. Go ahead and pet him some more if you want. He'd probably like that."

Tia rubbed Flynn's forehead and ears as he drifted off to sleep again. She whispered in his ear, "I'll stop by tomorrow after work, big guy."

7

———

Back at the precinct, Ethan rounded the corner to his cubicle. The ever-present mound of files had grown during his time out of the office. As much as he enjoyed helping out on patrol, the only way he'd solve the caseload on his desk was to have a week or two of uninterrupted work hours to follow leads and chase down witnesses. Actually, he'd prefer to just forget about patrol and dedicate himself to the job they'd originally hired him to do.

But he was having a hard time forgetting Tia O'Rourke. In the few times he'd talked with her, she'd smiled only once. Being a hard-ass didn't come naturally to her. It was challenging for him to reconcile Krav Maga with the woman who wore bunny slippers.

Not that he was all that great at reading women. God knew he'd misread all sorts of signals with his ex. He heaved a deep breath. His ex was a story he couldn't afford to focus on right now.

He glanced at his desk again. There was a new stack of files with Margie Plante investigation notes, and sticky notes scattered to the right of the folders. *Seriously?*

Sergeant Earl Thompson whistled from the far end of the room and waved Ethan over. "We've scored a meeting room. Grab a drink, and meet us in Conference Three."

"I see you've been thinking, Earl." Ethan held up the sticky notes. "Did you ever think of using a whole piece of paper instead of these?"

"No can do, Son. The thoughts come to me one at a time every few minutes. The sticky notes fit in my pocket. I've got to use what I have on hand to record the questions and ideas. I'm old-school."

Ethan grabbed his laptop and charger and strode toward the kitchen for a bottle of water. Everyone around here had their own form of brilliance. Earl was a master of puzzles, the yellow stickies being his puzzle pieces. It was Ethan's job to corral the messy process into a spreadsheet . . . eventually. But not until the tables in Conference Room 3 swam in a virtual sea of neon-colored notes.

Sometimes the meetings with Earl went on for hours. The man could focus on a fingernail shaving all afternoon if required. About the time Ethan would start going cross-eyed, Earl would be breaking his stride in mental alertness. The man was a fearsome mentor.

Working with Earl Thompson was like boot camp for detectives. He took no guff from anyone and expected discipline. The burly hulk with a buzz cut still participated in a grueling six-hour physical training twice a month with all his detectives, and he outlasted most of them. Ethan knew this for a fact. He'd participated in the last five hell workouts with Sergeant Earl Thompson and had barely kept ahead of the man thirty years his senior. It kept Ethan in shape for his Sanctuary missions. This afternoon would be the mental side of working out with Earl.

He entered the conference room and plopped the files onto the table. "Just us two today, Sarge?"

Earl kept scribbling a note. "Mulrooney's coming, but he's using the latrine first. Who contaminated the scene at Lieutenant Plante's house? The name's been redacted from all the printed material."

"A schoolteacher by the name of Tia O'Rourke. Nervous type. Almost backed out of the ride along at the last moment."

Earl's head shot up. "Tia? You sure?"

"I'm sure. Pretty, late twenties, red hair." *Absolutely no security around the perimeter of her house.*

An incredulous look crossed Earl's face. "The chief's niece?"

Ethan sat down and opened his laptop. "Yeah. Why, is that hard to believe?"

Earl started writing again. "Huh. The chief must've had her name stricken from the records. Going forward, make sure all the documents refer to her as 'the ride along' and not by her name."

Ethan glanced over the rim of his reading glasses. "Okay. Why?"

"Not my story, Son. Just do it for the chief. There's nothing illegal about protecting an innocent person who had a miserable ride along."

He nodded slowly. "No problem." *Even if it was odd.*

"And if you've got any sense, don't get distracted by her red hair. Hands off. Go sniff in another direction for a woman."

What the hell? "First of all, Earl, I wasn't sniffing but simply stating a fact. She has red hair. I need a woman in my life like I need a piercing on my trigger finger. One divorce is enough on my resume." *Sniffing, my ass.* "Chief sent me over there on Saturday to make sure her place was secure. I'm not doing that again."

Earl snickered. "Hellcat, huh?"

"I wouldn't go that far. She asked me to attack her so she could show off her self-defense moves."

He chuckled. "Good for her."

Ethan leaned back in his chair. "What does that mean?"

Earl plastered one sticky on the table and started writing another. "Like I said, not my story, Son."

Ethan shook his head. Why was he feeling defensive? "Any contact I've had with her has been at the chief's request." This time, at least. But he remembered kissing her senseless at that beach bonfire way back when. She'd been funny and carefree and was the most beautiful girl he'd ever met. Funny thing . . . that. Because she wasn't beautiful by magazine standards, but when Tia had smiled, she'd taken his breath away. She hadn't smiled on Saturday though, not really. It didn't take a rocket scientist to realize he'd been an annoying imposition to her.

"I understand. Sniffing comment withdrawn." Earl looked him square in the eye. "Relax. The chief and I appreciate how valuable you are. That's why he has you cover certain shifts and work with delicate people and situations."

Uh-huh. Well, there was nothing delicate about present-day Tia O'Rourke. And judging by the undertone of Earl's statement, the woman was a situation requiring discretion. Discreet, he could handle. But intimidated by her? No freaking way.

8

———————

Tia perused the school office, enjoying the funny and sometimes bizarre Pajama Day outfits. While she'd kept it low-key with her slippers, pigtails, and cartoon pajamas, the principal, Yolanda Decker, had gone all out with huge curlers that made her look like an antennae for space aliens.

Their friendship went way back. Yolanda had been Tia's fiercest supporter through her life-altering fiasco the past couple of years. Some teachers barely tolerated their principals, but Tia loved hers. It had been Yolanda who'd hired a substitute and promised she'd save Tia's job for her no matter how long it took. It had been Yolanda who'd handled the press with a firm hand and replied "no comment" to the invasive questions dozens of times. Yolanda had been principal at Sandy Beach Elementary for some twenty plus years, having been Tia's principal in fifth grade. Yolanda was good people.

Tia was playing catch-up after taking Friday off for the disastrous ride along. The butterfly shipment she'd been waiting for was somewhere in the school but not in or near her mail slot. Usually she'd email the office and wait for a reply, but she needed those butterflies for her second class of the day. Sighing, she got in line to wait. Tempting as it was, she couldn't take advantage of her personal relationship with the administration and cut the line. Her foot tapped impatiently.

Someone bumped her left side. "Oh, good morning, Miss O'Rourke. I see you're wearing the same clothes as when I left you." He gave her an ornery smile. "Did you happen to call the precinct and schedule my visit to your class yet?"

Tia almost dropped her coffee cup. *Ethan Kelley.* The reverberation of his velvet voice trickling down her neck and spine was delicious and downright unnerving. She rolled her shoulders to shake it off.

"Good morning, Detective Kelley. For your information, it's Pajama Day. That's why I'm wearing this otherwise-inappropriate outfit, and no, I haven't called the precinct yet. What brings you to our humble school today?"

"I just finished handling a truant situation with one of the older kids." He fastened a devious half smile on his face and winked. "I see you have coffee. Something you lacked Saturday morning, if I remember correctly."

"Ah, yes, you have seen me at my worst recently, haven't you?" She glanced into his eyes. They danced with humor.

He leaned slightly closer. "Is this your first cup or second?"

She inspected a hangnail on her pinkie. "Second. Why?"

"So you're in the proceed-with-caution stage of your day?"

"Yes, I suppose I am." Why was he doing this? The last time she'd seen him, he'd been frustrated as hell with her and had said he'd never bother her again. Why did she suddenly feel like they were sharing a cozy corner booth in a late-night diner?

Doris, the school secretary, who wore a pink Tinker Bell nightshirt and a velvet shower cap, pointed at her. "What can I do for you, Tia?"

She thought for a couple of seconds. *Why was she here? Ooh.*

Ooh. "Butterflies—a package was delivered on Friday, and I can't locate it."

Doris rummaged behind the counter and handed her a small parcel. Yolanda, the curler-wearing principal, had perched herself next to Doris and watched Ethan as she tapped her pencil on a pad.

Tia clutched the box to her chest. "Thanks, Doris, I appreciate your help."

"You two have a good day," Yolanda called out. Tia glanced at them as she and Detective Kelley left the office. Both women wore Cheshire-cat grins.

Tia huffed. "They heard our conversation just now."

He halted mid-stride. "So what? We had a friendly exchange."

She wheeled around and poked him in the chest with a finger. "Friendly exchange? They think you left my house this morning while I was in these pajamas."

He shook his head. "Impossible. I spoke very softly."

"Yeah, you did. So did I. But the principal wears one of those new miracle hearing aid things. I know she heard everything we said. People can hear the grass grow with those devices."

Ethan shoved his hands into his pockets. "Eh, I wouldn't worry about it."

"We've just been dumped into the Sandy Beach Elementary rumor mill, and I shouldn't worry about it?"

Ethan chuckled. "I don't mind. I haven't been part of a school rumor mill since middle school when I changed schools midyear and the kids thought I was a narc."

"Pfftt! You probably were a narc. And you should mind. This isn't the precinct, Detective, and I'm not your buddy. This is my place of employment."

"Now wait a minute. It was an honest mistake. How was I to know that Principal Decker wore a bionic hearing aid?"

She inhaled a deep breath. "My point is that you should've kept your mouth shut." Her head pounded. Honest to goodness. This was exactly the kind of unintended consequences she'd been trying to avoid for eighteen months, and no good-looking clueless detective was going to mess up the order she'd established in her life. "If you are done handling the truant situation, then please leave."

He gave her an *I'm watching you* sign with two fingers.

She responded with an unladylike *Slit your throat* sign with hers.

Storming down the hallway, Tia just knew this wasn't the end of the matter. It would take about a half hour for news of the office conversation with the drop-dead gorgeous detective to make its way around the school.

She had stopped at the restroom because she was still spooked about the possibility of having a full bladder with no bathroom available, when one of the first-grade teachers leaned out the door of her classroom and whispered, "You go, girl! I hear he's a real hottie!"

What? It'd only been three minutes. Tia walked fast to her classroom, clicked on her email, and opened one from her principal. It read:

My dear friend, if I were a younger woman, I'd have to mud wrestle you for him. I'll send an email and let you know when he's in the building again.

Yolanda had signed it with several variations of naughty smiley faces.

TIA'S CHEEKS heated when a couple of teachers gave her a standing ovation as she entered the teacher's lounge during second lunch. She started to explain the events culminating with the conversation in the office with Detective Kelley, but soon discovered her possible involvement with him enthralled her coworkers. Several of them had tried to fix her up with their grown sons or nephews last year.

Even Mr. Russo, the gentlemanly middle-aged music teacher, ribbed her. "Be careful, Tia. I hear he has quite a sidearm." Everyone chuckled. Mr. Russo didn't look half as deranged as the rest of the teachers. His version of Pajama Day was a pair of gray flannel pants and a long-sleeve Superman T-shirt. But Mrs. Spencer was the most authentic in her pajamas. She was seven months pregnant and wore Winnie-the-Pooh footed pajamas complete with the bulging tummy.

Tia laughed along with them. They weren't interested in the fact that there was nothing between her and Detective Kelley. There would never be anything between them. She'd make sure of it. The time for that had been fifteen years ago, and she hadn't seen him again until the ill-fated ride along. He could take his big muscles and his helping hands somewhere else. And from now on? He'd better keep his comments to himself.

9

———

Ethan climbed into his cruiser and grinned. He hadn't enjoyed teasing a woman like that in a *very* long time. Who'd have thought he'd run into her when she was wearing those ridiculous cartoon pajamas again? It was the most humorous opportunity he'd had in months, and it had simply plopped at his feet. *He couldn't ignore it.* Well, that and he absolutely refused to let the woman intimidate him.

There was something about her that was intriguing. What the hell had happened to her? She was mentally tough to be at work today ready to teach. Some people would need to take a week off and down a bottle of Valium after stumbling onto a murder scene the way she had.

He hadn't meant for anyone but her to hear his words in the office. The things he'd said were a *little* suggestive, but he was only having fun and trying to get a smile out of her. She beamed like sunlight when she smiled, and he'd just wanted to see it once more. But he hadn't intended to place her in an awkward situation with her coworkers.

Perhaps he'd do something to try to apologize. But the obvious flowers were out. That would only make the situation worse and really piss her off. Plus, there was no way in hell he wanted to give her the idea that he was even remotely interested, because he was not and never would be. Tia O'Rourke was the prickliest woman he'd ever met.

Yup. Flowers were out. But she did need one thing. He turned left and headed for the nearest hardware store.

ETHAN EYEBALLED the descriptions on the sides of all the coffeepot boxes. Which one to pick for Tia? He'd purchased a Keurig for his house, but not everyone liked the single-brew idea. He sauntered over to the customer service area and patiently waited for help from a clerk named Louann (according to her name tag), a plump and cheerful-looking woman in her fifties.

"Whatcha buying the coffeepot for?" she asked, clacking her blue gum fiercely as they walked together toward the small-appliance section.

"Excuse me?" *Weren't coffeepots for making coffee?*

"Well, Officer, is it for your lunchroom or your house?" She blew a huge blue bubble.

"I'm buying the coffeepot for a friend, and I'm not sure which kind she'd like to have. I was hoping you could help me narrow down the choices."

Louann sighed, popped the bubble with her finger, and stuffed the wad of gum back into her mouth. "You're buying this coffeepot for a *she*?" She cocked a hip. "You mean as in a *girl*?"

Ethan gave a nod.

"Oh my goodness, what the hell is wrong with you men these days?" Louann spat the words at him in staccato and shook her head. "Girls don't want men to give them coffeepots, buddy. Just because you guys like electronic things doesn't mean women like receiving them from you. God almighty, next thing you know, you'll be in here buying her an iron or a toaster oven."

She pulled a stepladder over and climbed the steps. "Ladies like to receive flowers or jewelry. Better yet, a trip to Cancun, but never a coffeepot. I'm just saying. Good-looking guy like you buying a woman a coffeepot? I can't believe it." She pointed to a big white box with a red coffee machine pictured on the front. "Here, give her this one. It's programmable and brews four to twelve cups and has a nice carafe that keeps the coffee hot for up to six hours. Maybe the carafe part will help you get lucky."

Louann hefted the box off the shelf and dropped it into Ethan's arms before she climbed down the ladder. "Let's go up front and make sure nothing's broken. The only thing worse than receiving a coffeepot as a present is getting a broken coffeepot."

Ethan pressed his lips together to keep from smiling. Not that he cared, but he wasn't scoring any points with women today.

"So, Officer"—she squinted to see his name tag—"I mean, Detective Kelley, would you like for me to gift wrap this coffeepot? We started gift wrapping small appliances for five dollars last year."

"Sure, Louann. That would be nice, if you don't mind."

"I suppose if the girl is going to receive a coffeepot, it had damn right better be wrapped." She proceeded to cloak the gift in a pretty pink-checked paper and added a matching bow. After completing the transaction, Louann handed him the receipt. With a doubtful smile, she gave him a motherly pat on his arm. "I hope this coffeepot thing works out for you, hon."

10

———

A spiky-haired blonde looked up from her computer as Tia entered Bayside Animal Hospital. "Tia, how nice to see you! Remember me?"

"Casey? Congratulations on the veterinary hospital and your engagement to Mike." Tia pulled her in for a quick hug.

"You here to see Flynn?"

"Yes. Is it okay to spend a few minutes with him?"

"Sure, follow me. He isn't sedated, and we have him in his own padded crate so he doesn't hurt his stitches. He's spent the majority of the day drinking water and eating again." Casey opened Flynn's crate and gave him a soft whistle, encouraging him to come out. The dog gingerly stood on all four legs, lumbered from the opening, and sat while Casey changed the dressing and rubbed ointment on a couple of his injured areas.

The phone rang in the office.

"Tia, do you mind watching Flynn while I answer the phone?"

"Sure, go ahead. I'll stay with him." She stretched out her hand to Flynn. He took a step in her direction and sniffed. Then to Tia's surprise, he took another step, whined a couple of times, and set his head on her knee.

"Aw, you poor thing," she whispered. "You're such a good dog. I'm glad to see you up and moving." She stroked the fur around his ears and forehead, careful to avoid his neck and torso, where the stitches were.

"Your lieutenant would be so proud of your valiant effort to save her from the freak that killed her. If she could, she'd make sure you had someone who would love you the rest of your days."

Flynn offered Tia his paw.

"They're going to find the bastard who took her from you, buddy. I just know the police will find whoever did this to you."

Casey was laughing in the distance with whomever was on the phone. Would the powers that be allow a civilian to have Flynn? Granted, she didn't have time to train a puppy, but Flynn was ready to go. And Tia really liked him and admired his bravery. But what if one of Lieutenant Plante's relatives wanted to take him? She could live with that as long as whoever drove away with Flynn would appreciate everything he'd done and be good to him.

Maybe she could talk to her uncle about adopting him.

No. Not after ignoring her family for so long. Tia peered into the dog's amber-colored eyes. "As long as you didn't drain my savings account every six months, you and I could be good friends, don't you think?" Flynn licked her hand again as she kissed the top of his head and scratched behind his ears.

Casey entered the room as she ended her phone conversation. "Well, I see Mike was right. This dog has taken quite a liking to you. He doesn't lick *my* hand."

Tia's eyes brimmed with moisture. "Hey, Casey, let me know if anyone tries to claim him, okay? I'll give you my phone number. How long do you think he'll be here?"

"I'm not sure. If he were a civilian dog, we'd let the owners take him home tomorrow so he could recover in his own surroundings. But this situation is different because he'll never go back to his handler's home. There's a local nonprofit animal-rights group that has offered to cover his boarding fees until this coming Saturday. After that, Mike and I have agreed to keep him here for at least another week, on the house. I'll tell you what—give me your number, and we'll touch base toward the end of the week."

"That would be great, thanks. Is it true that Flynn doesn't like to be groomed?"

Casey burst out laughing. "Oh, you have no idea. Margie brought him here for his shots, and it would take two or three of us to hold him down just to clip his nails afterward. He'd take the shots like a trooper, but he'd have none of the grooming. We haven't figured out why he hates it so much. Margie agreed one time to have him sedated so we could do everything all at once, but she didn't like anesthetizing him for a simple grooming. I don't blame her.

"She told us she'd configured something at home that would keep him still, and we taught her how to clean the ears, trim the nails, and give him a good wash and brushing in about thirty minutes. Margie was a resourceful woman who was full of laughter, and she loved her Flynn."

Tia's chest ached with emotion. If only she'd had a chance to meet Margie when she was alive. "Is he allowed to have a *t-r-e-a-t*? I'd love to give him one."

Casey placed a couple of soft dog chews in her hand. "You're welcome here anytime. We're open until at least six in the evening. Come with me, and I'll put your number in my phone. See if you can get him to follow us. The movement would do him good. He has a limp from his service years, and it's time he started walking more to keep his mobility intact."

Flynn gulped down one of the treats without even chewing. Tia called his name. He meandered his way to the lobby, where she gave him the other treat while giving Casey her number. Tia bent down and asked Flynn for his paw again, and he obliged her.

"Thanks for everything. I'll stop by in a day or two." The two women hugged a little more fiercely this time.

Tia gazed at the front window of Bayside Animal Hospital, where Flynn sat eyeing her car. He lifted his paw onto the glass. Damn, she was a goner for that dog.

11

Vince wiped the oil and vinegar from his chin with a wad of brown napkins. This sub was the best food he'd eaten since arriving from New York to pay Lieutenant Plante a little visit. Most of the food sucked down here. All the menus boasted superlative seafood added to eggs and dips and sandwiches. *Ugh.* These people loved their crab. They even put the crustacean on pizza. Every food had something called Old Bay on it, in it, or served on the side with it. They even put it in the mayonnaise and on their French fries. *Disgusting.* What a relief to find this dinky sub shop offering just one variety of fish and that being a tuna sub.

He'd opted for the Italian cold cut with oil and vinegar. It reminded him of home. But the bread was commercially prepared white fluff. It was nothing like fresh-from-the-oven bread in New York, made by artisans who'd passed their recipes down for generations.

Oh, the memories. He used to love delivering predawn newspapers in the Bronx neighborhood where he'd grown up. The scent of fresh bagels, real kaiser rolls, and Italian loaves with rosemary and olive oil had wafted in the air. He'd looked forward to delivering old lady Simon's newspaper to the back door of her bakery. Rarely mumbling a word to him, she'd snatch the paper from his hand and hand him a hot bagel in return. Those had been the good days.

But that was back then. He'd carried his dream of being a cop right through high school. He'd never wanted to date the head cheerleader. He'd wanted to be a cop. And dammit, he'd be one now if it weren't for that bitch Marjorie Plante. She'd been so high-and-mighty during his cadet interview, recommending he get counseling and reapply for the cadet program the next year. She'd even offered to take him to the shrink herself.

He should've never answered the questions about his mother and father the way he had.

Writing that his dad's name was Jim Beam and his mother's was Tia Maria had cost him dearly. He'd written it on the questionnaire as a damn joke, but Marjorie Plante didn't have a sense of humor. No, by-the-book Lieutenant Plante had acted all concerned about him. She hadn't understood humor even when it had hit her square in the face. Well, he'd kept his rage from her and had told her "yes ma'am" and had waited the year and had gone to counseling. But he never could obtain the clean bill of mental health the department requested.

Vince balled the paper sub wrapper in his fist and pounded the table. He'd be a real cop right now if it weren't for Margie Plante, and he'd done his best to look sincere when she'd opened the door to her house and he had pleaded for her help. There she was, looking all tan and fit and unarmed and concerned. She glanced behind her and said, "Just a minute," and shut the door without locking it. He let himself in and took over five steps later. To the credit of his inner genius, she'd attached her dog to that weird contraption in the corner.

Taking Plante down from behind was no problem. He had a foot and at least fifty pounds on her. That big old bust of some musician on the grand piano came in real handy. One pop to the head and she went down. The second and third blows were for sport.

But the most fun that day was hurting that dog. Oh, he'd considered just killing the thing after he'd found Plante's gun, but it was more fun to tease and kick him, dancing around just out of the animal's reach. *"Whatcha gonna do, Toto, bite me?"* That dog barked and snarled and pawed at the air like he'd tear him a new aorta if it only could.

The cops would never find him. He'd noted every touched surface before and after he'd offed her and had wiped everything clean. Carrying his shoes, he'd pranced out of the house wearing Lieutenant Plante's Nikes and strolled through her garden and through the cornfield beyond to his car a quarter mile away.

He smirked, tossing the sub wrapper in the garbage can just as the door opened and a patron entered the little shop. It was that dumber-than-dirt redheaded lady cop he'd seen in his binoculars trying to pee in Plante's backyard. Their eyes caught, and he gave her a little nod. *See how harmless I am?*

She ignored him, walked to the counter, and called out, "I'm here to pick up that ten-inch veggie sub with oil and vinegar, Pete."

"You got it, Tia. I'll be right out."

Pretty name. Vince's eyes wandered the shapely length of her body. She might lack brains but sure made up for it in looks. His fingers itched. What would it feel like to fist that curly hair and show her he was the boss? Licking his lips, he rose and headed out as the door chime announced his departure.

He glanced into the shop one last time. It wouldn't hurt a bit to take out one more lady cop. But you know, with that pretty redhead? He'd have to make her beg first. He knocked his fists together like a boxer. This little seashore town was starting to look like a lot more fun.

12

Sergeant Earl Thompson's foul mood preceded him as he grumped his way into C3 for the morning briefing. Dammit to hell, the presumed murder weapon—the bust from the piano—was clean.

He scanned the expectant faces of his waiting detectives. "Listen up, everyone. The only fingerprints we've found in Lieutenant Plante's home were the ride along's, those of an electrician who'd wired a new dining room chandelier a couple of days before the murder, and those of Sergeant Guy Evans from the NYPD." He cocked his head thoughtfully. "Now, why would there be fingerprints from a New York cop in Margie Plante's home?"

He rubbed the back of his neck, "The only distinguishable footprints leaving the home were in the backyard and fit Margie Plante's sneaker size, although we haven't found any athletic shoes on the premises that fit the imprint. In addition, there aren't any tire tracks except for police, ambulance, and the coroner's vehicles. And Margie's service weapon and ammo are absent from the gun cabinet, so whoever killed her is not only dangerous, but assumed to be armed." He handed the report to Ethan. "Keep reading, Son. Out loud."

"We've interviewed the neighbors. All of them are working couples who haven't seen a thing. Every single house has camera footage of their private driveways and porches, but none include a long-distance shot of the lieutenant's residence." He cleared his throat. "She had an alarm system but must've used it only at night, because there are no videos for the day in question."

Ethan took a sip of his water and continued. "The New York police are investigating any threats made toward Margie during her final ten years of service. It's a long list, but all but a dozen felons are still in prison or a halfway house. Officials up north are tracking the whereabouts of those dozen."

Earl swigged at his can of cherry ginger ale and motioned for Ethan to stop. "We're six days out from the lieutenant's murder and have diddly-squat in the way of suspects, unless we count Sergeant Guy Evans from the NYPD. As of a phone call I made five minutes ago, NYPD is questioning the sergeant to find out why his fingerprints are in Lieutenant Plante's kitchen, powder room, and on the ivories of her piano. Not the black keys, mind you, only on the white ones. He's been there—and recently."

Earl closed his eyes and considered out loud. "Who in the hell plays a piano and only touches the ivories? It doesn't make sense. But of course, Sergeant Guy Evans has the same rights as anyone else: innocent until proven guilty.

"Just a reminder for you newbies from up north. Worcester County is a big area with lots of farmland and little towns. The population this time of year is about twenty-five thousand, but it'll swell to a whopping quarter of a million in the resort area during the summer. We need to solve this murder by the first of May, before the influx of tourists arrives." Earl raised an index finger for emphasis. "That's only a month away."

He walked to the whiteboard at the front of the room.

"I want you to check out every hotel, motel, and quickie joint starting here." He made a small circle on the map. "Expand the perimeter as you need to. According to our profiler, we're looking for a hotel guest, most likely a single male, who's paying cash. The lack of evidence at the crime scene suggests our perp planned it. Otherwise, we'd have crime-of-passion evidence around the property."

"You're looking for out-of-state tags. Someone here to settle an old score, and with any luck, they've decided to stay until the funeral to admire their handiwork. Dismissed."

Ethan got up to leave.

"Not you . . . " Earl waved him over. "Chief wants you to visit Lieutenant Plante's K9. Ask the vet if there's any way the dog can attend the funeral and what we can do to make that happen. The dog is at Bayside Animal Hospital. Between you and me, the chief would love to have someone in the department sign on as the animal's new guardian, because the closest K9 unit is an hour away."

Ethan shook his head. "Well, it won't be me." Between his police work and Sanctuary missions, it wouldn't be fair to the dog if he adopted him. "Plante's dog has been retired for a couple of years."

Earl nodded. "True, but his sniffer isn't retired. Chief wasn't thinking of working him regular, but it sure would be nice to have him around and use his expertise if a child goes missing during the summer." He shrugged a shoulder. "If he's able to do it, of course."

"Yeah, okay, I'll stop by and see him. I don't know if the animal is even up and moving yet. He was in rough shape when we found him last Friday."

Earl picked up a yellow sticky note and held it out to Ethan.

"Chief gave me this note earlier today. He's assigned you as an escort to"—he squinted at the handwriting—"a Mrs. Bessie Stoddard during the funeral. She's Lieutenant Plante's great-aunt, the executor of her estate, and the only living relative Margie had. The aunt is in her eighties. Treat her like a dignitary, Son. Whatever it takes."

13

———————

Ethan cruised to a stop in front of Tia's Cape Cod. There was garden equipment strewn around the yard, and she'd spray-painted an outline on the grass to expand the flower bed. Ugh, it would take a lot of muscle and sweat to trench and remove the old sod. Tia knelt surrounded by containers of colorful flowers in the mulch in front of the house. He put his window down and turned off the engine.

She looked so content digging in the dirt. Every minute or so, she'd reach back, grab a flower, dig dig dig, and tuck it in. Once in a while, Tia'd toss her garden-gloved hands in the air and sway back and forth. He chuckled. She reminded him of the girl she'd been way back when. There must be music playing in her earbuds, because she didn't even know he was there.

He reached over and grabbed his sandwich. Might as well settle in and enjoy the show. He glanced at her leafing trees. A seventy-degree day like today would help them along, but there weren't any security cameras yet that he could see. She was so vulnerable back here on this street all by herself. Out of twenty or so houses, only three had year-round residents. He'd checked. The rest were summer rentals.

Ethan took a swig of his iced tea and smiled as her arms waved in a definite hip-hop beat. He'd bet a beer she knew how to cut loose on a dance floor. He hadn't gone dancing in forever. Maybe she'd go dancing with him? *Nah.* She'd made her feelings quite clear. *Bug off, buddy.* It was probably just as well considering his relationship track record.

This lunchtime view sure did beat his usual convenience-store parking lot. Cramming the last bite of sandwich in his mouth, he crumpled the wrapper, glanced at Tia, and whimpered. She was bumping and grinding on her knees with a flowerpot in each hand. The woman had the sweetest ass, and . . . he needed to make his presence known. He couldn't think about bumping and grinding all afternoon, especially when Tia had no intention of doing it with him.

He swung out of the car, grabbed the wrapped coffeepot from the back, and slammed both doors, hoping he'd made enough noise to command her attention, but no—she was still in planting mode. He loped up the front walk, set the box on the stoop, and waved. Nothing. She was completely immersed in her world and oblivious to her surroundings. Which wasn't good.

He didn't mean to scare her, but she wheeled around for another flowerpot, screamed, grabbed her garden trowel like a knife, and screamed again. Realizing it was him, she stood and hugged her middle.

"How long have you been there?"

"Only a couple of minutes."

Heaving a deep breath, she tossed the trowel aside. "Omigod, my heart is still racing."

Ethan shoved his hands into his pockets. "Yeah, sorry about that. I tried to get your attention, but you were really focused."

Her face darkened. "Are you here on official business?"

"Of course not, unless you've perpetrated a crime. Isn't today a school day?"

"Half day. The weather's so beautiful I couldn't stay inside, and I'm already late getting these flowers in the ground. I like gardening. It's relaxing."

He fake smiled. "Good for you. I think it's a pain in the ass."

Her eyes lit up. "Really? I can't imagine feeling that way." She yanked the gloves from her hands. "So why are you here?"

He pointed at the porch. "I needed to drop off that box."

Tia nodded knowingly. "My uncle again, or my mother. I'm sorry they're using you as their errand boy. You must be Carson's new favorite to send over."

"Well, not exactly . . . "

She tromped over to the porch. "Such a pretty wrapping paper. Hold the door, will you? I'll get it inside." She hefted the box.

Ethan glanced at his cruiser. The window was down, but the keys were in his pocket. "Sure, no problem." He jogged over and grabbed the door for her.

She spun around. "C'mon in. You gotta be wondering what's in here. My security system isn't installed yet, so there's no need to ask about it."

He wiped his feet and stepped inside, content to hang at the entrance while she tore the wrapping paper from the coffeepot.

Tia gasped when she saw the picture on the box. "Wow, it's red." Grinning at him, she popped the lid open and tugged at the Styrofoam mold surrounding the pot. "I wonder how they knew I needed a coffeepot? I haven't talked to them in weeks because they're so overbearing, you know?"

Well, no, he hadn't known until now. But every family had its own dynamics and—dare he say—dysfunctions. He'd tuck that tidbit into the part of his brain that already held hundreds of details about the folks around here. The lockbox with information and intimacies he'd heard on or off the job and would never share. Those tidbits came with the territory of being a cop.

Tia slid the coffeepot onto her counter, immediately filled it with water, and started a cycle. She scrunched up the wrapping paper and tossed it into the packaging along with the Styrofoam and cardboard. Picking up the little card, she proclaimed, "I'd better read the card. They've probably invited me to another Sunday dinner at the house. How can I say no to that when they bought me a coffeepot?"

Uncomfortable now, Ethan glanced around the place. "I see you've got different balloons."

She pulled the card out of the envelope as she waved his statement away. "Yup. I buy new ones every week or so, as soon as the old ones start to drop." One hand flew to her face. "Omigod, this beautiful coffeepot is from you?" Her cheeks pinkened.

He crossed his arms and nodded. "I didn't think you'd be home this afternoon and had planned on just dropping it off. You needed a new one, and I wanted to apologize for drawing attention to you in the school office." There, enough said. "Enjoy it. I should get going."

Tia walked around the counter and squeezed his arm. "Thank you, Detective. Thank you. I so appreciate the gesture and the, um, thought you put into it. I've been meaning to get one, and life's just so damn busy. It isn't even that hard to do, but I hadn't gone online and ordered it. I've been rushing through the doughnut drive-in several times a day to get a cup, but it never tastes like what I brew at home." She brushed the hair off her face. "I'm so embarrassed. I'm babbling. You didn't need to do this. Seriously, you didn't owe me anything."

He nodded and held up a hand. "Of course I didn't, but you needed a coffeepot, and it seemed like an appropriate mea culpa."

She beamed a smile at him, a real stunner. His heart

hammered in his throat, and his mind blanked. After all these years, the woman was still gorgeous—breathtaking.

"Please say you'll stay for a cup from the first pot. You aren't really a coffee lover unless you accept coffee from the first brew of a new pot. If you're in a hurry, I can give you a go-cup."

"A cup to go would be nice, thanks." He stepped away from the door as she added fresh water and grounds to the pot.

Tia waved an admonishing finger. "Be forewarned if you go back to the elementary school. They're still teasing me. According to the rumor mill, we're getting married on the beach and honeymooning in Belize." She laughed and gave him a deadpan look. "It's so ridiculous. I'm letting them have their fun."

His stomach lurched. Horrified, he shifted on his feet. "Wow. They move fast, don't they?"

"Yeah, well, it's their romance story, not mine. I think it takes a long time to build a relationship strong enough to endure a lifetime, you know? Plus, I'm not looking for a significant other anytime soon, anyway. I barely survived the last one."

Whoa. That was a whole lot of information he hadn't expected. He'd gotten out of his last relationship by the skin of his teeth, too. Still had the emotional scars.

She grabbed creamer from the fridge as the pot beeped that it was finished brewing. "That was fast. It's the perfect pop of color on my countertop, too." After pulling out two Styrofoam cups with lids, she waved him closer. "Here, fix your cup the way you like it. You want sugar?"

"Thanks, but no. I drink it black."

Tia shrugged a shoulder. "I think the fixings are half the fun." She snapped the lid onto her coffee and put the creamer away. "Well, back to my gardening, Detective. It'll be worth it once the flowers grow."

"I should get going, too. And call me Ethan."

"Oh." Tia chuckled. "Okay. Just remember I could still whoop your ass with my self-defense moves, Ethan."

Every time she challenged him, he wanted to poke her bear just a little bit more. It was damn uncomfortable being on the bottom in her eyes and didn't sit well with his personality. He held the door for her. "Thanks for the coffee."

"And thanks again for the beautiful coffeepot. It's very nice and extremely thoughtful of you." She gave him a little wave, slipped into her gloves, and dropped to her knees in the mulch.

Ethan noticed the big shovel used for trenching. He had a few minutes to spare, and his radio was quiet. Being twice her size meant he'd get it dug in half the time. He grabbed the shovel. "Hey, Tia." He pointed at the painted area. "Is this outline exactly how you want it?"

She barely looked at him, wiping her brow with an arm. "Yeah, but I won't get to that section until later."

"Okay." He started trenching what looked like a three-leaf clover outline. He was halfway done when she finally noticed him.

Pulling her earbuds out, she yelled, "Stop. You don't need to be doing that. You're in your work uniform."

He nodded. "Which means I'm wearing steel-toe boots. You're wearing tennis shoes. It goes a helluva lot faster in boots."

She tossed the trowel, scrambled to her feet, and trudged over to him. "I'm serious, Ethan. Put it down. You don't even like gardening."

"You're right on that one, but this is hardly gardening. It's digging. I do a lot of digging on the job. Doesn't bother me a bit." He placed a heavy boot on the shovel and stepped hard. "There's nothing wrong with being neighborly."

She set a fist on her hip. "But you're not my neighbor, and I don't want you to do it."

He squinted at the ire in her eyes and nodded. "And why is that? Most people would be grateful for a little help."

She pinched the bridge of her nose. "Because I'm not most people. I don't want to owe you a coffeepot or anything else because you helped me."

"I'm enjoying myself. You won't owe me anything. Not your time, not a coffeepot, and not even another kiss."

She threw her hands into the air. "Ooh, ooh, that's what this is about? You remembered the beach bonfire?"

His male ego enjoyed the fact that she remembered, too. "Girl, I'd have to be made of stone not to remember that evening. Why'd you take off like that?"

Tia made a goofy face. "My uncle was a sergeant back then. I would've been grounded all summer if I'd gotten caught underage drinking on the beach with a boy my parents hadn't met. I ran for my life, present and future."

He nodded. "I looked for you all summer, kept hoping I'd see you around."

She fidgeted with the tag on a glove. "Well, if it's any consolation, I kept an eye out for you, too."

"Have you ever wondered what might've been if we'd stayed in touch?"

She nodded confidently. "Oh, sure. We'd have enjoyed a summer fling and broken up, like most relationships at that age."

He glanced at her. "You think so? It took me a long time to forget you. I've still got the blanket." He raised a hand as he clarified, "The blanket belonged to Nan, and she left it in one of her linen closets. I considered tossing it, but it has such a nice memory attached to it that I let it stay."

Tia smiled. "While that is flattering, Detective, if we kissed today, there'd be nothing there. It all has to do with timing."

"Timing, huh? If you say so." He crushed a few more feet of

the edging while she stood by watching. "I'd have to put your theory to the test before I believed you. We were very well matched that night, if I remember correctly."

She rolled her eyes. "I'm telling you it wouldn't be the same today because we're different people. Trust me."

"If you say so. I think I'd rather find out and get it out of the way." He finished the last few feet of the trench and stood back to admire the outline.

Tia stripped off her gardening gloves and dropped them. "Okay, okay, I'll prove it to you. You'll see." She marched over, grabbed hold of his shirt, and pulled him down for a kiss.

For a few seconds, they both stood frozen like statues.

"See?" her lips murmured into his as she pulled away.

Not. So. Fast. He'd waited a long time for this kiss. He tugged her into his arms so his lips hovered against hers before gently tracing her top lip with his tongue, then suckling the bottom one, enjoying the cream and sugar of her caramel coffee-scented mouth. He pressed deeper long enough to tease a throaty moan from her, then ran his lips along her neck as she trembled against him.

Tia pushed away from his chest, shrugging. Without looking him in the eye, she stalked back to her trowel. "I told you we can't go back. It's just like kissing my brother, if I had one."

Uh-huh. Yeah, right. The woman had gripped his arms and melted like warm butter against him, participating with an eager abandon. Next time, if there was one, he couldn't guarantee he'd stay the consummate gentleman.

TIA GAVE one final wave as Ethan drove away. Lord have mercy. She crumpled to her knees in the dirt. The man could kiss ten times better now than he had at the bonfire. She touched a finger to her slightly swollen lips. Why on earth had she succumbed to the temptation and kissed him?

Well, she had been curious, and his nonchalant goading had irritated her enough to want to prove him wrong, but she'd misjudged the situation big-time. Her insides swirled like molten lava. What the hell was that about?

She couldn't get involved with Ethan Kelley. First of all, he was a detective. She'd be a fool to get involved with a detective again. And she'd promised herself many years of uninvolved singlehood ahead. And a red coffeepot, though a very sweet gesture, was a far cry from hearts and flowers. Not that she needed the typical romantic milestones for a relationship, but hold on just a blessed minute. Where was she going with this? Oh yeah, she wasn't looking for a relationship or planning to get involved with anyone. It wasn't personal against Ethan. She would take as tough a stand with any man at this point in her life.

But he wasn't any other man. He was someone she'd wanted to see, possibly kiss again, for years.

Stabbing at the soil and digging more holes, Tia shook her head. She'd probably made him feel like crap when she'd said it had been like kissing a brother. But he might have seen right through her words. If he had, she was the one who looked foolish. Tia crammed flowers into the holes, then roughly pressed the soil and mulch around them.

How dare he upset the order she'd reestablished in her life? If he knew how damaged she was, he'd run in the other direction. It would take her years to recover from her previous mistake, not to mention the surgeries she still needed to endure.

And he deserved so much better, because he was a really nice guy. Well, that settled that. There was no way in hell she'd let another kiss happen. Yes, it had been nice . . . more than nice. Maybe even life altering, sizzling, and other hot descriptive words she couldn't think of at the moment. She shoved her earbuds in and turned the music on.

She'd keep her wits about her and stay grounded, despite that when his five-o'clock shadow had grazed against her neck she'd nearly come undone. No more kisses for a long time.

Absolutely not. Period.

14

Tia stopped short at the entrance to the grand ballroom. The country club had a reputation for stunning decor and refined taste. They'd outdone themselves today for Lieutenant Plante's repast. The wafting scents of pink roses and eucalyptus blended with the aroma of the savory hors d'oeuvres the tuxedoed waitstaff served on silver trays. She'd never seen so many police brass in one place. The turnout for the repast was almost as large as the funeral's. A string quartet played soft music in the far corner. Tia caught Casey's short wave from a table across the room and briskly headed in her direction.

Casey rose, and after the two exchanged a quick hug, there were tears in Casey's eyes. "We saved you a seat at this table."

Tia looped her arm through Casey's. "Thank you. Are you okay?"

Casey lifted a shoulder. "I'm no good at funerals. This one is more difficult because I knew Margie personally." She took a sip of wine and swiped a tear from her cheek. "Flynn is sitting with Mrs. Stoddard, Margie's aunt. They're receiving condolences in the back of the room, away from the crowd. I'll walk over with you."

Tia's stomach flip-flopped. The last thing she wanted to do today was say goodbye to Flynn. Straightening her shoulders, she followed Casey. No way could Flynn leave without her at least requesting to keep him. While she understood the police wanting him here today in case the lieutenant's murderer had the gall to attend the service and repast, she couldn't help wishing he were resting somewhere cozy and warm with his furry friends.

A dozen NYPD officers surrounded Mrs. Stoddard, expressing their sympathies. A few even gave Flynn a quick pat on the head. Detective Kelley stood to Mrs. Stoddard's right, holding Flynn's leash. Ethan's dress blues accentuated his fine build, and really, she ought to stop noticing such trivial details about him. But he was so enticingly pleasant to look at even though she wasn't the least bit interested. Call it bad timing. Maybe she could fix him up with Sarah, the kindergarten teacher? At least then he'd be off-limits and she'd stop thinking of him as sinfully male. Tia shook off the ridiculous thoughts and peered around the crowd to get a look at her favorite dog.

He was lying on a big faux-fur rug with his head resting on his paws, but when she approached him, he lifted his head and barked. She got down on one knee and was rewarded with a face full of dog kisses.

Mrs. Stoddard leaned forward. "You must be the vet who's taken such great care of him."

Casey, who stood a few feet away, chuckled. "No, *I'm* the vet. Flynn tolerates me, but he loves her."

The older woman peered at Tia. "And who might you be, dear?"

"Tia O'Rourke." She reached over and held the woman's hand. "Please accept my deepest condolences for your loss, Mrs. Stoddard."

"Thank you, dear. Did you know my Marjorie?" She dabbed a tissue at her swollen eyes.

"No, I didn't. I was on a ride along with Detective Kelley when the disturbance call for Margie's house came in. I'm sure you're proud of everything Lieutenant Plante accomplished in her life, and I truly wish I had known her."

"Thank you, Tia. I appreciate your kind words. Flynn here seems mighty fond of you." She leaned over and gently rubbed the dog's ears. "He's almost as crazy about you as he was about my Margie, and that's saying something, because he adored Margie. He would have done anything for her. They were inseparable." She sighed wistfully. "They used to visit me all the time when she lived in New York . . . but enough of that. What do you do for a living?"

"I'm a third-grade schoolteacher and have been visiting Flynn after work. He's made great progress with his recovery each day. You could say we've bonded a bit. He's a brave animal, and I respect his service to your Margie and the citizens of New York. Are you taking him home with you tomorrow?"

"Oh, heavens no, dear, I'm eighty-six years old, and I moved into a retirement home a year ago. I'm still very active, but not active enough to take care of a seventy-pound German shepherd." She smiled at Tia with the kindest blue eyes that crinkled at the corners. "I asked my two sons and their wives if they would like to have Flynn as a family pet, and they both declined. You see, my older son is allergic to most dogs—it's a shame— and the younger son and his wife recently purchased two bichon puppies, so they have their hands full."

Mrs. Stoddard sipped at her tea. "I suppose there may be someone in the police department who would like to keep him and honor Margie's memory, but I'd like to see Flynn with someone he likes." She patted the seat next to her. "Please, sit with me a few minutes."

Tia scooted over, and Flynn followed, resting his head on her lap.

Mrs. Stoddard chuckled. "Look at that. He moves when you move, like he can't get enough of you. It's kind of cute, what with him being such a big dog and all." She leaned in as if she had a secret. "The detective who's escorting me today has been very kind to Flynn and me. And he loves dogs. We talked about it, but he said that with his work schedule, he wouldn't have the time to devote to an older animal. I'm not sure if I believe him, because he certainly has been attentive today."

What? Tia rubbed her forehead. *Omigod.* Mrs. Stoddard was considering giving Flynn to Detective Kelley? To Ethan? *Nooo way.* The guy was nice, and seriously the best kisser, but she had been the one visiting Flynn for well over a week. Adopting a house-trained dog had been on her wish list for quite some time. For heaven's sake, it was high time she started verbalizing the things she wanted in her life.

She turned to face Mrs. Stoddard. "I've been hoping for a chance to speak with you, because I'd really like to keep Flynn. I have a house with a backyard, and we're already pretty good friends."

The old woman patted Tia's hand. "I'm delighted to hear that, but he's an awfully big dog. Are you sure you could handle him?"

Tia smoothed her skirt and sat up. "Mrs. Stoddard, I teach, fix boo-boos, and encourage twenty-two third graders five days a week. If I can handle that responsibility, I'm sure I can handle Flynn."

The elderly woman regarded her with an appraising gaze. "Well, dear, when you put it that way, you're almost overqualified." Folding her arms, she continued, "You're about the same size as Margie, but my niece came across as bigger because she was so tough from the police work."

Tia laughed. "I'm a shrinking waif?"

"Goodness, no. But Flynn reacts to commands from a trained officer, so to speak. I've seen my Margie bark orders at him until he settles down."

Tia thought on the older woman's words. She hadn't seen the police-trained side of Flynn yet. "I'm willing to learn, and I'm sure I'd figure out how to take care of him."

"You look like a smart girl," the older woman commented thoughtfully.

"Mrs. Stoddard, as much as I would like to be Flynn's new person, I also want you comfortable with your decision." Okay. She'd said it. There was no point trying to convince the woman against her will. It would only bite Tia in the ass later.

"Yes, well, Flynn was incredibly important to Margie. But the fact that he's bonded with you is noteworthy." She gave Tia a wink and turned around. "Detective Kelley, would you please get the New York police commissioner for me?" Ethan nodded, passed the leash to another officer, and left.

The police commissioner shook a few hands on his way over and sat down at the table with a sincere expression on his face. "What can I do for you, Mrs. Stoddard?"

"Commissioner, I was just talking to Tia here, and she's developed quite a rapport with our dear Flynn. I think we should let Tia have him as her pet. Do you know of anyone else who might have their heart set on keeping him?" She patted Tia's arm gently.

The commissioner frowned at Tia and then Flynn. "Mrs. Stoddard, Flynn is a trained police dog, albeit retired. I was thinking he might come back with us tomorrow. Officer Pinkerton has expressed an interest in keeping him with the other two retired K9s under his care. Unless you strongly object, I think it would be a nice living situation for Flynn."

The woman pursed her lips. "Does Flynn know Officer Pinkerton from when he worked with Margie in New York?"

"No, ma'am. Marjorie and Officer Pinkerton knew each other, but their dogs did not socialize or train together, because they served in different units."

"Well, Commissioner, I think we should spread the wealth around a bit and allow Flynn to live with Tia. They are already acquainted, and Tia could take a crash course from one of the officers on how to work with him and any commands she will need to use or avoid."

The commissioner shook his head doubtfully. "It's a nice thought, but Flynn is not only a K9, but he's also been deeply traumatized by Margie's passing."

Tia inhaled a sharp breath. She'd identified with the dog's physical wounds, but hadn't stopped to think about the mental trauma. There was another thing she had in common with Flynn.

Not to be ignored, Mrs. Stoddard waved a crooked finger at the commissioner. "You know, Margie left me in charge of her will. God knows I never expected to be her executor considering our age difference, but I have the right as her next of kin to make the decision, don't I?"

The commissioner set his lips in a grim line. "I suppose, but I need to make sure that whoever has Flynn is fully prepared for the responsibility."

Mrs. Stoddard's face lit up like a light bulb, and she gave Tia a conspiratorial wink. "Detective Kelley?" She pointed at him. "You can help Tia. That way, someone from the local police department will have their finger on Flynn's welfare, and Tia will have help when she needs it."

The commissioner nodded. "Since you put it that way, Mrs. Stoddard, I'd abide by that decision and would be more than happy to expedite the situation any way I can."

Mrs. Stoddard peered at Tia and beamed. "See that, dear? The commissioner agrees with me. And it's obvious that Flynn really likes you. You're the perfect fit to be Flynn's new owner, and with Detective Kelley's help, you'll do great. I think this was somehow meant to be since you and the detective were the first to know that my lovely Margie was gone. It's as if she passed his leash to you."

Tia's mouth fell open. Oh, this would never work. The stunned look on Ethan's face spoke volumes. She shook her head at him as subtly as possible.

He took the cue and jumped into the conversation. "Um, ma'am, I'm not a K9 officer, and like I explained earlier, my work schedule doesn't allow me much time to devote to a dog."

Chief Carson piped in. "You can take time off from your cases to help Tia, Detective."

Tia wheeled around. When in the hell had her uncle joined the conversation? She nodded mutely and forced a strained smile. There had to be another solution that would appease the elderly woman and the commissioner. Sharing Flynn with the detective was preposterous. The very idea—blatantly absurd. She glanced at Ethan. He wasn't smiling, either. Maybe she could think of a way to circumvent Mrs. Stoddard's misguided plan later.

Detective Kelley didn't even want a dog. He'd said so himself. And she didn't want to be around him, because he was so freaking sexy. And the only reason he'd offered to help at the house was because her uncle had sent him over. The sooner she let Ethan know she didn't need him involved in her or Flynn's life, the better it would be for everyone. Her mind raced. Poor Flynn. All he really needed was a warm fireplace to soothe his bones and one person to love him.

Mrs. Stoddard reached for her cane and wobbled to her feet. She motioned to Tia and Ethan. "Don't go anywhere. We'll meet back here in a half hour to sign the papers and turn Flynn over to your care. My lawyer's here."

Tia's eyebrows lifted. "Papers?"

"Yes, dear. Margie left Flynn a trust fund of sorts for his geriatric care. You and the detective will both need to sign for it." She scrutinized each of them before stepping away. "I hope you don't have a problem sharing a checking account with Flynn as the beneficiary."

As soon as the older woman left, Ethan's shoulders shook with mirth. He cleared his throat and leaned toward Tia. "I suppose we should get together for coffee tomorrow to discuss the care of our boy."

She shot him a withering glance.

"You definitely need to call me Ethan now that we're personally involved. We're sort of joined at the fur." He threw his head back and laughed. "I need more work like I need a hole in my head." Wiping the fun from his eyes, he coaxed, "C'mon, Tia. You've got to laugh."

She tapped a foot. "I really don't want to share Flynn with you. We need to come up with some kind of mutual agreement."

A teasing grin crossed his face. "Already trying to keep my boy away from me? Don't make this a custody battle."

She turned away to hide her smile. He was kind of funny, but honestly, this was no laughing matter.

Ethan stepped in close enough that his breath grazed her neck. "We'll set up visitation times tomorrow. Don't make me get my lawyer involved."

Delicious chills tickled the length of her back. She longed to angle her neck so he'd do it again but squashed the urge.

God help her. She'd gone from the frying pan straight into the fire.

15

———

The chief's administrative assistant leaned her head into his office. "There's a woman on line two waiting to speak with you. She insists you are the only person she can talk to about whatever . . . "

Carson gave her a sideways glance and a nod. He reached for the phone, propped it under his chin, and pushed the button as he tossed a stack of reports onto his desk and prepared to review them. "Chief Carson here, what can I do for you?" He thumbed through the folders while waiting for a response.

"Chief, thank you for taking my call this morning." The voice on the other end was sweet. "My name is Mabel Hawkins, and I'm married to retired Colonel Arnie Hawkins. We live over on Bay Street."

"Yes, Mrs. Hawkins, how are you today?" Carson frowned when he opened Earl Thompson's report and a smattering of neon sticky notes greeted him.

"I've been better. I must speak to you about one of your young officers."

"Oh? Tell me about it, Mrs. Hawkins." Carson sighed, leaned

back in his chair, and yanked on his tie to loosen it a bit. Hopefully the cadets weren't speeding again.

"The other day, an officer in an unmarked car stopped my Arnie and me." Her voice trembled with emotion. "The officer said my husband was speeding, driving thirty-five miles per hour in a twenty-five mile-per-hour zone. Well, of course, Arnie hadn't realized he was speeding, and he apologized to the officer and told him he'd be more aware next time he drove through that shortcut. He was very respectful to the officer. We were shocked because neither of us has been stopped by a traffic officer since the nineteen eighties. Nowadays, we wonder if we are driving too slow, because people are always passing us." She chuckled.

Carson took a swig of his tepid coffee and waited for Mabel to get to the point.

"Well, to make a long story short, that young officer insisted Arnie get out of the car. Arnie has bad arthritis, and it takes him a while to stand up straight after he's been driving me around doing errands. But my husband complied, and when he was standing up, the officer grabbed Arnie by his jacket and shoved him face down against the hood of our car. And then he used his nightstick to hold mu husband down at his shoulders while searching his pockets and lecturing him about the speeding laws in town. Arnie was hurt, and furthermore, he had already apologized to the policeman."

Carson sat forward in his chair. This didn't sound like a routine traffic stop. His officers didn't carry nightsticks anymore and seldom asked people to vacate their vehicles unless they suspected drugs, drinking, weapons, or a serious offense. "Then what happened, Mrs. Hawkins?"

"The officer told me to shut up because I was crying, and I thought Arnie was going to punch the officer when he spoke to me so harshly. He let my husband go after ten minutes and a second tirade. Poor Arnie was so humiliated. He's never broken a law in his life, and my wonderful husband fought in Vietnam for six years. He shouldn't be treated poorly by any person, especially an officer of the law."

"Mrs. Hawkins, would you go get the ticket or warning the officer gave you and read the number in the right-hand corner to me, please?"

"Well, that's the thing, Chief—the officer didn't give us a warning or a ticket. I never even got his name. He has a streak of mean in him though. I don't ever want to see him again. Arnie doesn't even want to drive to bingo this afternoon. I can tell he's nervous about encountering that cop again."

Carson rubbed his neck. He asked Mrs. Hawkins for her address and phone number and the location of the traffic stop while promising he would get back to her as soon as he'd located the officer who had initiated it. "I'm very sorry for the way your husband was treated. Just sit tight, and I'll gather more facts from my end."

He was already searching his computer for traffic stops in the general area she spoke of when he hung up the phone. He pushed the intercom button, and his assistant answered.

"Yes, Chief?"

"Please locate Detective Kelley and tell him I need to speak with him as soon as possible."

"Sure, I'll find him right away."

Carson moved from one program to the next looking for the encounter Mrs. Hawkins had described. There were no records of any stop in the past two weeks in that area. Then he looked up Arnie Hawkins's license plate number and endeavored to trace the traffic stop from that angle. Nothing. According to the database, Arnie Hawkins hadn't been stopped since the late nineteen nineties, and that was for a burned-out brake light. What the hell was going on?

~

MABEL HAWKINS REMINDED Ethan of his grandmother with her gray bouffant hair and pearl earrings and necklace. He carried the silver tray laden with china coffee cups and fixings to the living room to set it on the glass table for her as Colonel Hawkins muted the baseball game between the Orioles and the Nationals.

"You know, Detective, I don't think I was speeding the other day. My Mabel chastises me all the time for driving like an old person. It upsets her that the younger generation passes us on the road every chance they get. But I had enough of driving fast in Vietnam. Sometimes, the situation in the jungle would change so fast we'd hightail our asses out of there with guys hanging off the vehicle. It was life or death back then. Nowadays, I like to take my time on the road—I'm not as quick as I was in my seventies."

Ethan joined the conversation. "Speaking of getting places, would you and Mrs. Hawkins like it if I drove you to bingo? It starts in a half hour, and on behalf of the department, I'd like to drive you there and home again. No sense staying here and missing the fun events you enjoy, when you have a chance to ride in the cruiser with someone else doing the driving."

"Well, I don't mind missing bingo once in a while, but Mabel here, she enjoys it so much I'd hate to see her miss it. All of her girlfriends play, and their husbands, too. What do you think, honey pie? Shall we let this nice officer drive us to bingo?"

"I'd love to go, Arnie, as long as you come with me," she said, and took a sip of her coffee.

"Okay, it's settled, then. Let's get the photos of my bruises done, and we'll make like a ripe coconut and split."

Mabel giggled at his less-than-stellar comparison.

Ethan helped Arnie remove his shirt and took photos of the

bruises on his chest and back from his encounter with the mysterious policeman. After returning the silver tray to the kitchen, he turned the lights off and locked the door as the Hawkinses made their way to his car.

He pulled over and parked the cruiser at the exact location the colonel said the traffic stop occurred, got out, and walked around looking for tire tracks. Yesterday's rain had washed the evidence of any imprints into the gutter. He leaned in the driver's-side window he'd left open. "You're sure this is where you were stopped?" Ethan inquired.

"Absolutely, Detective. You want me to get out and look with you?"

Aw, please no, it took ten minutes to get you in the car and comfortable. "No, Colonel, that's okay. I'm going to spend a minute or two and take a look around." Ethan walked up to the intersection and back again.

What an odd place for a police car to pick off speeders. The department never used this location as a speed trap. It would be silly. The retirement community was only two blocks west, and the neighborhood was among the quietest in the area. The only calls they ever received out here were from elderly people who needed medical attention. According to Chief Carson, there hadn't even been a fender bender this way in over a year.

Ethan climbed back into the cruiser and headed for the bingo hall.

"He didn't wear a black armband like you have on. I suppose that's to honor Lieutenant Plante, right? Lovely woman she was. I only met her once at the VFW hall. She was standing behind the buffet line cutting the prime rib."

Ethan turned the fan down. "Excuse me, sir? Would you repeat what you just said?"

Arnie fiddled with his hearing aid and raised his voice. "I said Margie was a lovely woman and the officer who stopped us wasn't wearing a black armband like you have on. That's another thing he should be reprimanded for when you figure out who he is."

That's what I thought you said. No black armband. How could an officer forget to wear his armband? They were standard issue for the next three months in honor of Lieutenant Plante's lengthy service to the people of New York. The cadets had even put a couple of extra armbands in each cruiser glove box in case an officer left his home. Carson had also made sure there was an extra box of armbands in the locker room. There'd be no excuse for not wearing one. Hell, if someone showed up without it, they'd be busted at roll call.

So then, who was out there stopping the public for traffic violations?

16

Tia scrawled her name on the trust-fund check and slid it across the counter to Casey. "Thank you for everything. You and Mike have worked miracles for Flynn. I'll take it from here." She grinned. "I can't wait to show him around his new home."

"He's a wonderful dog, Tia, and it's been great catching up with you after all these years." Casey glanced at the check. "Will Detective Kelley be stopping by later to sign this? There's a spot for him to sign."

Tia rolled her eyes. It was ridiculous that the lawyer had set up Flynn's trust fund this way. "I will call Ethan after I leave. He can come over later to sign it."

Casey giggled. "You didn't remind him on purpose, huh?"

Tia pasted a nonchalant smile on her face. "You got that right, girl. The less I run into that man, the better for me. But I will call him within the hour so he knows his signature is required."

Casey nodded. "Got it. No problem. Feel free to call us if you have any questions about Flynn's care. We're happy to help."

Tia mumbled her thanks and turned around as Detective Kelley whooshed through the front door.

"Sorry I'm late, ladies. Just finished a wellness check on one of our senior citizens." His radio squawked insistently, and he lowered the volume. "Where's the check I need to sign?" He smiled warmly at them.

Tia shook her head. She should've known he wouldn't forget. From what she'd seen, the man was annoyingly organized.

Casey held up the check and handed it over with a pen. "Here you go, Detective."

"Please, call me Ethan. We're just one big happy family around here, aren't we?" His gaze landed on Tia.

Tia nodded insistently. "I can take it from here. Thanks for taking care of the check."

A bemused expression flitted across his face. "Of course. We're in this together." He bent down and scratched Flynn's ears. "Are you ready to go for a ride in the cruiser, big guy?"

No freaking way. "He's riding with me to my house."

"Of course he's going to your house. But his new daddy worked patrol today. I thought I could at least give him a ride home."

Tia folded her arms. "No, he's riding with me. You have no idea what kind of reaction he'll have riding in a police car again."

"He'll be fine and a hell of a lot more comfortable than riding in your little Kia Soul. In case you haven't noticed, Flynn here's a big boy."

Her cheeks were getting hot. "I emptied the back seat and made a comfortable space for him. I've got it under control."

"Did you get a car seat yet?"

"No. I haven't found one I liked." Which was partially true, because she wanted one decorated in doggie paws. Tia frowned.

"Don't you worry about him. I'll drive slow and avoid the potholes."

Ethan took the leash from her hand. "Let me walk you out at least. Thanks, Casey." He held the door. "Aren't we the most perfect-looking pet parents?"

She was barely able to keep the laughter from her voice. "Stop it, Ethan." Why did her emotions ping-pong every which way when he was near? Just like the day on the beach, but at that point in her life, she'd thought she'd found her soulmate. So much for teenage crushes. Tia opened her car door, and Flynn ambled inside.

"His tail is sticking out," Ethan noted.

"I won't shut the door on his tail. Seriously, I've got this."

He rubbed his hands together. "I bought him a big comfy dog bed."

Tia rolled her eyes. "So did I. Keep the one you bought at your house in case I go out of town some weekend and can't take him with me."

"Long-distance relationship, huh?"

"That's none of your business, but since you asked, my best friend lives in Baltimore, and I'm not sure her building allows pets."

"Well, you might want to take him with you regardless of the rules if you're going to Baltimore. He'd be the one taking care of you."

She shot him a sideways glance. "Detective, for your information, most of Baltimore is really nice."

He cocked his head and winced. "You're right, but like any city, it's no place to let your guard down."

She changed the subject. "I hired a company to deliver all-natural food once a week for Flynn and picked a plan with his nutritional needs in mind."

"You're the perfect dog mother, Tia. I bought him a gigantic package of rawhide bones. They're in my cruiser trunk. Lieutenant Plante had a bucket of them in her pantry. I figure it'll save your shoes from becoming tattered remnants."

"Oh, good. I hadn't even thought of that. Do you want to put them in my front seat and get back to work?" *Please say yes.*

"No, as of ten minutes ago, I'm on dog duty per your uncle's request. I'll follow you home and make sure Flynn settles in okay. Besides, the chief wants a weekly report on the dog's recovery."

Damn. She couldn't even get a pet without her uncle being involved. This was a new level of overbearing, even for him. She took a deep breath and shut the car door. "Please note for your report that Flynn's tail remained intact." Her mouth twitched with amusement as she climbed into the car. "I'll see you back at my place."

ETHAN ARRIVED at Tia's a few minutes before she did. The yellow Cape Cod had blue shutters and a nautical wreath on the storm door. From the street, it was cute as a button with trimmed hedges and planters full of pansies by the front door. The seasonal flowers she'd planted a week ago made the place beam with a colorful, happy vibe. He paused a moment, remembering their kiss in the garden. Something deep inside him craved an encore, and he'd been looking forward to seeing her all day long. He'd even mentioned it to his best friend, Mac.

Walking the perimeter of the house, he checked to see if she'd installed any security cameras yet. Nope. He stuffed his hands into his pockets. Tia would get upset if he mentioned the security issues again, so he'd keep his mouth shut and eyes open.

Ethan set the bucket of rawhide chews on the front porch as she pulled in. Swinging her purse over a shoulder, she hoisted the mammoth dog bed onto the other and opened Flynn's door.

"Let me help you with that thing." He lifted it off her shoulder.

"Thank you, but I had it," she replied flatly.

"I may as well make myself useful. You get the dog." He held the storm door while Tia ushered Flynn inside, and then left his boots on the porch. "Where do you want Flynn's new bed?"

"Over there by the fireplace."

Ethan dropped the huge cushion into place. Flynn trotted over, sniffed, pawed at the cushion for a minute, did the dog-turning-around-and-around thing, and lay down.

"Have you thought about where you'll put his food and water?"

She gave him the once-over. "Yes, in the kitchen by the microwave cart. You're looking rather relaxed, Detective. Why'd you take your boots off?"

"They're full of mud. I spent part of my shift walking the fallow fields behind Lieutenant Plante's house searching for anything we might have missed."

Tia opened a drawer and tossed him a towel. "My porch is a practice-landing site for seagull droppings. Bring the boots inside, and set them on this."

He caught it one-handed with a laugh. "Thanks, the boots thank you, too."

"How's the case going? Are you closing in on a suspect?"

Ethan set his boots inside. "Confidentially?"

She peered at him from the kitchen. "Okay, confidentially. I know what the word means."

He nodded. "We have a suspect. Personally, I don't think he'll pan out. Otherwise, no fingerprints, no DNA, and no idea. This isn't what the public wants to hear. Whoever did it should be locked up by now."

"Did your crew find whatever it was I kicked across the kitchen?"

Ethan paused, maintaining a blank expression. "There's no mention of that in the reports. What was it?"

"Beats me. I came in the back door, and my foot caught something and sent it flying. At the moment, I was seriously invested in not getting caught and finding a bathroom."

"Did you see where it went?"

Tia shrugged. "Under the counter or maybe an appliance? I'm pretty certain I told your guys about it when they interviewed me at the hospital. Whatever it was hit something hard, and the skidding noise stopped." She shoved a mug of tea into the microwave.

"Would you happen to have a coke?"

Tia raised an eyebrow. "In the fridge, help yourself. You're getting a little too comfortable here, Detective."

He opened the refrigerator door and stood back. "Don't worry. I know my place. If I get out of line, you'll kick my ass."

"You don't believe I can?"

"After checking with a recruit who said he used an ice bag on and off for twenty-four hours, I know you can."

An evil chuckle rumbled from her throat. "I couldn't do that eighteen months ago."

"Very impressive. You want some carryout? I'm used to eating after work."

"Now you're wayyy too comfortable."

"Actually, I'm concerned for your health. There are soy milk, strawberry jam, a horseradish dip, dog food, and three beers in your fridge."

She laughed. "Admittedly, I need to place an order for grocery delivery, but I'll pass on the carryout."

Ethan opened his phone and started typing. "Do you eat Thai?"

"If I were eating carryout—which I'm not—I'd pick Thai over Chinese any day."

He tapped a few more times and closed his phone. "What precipitated you learning Krav Maga?"

Tia touched a hand to her throat and turned away. "Nothing, really. I wanted to learn self-defense." She spun around to face him. "Tell me, Detective, do I come across as incompetent?"

Oh, hell. This *had* to be a trick question. "No, why?"

"Because . . . empty refrigerator aside, I handle my life quite well. But my uncle keeps sending people, mainly men, to check on me. I'm thirty-one years old and have been taking care of myself for years. And it baffles me that even Mrs. Stoddard insisted I have a chaperone to take care of a retired K9. You can't blame me for wondering if people view me as incompetent." She rubbed her arms and leaned against the counter, waiting for his answer.

Definitely a trick question. He wasn't getting involved in a dispute between her and Chief Carson, and damn, he wanted to massage her shoulders and soothe the worrisome question away. "I think Mrs. Stoddard was deferring to the police commissioner's hesitation about a civilian handling a retired K9. I can't comment on the rest of it, because I have no insight into your uncle's motives."

She nodded slowly. "So you never looked into Flynn becoming your dog?"

He shook his head. "Oh no. I was as surprised as you at Mrs. Stoddard's decision."

"You never said anything to my uncle about Flynn?"

"No. He mentioned the dog to me as a good resource for this area because the closest K9 unit is over an hour away. I think the chief is interested in Flynn helping out here or there over the summer should the need arise."

"What kind of need?"

"Missing persons. Especially kids. Perhaps the reason we both were designated as Flynn's caretakers is the trust fund the lieutenant left for his geriatric care."

"Meaning what?"

"Well, there's over a hundred thousand dollars in the fund. Veterinary-care costs are through the roof. Flynn is eight with a general life expectancy of nine to thirteen years. Maybe Stoddard and the commissioner figured the money was safer if we had to agree on expenses."

She nodded. "What do you think about getting pet insurance for him?"

"I suppose, if that's what you want to do. I haven't had a pet since I was a kid, so I have no idea if a policy would be worth it."

For a minute the room was quiet with the exception of Flynn's snoring. "You're plenty competent, Tia. I think it was about the money and Flynn's training." He reached into his shirt pocket and pulled out a laminated card. "Here are the commands he knows. Whatever you do, don't say this one"—he pointed to a word on the card—"unless your life is in imminent danger."

"Why? What does it mean?"

"It's German for *attack*—and he will."

The doorbell rang. Ethan glanced out the window. "I'll get it. It's for me."

After handing the delivery kid a tip, he returned with two bags and set one on the counter. "Call me presumptuous if you want, but this bag of Thai is yours." He smiled. "Maybe place that online grocery order while you're eating."

Tia stood motionless in the middle of the kitchen. "Oh, um...."

He leaned forward and spoke in a hushed whisper. "It's just food. It won't bite."

She laughed nervously. "Right. I'll get some plates and forks."

He strode in the direction of his boots. "None for me. I'm leaving."

She chewed her lower lip for a few seconds and hurried to a cabinet. "No, don't do that, Detective. By the time you get home, it'll be cold."

"I reheat meals all the time, not a big deal."

She wheeled around with plates and silverware in her hands. "I . . . I insist."

Ethan set his boots back down on the towel. "Are you sure? Do you have more questions about Flynn's commands?"

She managed a tremulous smile. "Probably. I haven't even read the list yet, and we both know Thai is better when it's good and hot."

"Okay." He sat opposite her at the small kitchen table and started spooning noodles into a bowl.

"How is Flynn still sleeping with the scent of good food swirling around?"

Ethan glanced up from his plate. "First day home from the hospital is always a sensory overload. Look at it this way: If he weren't comfortable, he wouldn't be able to sleep."

"Yeah, I guess you're right." She pointed at her food. "This is great, by the way. But you need to stop buying me things. First there was the cup of coffee, then the coffeepot, and now this."

He thought a minute. "The cup of coffee was a bribe so you'd let me in to check your doors and windows. The coffeepot was because I gave your principal the wrong impression, and tonight is a welcome-home dinner for Flynn."

She smirked. "Is that what this is, Detective?"

"We're pet parents now and sharing a checking account."

She leaned back in her seat and gave him an appraising look. "Is there a Mrs. Kelley who'll be upset I ate Thai with her husband? Or worse yet, be livid that I kissed him on the front lawn?"

He gulped hard as the spicy Thai warmed his throat. "Not anymore and I just might keep it that way."

Tia's eyebrows drew together. "That's a shame. I was hoping to introduce you to one of my teacher friends. She likes you law-enforcement types."

He coughed on a noodle. "I wouldn't recommend it."

Tia stabbed a couple of snow peas with her fork. "What if she comes to visit and just happens to meet you?"

He dropped his fork onto his plate and leaned forward. "Don't."

HIS EYES HAD TURNED dark and brooding. She must've hit a nerve. Tia looked down at her food. "I apologize. I, um . . . it's just that she's a lovely person and looking to settle down. I didn't mean to be pushy."

He gave her a curt nod and picked his fork up. "I'm divorced and still working through it. If I decide to change my marital status, I assure you I am quite capable of finding my own woman. How's your love life?"

Ouch. He'd turned that table, and she deserved it. "Um, no divorce but I was clueless to things that were going on in my last relationship. I'm definitely staying single for the long term." Dabbing her mouth with a napkin, she snuck a peek at his eyes. They'd softened a fraction. "That's part of the reason I wanted a dog. You know . . . company."

He leaned back in his chair. "And the added security doesn't hurt a bit while we're catching Lieutenant Plante's killer."

Tia shifted uneasily in her seat. "Yes, that too."

He abruptly snapped the lid onto his unfinished Thai and slid it into the bag. "You think you'll be all right with Flynn tonight?"

"Oh, sure. We're buddies. No need for you to hang around."

"All right. I promised my grandmother I'd take her shopping after her dinner hour."

"That's nice of you. Does she live nearby?"

"She does. Over at Happy Acres Retirement Community."

Tia wrinkled her nose. "Really? I volunteer there on Thursday evenings. What's your grandmother's name?"

"Nancy Ryan. She has an apartment there."

Tia sat back and stared at him. "Nan? Your grandmother is Nan?"

He cocked his head. "You know her?"

"She's in my Thursday reading club. I love her." Tia shook her head. "What a small world. Is she why you moved here a year ago?"

He nodded. "More or less. After I moved back, Nan informed me of her move to Happy Acres and turned the house over to me."

Tia grinned. "She's a real spitfire. Her love for life is an inspiration."

Ethan rocked back on his heels and smiled. "Yes, she is. I'm planning an eightieth birthday party for her. Her wish list is a bit bizarre."

"Meaning?"

"Confidential," he winked.

"Oh, come on. I know how to keep my mouth shut."

He shook his head and chuckled. "She wants to be arrested on her birthday."

"What?"

"Seriously, it's on her bucket list."

"Why?"

"Even though she participated in the big protest demonstrations of the nineteen sixties, she was never arrested for anything."

Tia giggled. "Wow. That's an unusual request. How are you going to pull that one off?"

"With your uncle's blessing—I hope." He rose and set his plate in the sink. "Call me if you need help with our boy tonight. Nan runs out of steam after a couple of hours at the outlets. I should be home by eight."

Tia rolled her eyes. "I'm sure he'll be fine. Thanks for the supper."

Ethan paused while putting his boots on. "I'll be in and out of town for the next two weeks. You want me to cosign another check just in case?"

"That's okay. I'll front the money if needed, seeing as I planned on spending my own to take care of him anyway. Going somewhere special?"

He shook his head. "No. Maybe. I'm on call for my second job. Sometimes I need to leave town on the spur of the moment."

"What kind of job?" She wanted to withdraw the question immediately. It sounded like she was prying, and as much as she wanted to keep her distance from him, her curiosity had overwhelmed her good sense.

"I work with young people, help them get their lives restarted after a trauma."

What a rewarding side hustle. She kept her mouth shut this time.

"See ya. Let me know if you need help with Flynn or a break from the dog-mom routine. Otherwise, I'll stay out of your hair." He slipped out the front door and strode to his car.

Tia glanced at Flynn and then out the window as Ethan pulled away. She rubbed her hand against her breastbone. It was the weirdest damn thing. The house felt kind of empty without him.

17

———————

Tia had been so tempted in between bites of noodles to reminisce about the bonfire with Ethan. He'd been her first real kiss and a doozy at that. He'd wrapped the blanket around them both, and they'd kissed and talked for hours. She'd always regretted bolting when the cops had shown up, because she hadn't gotten his number or even his last name. All summer while working at the ice-cream place on the boardwalk, she'd hoped to look up and see him standing in line. But it had never happened.

Tia whistled for Flynn and headed for the stairs. Time to show him his new digs and the second plush bed she'd bought for him up in her room. He lifted his sleepy head and lumbered toward her, gingerly picking his way up the steps. Poor guy. He had to be sore from the surgeries and trauma he'd endured. Later on, she'd give him one of the pain relievers Casey had included in his take-home bag.

She opened the bedroom doors, the linen closet, and the bathroom door. Might as well let the dog sniff and discover the sights and scents of his new home. Thank goodness she hadn't brought Ethan up here to see this dog bed. Her room was a disaster. She flung open the closet door and tossed dirty towels and clothes down the enormous laundry chute in the floor of her closet. While not pretty, it sure was functional. After stripping the bed, Tia lobbed the sheets and blanket together. The weather had warmed enough for her to bring out the summer bedspread, so next went the down comforter. It disappeared from view, sliding all the way to a drop about three feet above her clothes washer, and landed with a little thud. The chute was one of her favorite features of the house.

Flynn growled as she pitched more dirty clothes over his head and down the cavernous slide.

Tia stopped.

The dog got down on all fours and combat crawled to the big hole, growling all the way. He even went so far as to let his front paws hang over the edge while he investigated. Whining, he shimmied backward.

Whoa. Her new housemate didn't like dark holes?

Tia walked around the bed, throwing dirty pillowcases down the opening as he paced and barked. When she hung a jacket in the closet, the dog lunged in front of her to keep her away from the hole.

Oh, she'd have to work with Flynn on this because those closet doors were open more often than not. She couldn't have him freaking out every time she needed clothes or dropped some laundry.

After grabbing a chewy treat from the new jar on her nightstand, Tia shut the closet doors and got down on one knee in front of Flynn. "Here, boy, you're a good dog." Ruffling his fur, she stroked the concern from his furrowed brow. "We'll have to compromise on the laundry chute, my friend, because I really like it."

She'd ask Mike and Casey if they had notes on his background. Maybe there was a simple explanation for his behavior.

~

ETHAN STRODE through the precinct doors and headed for Conference Room 3. As he'd suspected, Earl had already parked himself at the massive conference table. A long whiteboard hung behind him. The sticky notes covering the board gave it a rainbowlike appearance. It'd be a great day if Earl's notes yielded a suspect by day's end.

"Morning, Earl."

"If you say so, Son."

"Does Tina still have you eating egg whites and sprouts?"

"Shut the eff up."

Ethan pulled two huge bagel sandwiches from his bag and slid one the length of the table with the precision of a bartender delivering a whiskey neat. It landed three inches from Earl's scribbling hand.

The older man's face broke into a grin as he lifted the wrapper. "*Now* it's a good morning. And to answer your question, Tina made an egg-white, kale, and blueberry shake for breakfast. I poured it down the garbage disposal the minute she left for work. She's determined to treat my slightly elevated cholesterol with a clean diet."

"That's what you get for marrying a woman some twenty years younger than you, boss."

"Stuff it, kid." Earl held the breakfast sandwich to his nose and inhaled. "Sausage, egg, and cheese. This is what breakfast should smell like." He took a bite and closed his eyes. "Thanks. I've been up since four thirty and running on coffee."

"Turkey sausage, and no problem. By the way, I saw the ride along late yesterday, and she mentioned kicking an object when she entered Margie's kitchen, but the evidence files make no mention of it."

Earl took another bite of sandwich. "Did you check the inventory log?"

Ethan nodded. "Yeah, of course. I stayed up late last night looking through all the files. There's no info about it. Tia said she'd told whoever interviewed her at the hospital about kicking something across the room."

Earl took a swig of his coffee. "First I've heard of it. Who turned in the report?"

"Carmichael, and he's a thorough investigator."

"Maybe the ride along *thought* she told the interviewer. She was treated for shock."

"Possibly, but she was quite certain that it came up during the conversation. And considering her relationship to the chief, she'd understand that details like that are important, shock or not."

"True. But we haven't found anything unusual inside the crime-scene perimeter. The struggle took place in the great room. That's thirty feet away." Earl tapped his pen on the table and ruminated while he finished his sandwich. "Wanna take a ride to Glen Cove Road and look around?" He crumpled the wrapper into a ball and tossed it at Ethan.

Ethan lobbed their garbage into the can. "I was hoping you'd say that. You want to go now?"

Earl patted his middle section. "Yup. I'm all fueled up. Go sign out a vehicle."

"Let's take my truck. It's ready to go."

"Make sure you bring camera equipment."

"Got it."

"And leather gloves in case we need to move heavy shit."

"Got that, too."

Earl rose and slipped into his winter jacket. "You think you'd bring me another one of those sandwiches tomorrow? I'll buy."

Ethan held the door open. "Sure. Why don't you just take the cholesterol med the doctor gave you and forget about it?"

"Bug off, Son. Getting older ain't for pussies. It seems like every time I go to the doctor, I walk out with some new medication. It's out of hand. I eat decent, work out, got a good body-fat ratio, but my cholesterol continues to rise."

"I think they call it heredity, Earl."

"Well, screw that." He stormed out the front doors of the precinct. "They say too much medicine can affect how the equipment works."

Ethan barked a laugh. "That's what you get for marrying a woman only a few years older than me. She's a lot to keep up with, I'm sure."

Earl slid into the passenger side of the truck and shut his door. "Just for that, I'm gonna make your life miserable at the next hell workout. You wait, Son."

"You've always exceeded my expectations, sir. I'll look forward to it."

Earl ran a hand across his head as they pulled out of the lot. "I need a haircut."

Ethan glanced over. "It's a half inch long, sir."

"Like I said—I need a haircut."

THEY PULLED the crime-scene tape off the front door, slid into their paper booties, and stepped into Plante's home. The chill in the air hung like a warning. Something sinister had happened in those rooms.

"You got any idea when Mrs. Stoddard is listing the house? Because there's no way anyone's going to buy it looking like this." Earl frowned and shook his head. "You know, I can handle any crime scene no matter how horrific, but once I've done my job, I hate going back to the place. It's always been that way for me. It's hard for me to take once the crisis is over."

Ethan studied the framed pictures on a mahogany bookshelf, snapped a few pictures, and put his phone away. "I believe Mrs. Stoddard has turned the details of the sale, including the cleanup, over to her lawyer. They haven't started yet because forensics hasn't signed off on the property. You know how they like to wait as long as possible just in case they need another run-through."

Earl heaved a breath, flicked on the overheads, and fired up his flashlight. He scanned the entire kitchen floor. "I don't see a damn thing down there. Did Tia mention if the object she kicked was heavy or lightweight?"

"No, she simply remembers kicking something right after entering this kitchen. She said the sound stopped abruptly, so it couldn't have gone far." Ethan got down on all fours and prowled the gleaming wood floor one sector at a time.

Earl followed suit. " Hell, I didn't bring my kneepads. There are four floor vents. Let's check them."

They crawled for several minutes in an eerie quiet.

Ethan broke the intense silence. "There's nothing here. You find anything?"

Earl cackled. "I'm cashing in over this way. The vents produced three toothpicks, a penny, and a couple of dust bunnies. This is the cleanest kitchen floor I've ever seen." He rose up on his knees. "You brought the leather work gloves, right?"

Ethan pulled a pair out of each pocket. "Here you go. What are we moving?"

"The refrigerator, Son. Tia's a smart woman. I've known her her whole life. If she says she kicked something, then I believe her." He stood up. "Try to shimmy that fridge out from the front."

Ethan gave the refrigerator doors a pull, and the huge unit slid several inches before it stubbornly stopped. He hugged it from the front, and through the process of drag and tug, he got it out except for the last few inches. Earl joined in, and together they got the unit completely out.

Their flashlights illuminated the floor behind the fridge. "There we go, a plastic spatula. Let's bag it just in case, but that utensil probably dropped off the counter when Margie was cooking." Earl snapped a photo of the spatula and placed it in a thick tamperproof bag.

Ethan grabbed one side of the fridge. "Help me slide this behemoth back in place." With a few grunts, the unit begrudgingly slid back.

"Are you thinking what I'm thinking?" Ethan asked.

"Yup. We gotta pull the range out, too. It's a Chambers gas stove from the previous century and is sure to weigh a ton. Look at that—it's even got a thermowell with a pot for cooking corn or crabs. You ready?"

Ethan stretched for a few seconds. "As I'll ever be. Let's go." It took them five minutes, a few cuss words, and a good sweat, but the aging gray combination stove and oven rested in the middle of the kitchen floor. Ethan aimed his light toward the cavernous space behind it. "There's nothing back there."

Earl got down on all fours and cast his light under the stove. "There's something caught on the slide mechanism, probably why it was a bear to pull out. I mean, aside from the fact that it's the weight of a heifer." He wiped his brow with a sleeve. "We gotta tip it back a couple of inches so I can get at it."

Ethan shook his head. "Are you trying to kill me? This cast-iron mother must weigh three hundred pounds."

"I know. That's why I make our crew participate in hell workouts. We gotta do the hard stuff or go home. Let's slide it back a foot so that when we tip it it'll rest against the counter."

Ethan inhaled quickly through his teeth while Earl let out a string of coaxing curses until the stove rested at a slight angle against the countertop.

Earl slid a few cookbooks under the unit in case it rocked. He traded his leather gloves for a fresh pair of latex gloves and illuminated the underside. Stretching his arm, he captured a compact shiny metal device about four inches long between two fingers. "I found something. Looks like a penknife." He dropped it into the evidence bag Ethan was holding.

Ethan held it up to the light. "That's not a penknife. It's a miniature lock pick set and probably the item Tia kicked across the floor, judging by how it was jammed in there. We'll let forensics check it out. I'll bet you a beer after our next workout that Margie Plante's fingerprints are nowhere to be found on this thing."

"Don't count your chickens," Earl chirped.

"Yeah, I know."

"Let's get this stove back in place. I've been meaning to ask: When's the last time you checked on Harlan Brinker?"

Ethan grunted as he shoved the oven backward. "I saw him a few days ago, after I went to see the Hawkins couple. Mabel inquired about Harlan because she knows him from church. Then she asked if I'd deliver a frozen lasagna she'd made for him. He seemed pretty good. There was food in the fridge and a forty-pound bag of dog food in the pantry, even a bowl of fruit on the kitchen counter. I was a little late meeting Tia at the vet to pick up Flynn because I'd stopped to see Harlan, and you know Harlan. He can talk your ear off."

Earl nodded. "Thanks for checking on him. I'll go next week and take a pie from the farmer's market that just reopened in the Pines. He's had a rough year since losing his wife, and not having any family nearby to look after him makes it that much harder. I had to show him how to use the washing machine and dryer a while back." Earl took off his gloves. "Helluva thing Mrs. Stoddard did, making you co-owner of that dog. Talk about getting blindsided. I guess you're spending some time over at Tia's, huh?"

Ethan shifted on his feet. "A little bit, but I've adopted your attitude about her."

Earl glanced over as he removed his paper booties. "Yeah, what's that?"

Ethan chuckled. "It's not my story, Son."

Earl laughed. "There you go. The best way to get through this life unscathed is to face forward and keep your nose out of other people's business. It isn't always the easiest thing to do though, Detective."

18

Tia turned the radio down once she saw the police lights in her rearview mirror. Surely the lights weren't meant for her . . . but the vehicle directly behind turned left, and the cop car stayed on her tail. Turning on her right blinker, she slowed down and pulled as close to the curb as possible. This wasn't the safest place to pull over on this road. It had no shoulder lane and irrigation ditches on both sides.

Only a minute ago, her speedometer had been reading in the thirty-mile-an-hour range. Maybe she'd been off a little, but she hadn't been driving fast or stupid.

Tia fumbled for her license as the officer approached her car. She didn't recognize him. Of all the crappy luck, to end up with an officer she didn't know. Flynn was dozing in the cushioned back-seat domain she'd coined *the boot*.

Why had the cop stopped her? Tia let her window halfway down and turned the car off.

"Evening, ma'am. May I see your license and registration please?" The cop aimed his flashlight at her face, effectively blinding her.

"Certainly, Officer." She shielded her eyes from his invasive flashlight. It wasn't dusk yet and the sun was still out. "I need to go in the glove box for my registration."

"Slowly, please."

The registration and insurance information were in an accessible pouch, and Tia quickly handed them over. She was just about to ask the guy if he would aim his flashlight away from her eyes when there was a low, primitive growl—an unearthly sound, unlike anything she'd heard before.

Flynn suddenly leaped into the front seat and landed with paws on her back and legs, barking and seething like a feral animal.

What on earth?

She was pinned and unable to move. His claws tore at her blouse and the bare flesh on her thighs as he repeatedly snapped at the officer through the half-open driver's window. He relentlessly crammed his snout and scrabbling right paw through the small opening.

She caught a glimpse of a baton in the air and grabbed the dog's torso, heaving with all her might to shove him out of the way. Flynn wouldn't budge, and the baton clipped his front paw. He whimpered only a second, then resumed growling and scratched at the door like his life depended on getting outside.

The officer continued jabbing at the driver's side window with his baton. Flynn took several hits to the mouth and head, but kept snarling.

"Your fucking dog bit me. Subdue him, or I will."

"I'm trying," she shouted, although she doubted he heard her over Flynn's carrying-on.

The next time the baton came through the opening in the window, Tia grabbed it with both hands and yanked with all her might. It broke free from the officer's grasp.

Flynn scrambled into the passenger seat, clawing at the windshield. Tia pulled him back by the harness. Why was he doing this? He'd barely finished recovering from his injuries. He'd never disobeyed her before now.

The dog wheeled around and growled at her. She froze. Flynn uttered the most soul-wrenching whine and stared right into her eyes.

What is it, buddy?

He was trying to tell her something, but she had no idea how to interpret his signal. Flynn ripped his gaze from her eyes, clamped down on her leather purse, and shook it violently.

The officer banged on the passenger window of the car. "Subdue your fucking dog, lady." As the guy walked the perimeter of her car, Flynn leaped from seat to seat, snarling like a wolf that'd picked up the scent of blood. Tia pressed the lock button. If the man opened the door, he didn't stand a chance. He had no idea Flynn was a trained K9.

The officer slammed his fist down on the hood of her car and held up a bleeding hand. "See this? Get the fuck out of here. If I ever see that dog again, I'll kill it."

She didn't need telling twice. Tia tossed the cop's baton out the window. Flynn was still growling as the officer climbed into his car and turned off his police lights. Her hands shook while she jammed the key in the ignition. The car lurched forward, throwing gravel, and she sped down the road.

A mile later, Tia pulled into a convenience store and parked in the back lot. She faced Flynn, who still stood in the front passenger seat.

"What in the hell was that about? Get in the back seat!"

Oh my goodness, she shouldn't be screaming at him. If only she could've read his mind back there. That look was a genuine plea for . . . what? What? Shit. She didn't know, but something. The dog lowered his haunches onto the passenger seat and set his head on the dashboard.

"No, Flynn! Get in the back seat," she yelled, pointing. He

barked once and stared at her but didn't move. He looked like he had no intention of sitting in the back ever again.

~

ETHAN GOT out of his truck at Tia's house and peered inside her half-open Kia window. Flynn was sitting in the front passenger seat. "Are you all right?"

Tia lifted her head from the steering wheel and ran a hand through her hair. "Yeah, I think so. I'm not sure if I've lost control of him, and I wanted you here in case he tries to bolt when I open the door." Tossing a hand in the air, she gave a bitter laugh. "You're his dog father. Maybe you can make some sense of his behavior today."

"What happened?"

"We were stopped by a patrolman out on Holly Knoll Road. I still don't understand why the guy stopped me. I *know* I wasn't speeding." She jerked her head in the dog's direction. "But Flynn decided he didn't like the cop and totally lost his cool. He bit the man's hand and then the cop hit Flynn with his baton." She hugged her chest. "Flynn whimpered when the baton hit. I have no idea how bad he's hurt. Would you help me get him out of the car? For all I know, he'll run. He hasn't been obeying me since the traffic stop."

Ethan shoved his car keys into a pocket. "Where's his leash?"

She leaned over and reached toward the passenger floor. The back of her light-blue blouse had blood spots all over it. Good God, what the hell had happened to her back? "Here it is." She held it up.

"Clip it onto his harness, and feed it to me through the passenger-side window. That way, I'll have control of him and you can get out."

She nodded, let the passenger window down a few inches, and tossed the thick leash in Ethan's direction.

He caught it. "Okay, I've got him. Take your time and get out. Maybe you could open the front door for us?"

Tia gathered her things and made a beeline for the door. Within seconds, she was inside.

Ethan braced himself, opened the door, and whistled for Flynn. The dog stepped onto the blacktop, limped to his favorite tree, and relieved himself. Then the sniffing began. Ethan walked the perimeter of Tia's house, allowing Flynn to lead the way with his nose to the ground. Every direction the dog tugged, Ethan followed. Flynn widened his search the second time, sniffing back by the fence line and in the pine trees framing the property. Seemingly satisfied, the dog headed for the front door.

Ethan sat down on the front stoop and examined Flynn's paws. He had three broken claws, which explained the pronounced limp that had persisted throughout the sniffing tour of the yard. While Ethan ruffled his coat and praised him, Flynn recoiled at a stroke to his snout. A trip to the vet would be a good idea.

He looked the K9 in the eye. "I don't know what freaked you out, but whatever it was, you were working, huh? Let's go see how your girl's doing."

He found Tia in the kitchen with one bare leg propped up on a kitchen chair. Ethan stood back and enjoyed the view. The woman had gorgeous legs, long and shapely, supple and strong. Their kiss in the garden had been hot, but then she'd tried to fix him up with one of her teacher friends. He could only conclude that she wasn't interested in him. Ethan turned away. This weak moment would pass even though his resolve to resist her was slipping, bit by tempting bit. *Nice legs. Now move on.* His dick protested, but such was life.

Tia hissed through her teeth as she dabbed peroxide on the gashes above her knee. "Son of a gun, that hurts."

Ethan took a quick look at her leg. "Some of those cuts are deep. You might need stitches."

She waved him off. "Don't say that to me. I do not need stitches."

"Can I get you a warm towel or something?"

Tia glanced at him. "No, thanks. It's enough that I interrupted your day because I can't control my dog. Thanks for coming over. I didn't want him getting loose and hurting someone or himself. I've never had an animal lose their crap like that."

"Exactly what happened, and how did you get those cuts?"

She threw her hands in the air. "How? I'll tell you how. You know those movies that are set in a big city, and the cabbie is sitting in the car just minding their own business in front of a building and then wham, a body falls through the windshield? Well, that's how I got these cuts. The officer approached my window, I handed him my license and registration, and out of nowhere Flynn growled like a seething werewolf and leaped over the seat landing half on my back and his other half in my lap. I've never heard an animal sound that threatening in my life. I definitely picked the wrong day to wear a skirt and blouse to school."

She snatched a clean towel from a drawer and murmured, "But it was such a pretty day, you know? There was that hint of a warm spring in the air, and I woke up to the faint scent of my lilac bush in the backyard. I don't want to be mad at Flynn, so it's the lilac bush's fault I have cuts all over my legs."

"How could you possibly smell the lilac bushes from inside?" He already knew he wasn't going to like her answer.

"Because I sleep with the bedroom window open a few inches."

Ethan shook his head. "Tia, there's a murderer out there. Have you no sense of self-preservation?"

"Really?" She cocked her head thoughtfully. "So I shouldn't sleep with my second-story bedroom window open? Do you think the murderer has climbing abilities, too? Let me tell you something. I allowed another person to control my life once upon a time. Never again. If the sick creep who killed Margie Plante wants to scale the side of my house to get to my open bedroom window, then he or she will eat the barrel of my shotgun."

"Shotguns are slow when the seconds count."

"Then I'd use the handgun under my spare pillow."

Whoa. Touché. His resolve to stay single slipped and fell on a banana peel. How hot would it be to remove a gun from her bed? Scorching. Whew! Good to know in case he ever stayed overnight. A guy could dream. He would be prudent to disarm the bed first.

Ethan shook off the mental picture. There was no way they'd ever sleep together.

He changed the subject. "How's your back?"

"It hurts. Flynn and I were a tangled mess after he leaped into the front seat. Why?"

"There are bloodstains on your blouse. Maybe take it off so I can see how bad you're hurt, and I'll clean you up."

She arched her eyebrows. "I'm not taking my blouse off."

He dipped his head and silently counted to three. "Not like *take it all off.* You can cover up with something, but if you aren't willing to go to a clinic, someone has to disinfect your back."

Her mouth rounded to a perfect O. "Gotcha. Right." She went upstairs and returned wearing a high-neck backless beach cover-up.

Come to think of it, he'd never seen her with a button undone or showing a hint of cleavage. It was unusual behavior for a woman as attractive as her. He hadn't thought much of it until now, but she almost always wore a turtleneck, a button-down, or a zip up that completely covered every inch of her front. Why? And the last thing he needed to be thinking about was her chest, so he chucked the thoughts into the recycle bin with the previous leg thoughts and hoped he could forget about the freaking gun in the bed, because last night he'd relived every sexy detail of the yard kiss and hadn't been able to sleep.

Sliding onto a counter stool, she held out a pair of latex gloves and the peroxide. "Go easy. I looked in the mirror. There are a lot of them, and they hurt."

He grabbed a wad of cotton balls and counted the dime-size cuts on her back. There were twenty-three of them to be exact. After soaking the cotton in peroxide, he dabbed at the dried blood. "Flynn didn't mean to hurt you. He was working and even investigated your yard before he came in tonight."

She gasped when the peroxide bubbled. "What do you mean . . . working?"

"He was protecting you and didn't have enough room in the front seat. A dog like him will lay his body across yours to shield you."

"It was just a traffic stop. Why on earth would Flynn feel the need to protect me from a police officer?"

"I'm not sure, but I have a working theory."

She glanced over her shoulder. "What kind of theory?"

"It was on the late news last night. Someone impersonating a policeman has stopped a number of our citizens. He's roughed up a few people, threatened and taken money from others. Dispatch has no record of these stops. Every officer lets dispatch know their location when they initiate a traffic stop. It's for their safety in case they need backup or someone needs medical care. I called dispatch, and there haven't been any recorded traffic stops on Holly Knoll Road in the past eight hours. "

Her body went rigid. "What?"

"For a couple of weeks, we've known we have a murderer and an imposter cop out there. We've been treating the cases as separate incidents because until now, there wasn't a point of intersection to tie them together." He reached for a fresh clump of cotton balls. "Flynn is the only one who knows who killed Margie Plante, and let's not forget that the killer also beat him within an inch of his life. A smart dog like him won't ever forget the scent or the voice of that killer."

"Stop." Tia spun her counter stool around. "So Margie's killer and the guy who stopped me are the same person?"

The shock on her face was obvious. He'd go easy. "It's possible. Let's just say I'm thinking it through at the moment. Why else would Flynn go berserk over something as benign as a traffic stop? My theory makes sense."

Tia shook her head slowly. "I may have been stopped by Margie's killer. I'm glad I didn't know then what I know now."

Ethan cocked his head. "Why was Flynn with you? Didn't you have school today?"

"Yes, I had school, but I ran home afterward, picked up Flynn, and took him to Harlan Brinker's farm to run with his hounds. Flynn loves those dogs, and the socialization and exercise do him good." She shook her head. "All this happened because I wanted to be a good dog mom."

His fingers had stilled. "You know Harlan?"

She laughed. "Duh—I'm a local. Everyone knows Harlan. I baked an apple cake for him last night and dropped it off while the dogs had their run. Harlan loves my apple cake."

"You bake?" He couldn't believe it. Where the hell did she keep the milk and eggs? The refrigerator was always empty.

Her voice lowered to a scold. "Yes, I bake. I've even been known to mix pasta salad in a bowl and use a cast-iron skillet on occasion. But it's more fun to bake for somebody else. When I bake for myself, I eat the whole thing and worry about getting fat."

Fat she was not, but he understood the sentiment. "Well, anytime you feel like baking, just let me know, and I'll pick up the ingredients and eat the finished product with you. Then we'll only get half as fat together." The word *together* stopped him from teasing her more. What was happening to him? He hadn't wanted *together* with anyone since his divorce. He thought back to what they'd been talking about before Harlan and the apple cake.

"Did you get a good look at the guy?"

"Not really. He approached me from behind—came up alongside my window and blinded me with his flashlight even though it was daytime." She closed her eyes and paused a moment. "I guess I did get a brief look. It was when he walked around the car screaming how Flynn had bitten him and I needed to subdue my dog. At one point, he smashed his hand down on the hood of the car." She turned around, set her elbows on the counter, and rubbed her forehead. "All I can remember about his looks is that he's tall and has a sharp nose. His hat covered most of his features, and he wore sunglasses. The mirrored kind."

That was something. "Did you notice if he was overweight, had a paunchy gut?"

"No, he wasn't heavyset. He was kind of like you but not as built."

A surprise jolt of lust coursed through his abs. "You think I'm built?"

She laughed. "He didn't have a broad chest and big arms like you do. He definitely wasn't as muscular as you."

"You've noticed my muscles?" He couldn't resist pushing the issue a little.

Tia rolled her eyes. "Stop fishing for compliments. You know you have muscles. It's obvious you work out."

"I stay in shape for my job, but I had no idea you were looking."

"I'm not blind, just keeping my distance."

Ethan soaked a few more cotton balls and kept dabbing. "And why is that?" Ooh, he was playing with fire now.

She sighed deep and long. "A year ago, I was in a very dark place, and I'm not going back there. Besides, you've probably heard all about it at the precinct since you've been there a year."

"Haven't heard a peep."

"Well, that's unusual for gossip central, but encouraging. Maybe it's all behind me." She shivered. "Are you almost done? I'm freezing, and I should check Flynn."

He disinfected the final two cuts. "All done. Flynn's got three broken claws and flinched when I touched his snout."

She slid off the kitchen stool. "Poor thing. I tried so hard to keep him from the window, but the baton clipped him a couple of times in spite of my efforts."

"Now that we know you're okay, we should get him to the vet."

"Yeah. I'll go change and call Bayside to see if we can come in." She wheeled around. "I can go myself. You probably need to get back to work anyway."

After a weird incident like this, she wasn't getting rid of him easily. "I'm the dog daddy, remember? I'll go with you. We'll use my truck. I'll arrange for forensics to dust the hood of your car for fingerprints. You said the cop placed his hand on it."

"Yes, that's right." She got halfway up the stairs and leaned over the banister. "Do I need to go to the precinct and give a statement?"

He whistled for Flynn and thought a second. "No. I'll take your statement here." Her relief was damn near palpable as she continued up the stairs. One of these days he would find out what had happened to her and why the precinct and interviews were such touchy subjects.

The house was quiet when she returned downstairs. "Ethan, when they come to dust the car, please, no police lights. My neighbors will be full of questions tomorrow if there's a big scene."

Yeah, well, she only had two neighbors this time of year, but he'd keep that info to himself for the time being. "You wouldn't happen to have a floodlight to illuminate your driveway?"

She nodded. "It's got an automatic sensor. I'll set it on the constant mode." Tia grabbed her purse and locked the door on their way out.

Flynn limped in discomfort, and Ethan picked him up and carried him to the back seat of the truck. As they pulled away, he turned to Tia. "You said you gave the cop your license and registration. We should dust them for prints as well. Maybe later I'll run them to the station."

Tia gave him a deer-in-headlights kind of look. "Would you mind turning on the inside light?" Methodically rummaging through her purse, she murmured, "I never got them back. Oh no . . . that cop guy still has them."

Ethan nodded slowly and turned onto Route 90. "No problem." But hey, it was a huge complication because now, the guy had her address.

19

───────

Vince shoved his swollen, aching hand into an ice bucket and cursed. What were the odds? What were the odds of him stopping, of all the people in this sleepy county, that one redheaded lady cop on a country road? And what were the odds that she'd have Plante's dog in tow?

He should've killed that thing the same day he'd taken care of the lieutenant. That damn animal had spooked him ever since his first cadet interview. It had been hard enough sitting there in the big office with Plante at the huge desk and him in the little chair while the dog lay right by the window watching his every move.

When Plante asked about his father's name being Jim Beam, that freakin' dog sat up and growled. Plante gave the animal some kind of hand signal, and he lay down again, but the K9 watched everything like a beast eyeing a raw steak on a counter-top. That creature gave him the willies. He hated Margie Plante and her pity, but he hated that dog more. His world would be a safer place once he got rid of it.

The red-haired lady cop must've been driving her personal car, and it didn't have a dashcam. He'd checked. It was a good thing, too, because he would've had to kill her right then. Killing on the fly was not smart. Too many things could go wrong when acting on impulse. He'd planned Plante's death for weeks. But that dog? Next time he saw it, it was going down whether he had a plan or not.

He tossed the redhead's license on the little table. It was hard to believe she was a cop. She sure didn't act like one. He'd waited for her to pull a service weapon on him during the traffic stop, but she never had. She'd been just as shook up as he'd been. It had never occurred to him before now, but maybe she wasn't a cop? He flicked a blade of grass off his shirt. It didn't matter. She had Plante's dog, so she worked with the cops one way or another.

Once he finished moving, he'd take care of the dog. It'd be easier now that he knew where the animal lived. He'd watch for a while, get a sense of the redhead's routines. That way, he could take the both of them when they were unaware.

MIKE STOOD and rubbed his chin after examining Flynn in the lobby of Bayside Animal Hospital. "You probably don't want to hear this, but I should anesthetize him. I already know he won't let me trim his claws. Plus, I need to get inside his mouth and see how many teeth were damaged."

Tia got down on one knee and stroked Flynn's fur. "Okay. Do whatever you need to so he feels better."

"Look, you two. Flynn's injuries are consistent with animal abuse. What happened?"

Ethan widened his stance. "Flynn was working when he sustained these injuries."

"Working as in rendering assistance as a K9?"

"Exactly. He had a run-in with a suspect."

Mike nodded. "Okay. I believe you, but just in case, will your boss back you up?"

"Of course. I'll leave a business card."

"Please understand, Detective, I'm required to fill out reports. Sometimes I get questioned; other times I don't."

Tia handed Flynn's leash to Mike. "I'd like to stay with him."

"Honestly, there's no need for that. Go enjoy the rest of your evening. He's comfortable with me, and though he is injured, it's nothing life-threatening. I'll take him right back and get started. As long as the X-rays don't show any extensive damage, I'll put him under and fix him right up. Casey's on her way back to help out. I'll call you later. Plan on picking him up tomorrow, say midafternoon."

Concern creased Tia's brow. "Okay. We appreciate your help." She stroked Flynn's fur a couple of times and turned to leave. "Hey, Mike, one question . . . there's a laundry chute in my house, and Flynn hates the thing. He's afraid of it, doesn't want me near it. Do you have any idea why?"

Mike thought a moment. "The only explanation I can offer you is that he was shot in a dark sewer tunnel, and Margie took a beatdown in the same tunnel while chasing drug suspects. It's the bullet that gave him the limp he has today. Other than that, I wouldn't know."

Ethan held the door for her. "You know, T, maybe consider staying at your mom's or Carson's for the next few days."

"It breaks my heart to leave him here again." Tia swiped at her cheek. "Why should I stay with my mother?"

"Because the guy who stopped you has your address, and Flynn's laid up and can't protect you, and I need to go back to work." Damn if Mac hadn't been lighting up the Sanctuary burner phone in his pocket every minute or two, which could only mean one thing. They were going ahead with the mission tonight.

"First off, I'm a grown-ass woman and well equipped to take care of myself. Secondly, and this may be a news flash for you, but my mother and Carson live together. Talk about getting tag teamed. There's no way I'm spending the night there. I love them both, but I'm capable of handling this on my own, even if it does make me a little nervous." She strode to the passenger side of his truck and climbed inside.

He stood outside the vehicle a moment checking the texts on his burner. He'd been right. His Sanctuary unit was on the move. He texted Mac.

Got a witness needing protection. I'm not available.

Mac replied.

Yup, I heard the whole convo. Feds will sit on her house all night.

One side of Ethan's mouth quirked up.

That's some sensitive equipment you're sporting.

Mac fired back.

Uncle Sam's a badass. Get moving.

Ethan hopped in the truck. "You sure you're okay being alone tonight?"

"I'll be fine. Got a date with a frozen pizza and a big stack of tests to grade. Flynn'll be pissed he missed pizza night. Last week he loved the crusty bones."

"Maybe leave the floodlight lit in the driveway."

"Yeah." She sighed wistfully. "Poor Flynn. The big dog in the sky needs to cut him a break."

Ethan smiled. "Let's be thankful he didn't cross the rainbow bridge."

Tia laughed a little and shook her head. "You're something. I hardly ever meet a person who's on the same wavelength as me. My friends Mo and Sarah understand me, but they're about the only ones. You really ought to meet Sarah, Ethan . . ."

"Don't." He didn't apologize for sounding harsh this time.

She turned to face him. "Why not? She's very nice and pretty, too. And you're a decent guy, a good dog daddy, a respected sworn officer."

"I'll find my own woman when I'm ready." And he was still chewing this over in his head, but if anyone could motivate him to cancel his self-imposed moratorium on serious relationships, it was the woman sitting next to him.

Tia snickered. "Yeah, right. Sometimes you have to try more than once to get a good fit."

He stopped at a red light and gazed at her speculatively. "Do you hear yourself? Are you ready to try again after whatever the hell you went through?"

She lifted her chin and stared out the window. "I've got a lot more to fix than you do. And there are some things I can't magically erase. I've just gotta live with them."

Twisting the thin leather strap of her purse between two fingers, she murmured, "I guess I'm a little like Flynn . . . at least I didn't cross the rainbow bridge trying to get out of the situation I got into."

Ethan pulled into her driveway and parked.

Tia grabbed her things and jumped out. "Thanks for helping me today. Flynn thanks you, too. You don't need to come in. I've got it."

He flung open his truck door. "I'm coming in. It's not up for discussion. You stay in the kitchen while I clear the house. Then I'll leave."

She rubbed her forehead with a finger. "Okay, if you insist."

"While you're in an agreeable state of mind, and because you won't stay with your mom and Carson, would you consider sharing phone locations with me?"

She rolled her eyes. "Is that really necessary?"

"You're on your own tonight without Flynn. And if you need something—anything—we can find each other quickly."

"For heaven's sake, I'll be fine." She smoothed the hair off her face. "But I do understand your concern, because that creep has my license, so okay, I'll share my location with you as long as you reciprocate. And it's temporary, until Lieutenant Plante's killer is caught."

"Agreed. Thank you."

He cleared the house, sent her a share location request, and spied her phone on the hallway credenza. She'd probably get busy and forget to accept it. Grabbing the phone, he swiped at her screen, tapped twice, and approved it on her behalf. There. All done. He locked the door behind him as she placed a frozen pizza in the oven.

What on earth had happened to her? It had to be a matter of public record. He could look her up in the system and find out every sordid detail.

But after getting to know her a bit, he didn't want to invade her privacy by reading the CliffsNotes. No, he'd wait. Maybe one of these days she'd open up about it on her own.

He drove by the Feds near her house and gave them a two-finger salute. Tia wouldn't be crossing any rainbow bridges tonight. They'd make sure she stayed safe.

20

Ethan rubbed the temporary-hair-color gel into his crew cut and slicked it back with a comb. His usual light brown instantly turned almost black. It'd do. He lathered his face and proceeded to shave his beard and mustache. Easy come, easy go. They would grow back. Tonight, he couldn't look like himself.

He was one of four men in the Sanctuary locker room transforming themselves into someone new. Crisp tuxedos hung in a neat row on a clothing rack above complementing wing tips. They'd used this chameleon smoke-and-mirrors routine many times before. At least tonight he didn't need to endure a new nose affixed or contend with prosthetics in his mouth to change the shape of his jaw. This job required simple hair color, contacts, eyebrows, and a clean-shaven face. He was down with that.

Mac stepped to the center of the room already wearing his wino getup. Because Mac's past included way too many glossies on magazine covers, he always dressed as a local drunk, nondescript and harmless. Few people knew he was the brains behind the Sanctuary missions and, when needed, the eyes behind the sniper rifle. Mac cleared his throat, and the room fell silent.

He held up a spray bottle. "Before I douse myself with this eau de garbáge, I want to go over the details one more time. Ethan and Gus are running point tonight as emissaries of a Russian mafia boss in search of new women for his entertainment. Derek's manning the van and computers. He'll take down the live feed in the club hallway and the loading dock. Beck and Mooney?"

They both raised a finger.

"You're sitting at the bar and will clear the hallway of possible collateral damage when the plan goes down. Try not to look delicious, you two. We wasted a whole minute last time waiting for you to unwind yourselves from the ladies." The locker room broke into catcalls and off-color jokes.

Mac slashed a hand, and the place quieted down. "Our mission this evening is to visit The Pink Owl, owned by one Pavel Romanov, entrepreneur and human trafficker. Mr. Romanov will be our guest until we locate his latest shipment of trafficked women. Our source says he introduces the ten p.m. male strip show every night. Our only occasion to nab him will be in the hallway to his private quarters after the intro. Two Serbian fighters serve as his bodyguards. Expect the unexpected." He looked up from his notes. "We're not playing nice. Sanctuary paid the money for five of Romanov's captures a few hours ago. Our job is to find those women and make sure they get their lives back. We've practiced the logistics for this a dozen times. Our federal contact at The Pink Owl wants out. Gus and Ethan will make sure said contact is clean and extract her." His eyes roved the crowd. "Any questions?"

The room remained silent. "Remember the rules of engagement tonight. No live bullets unless absolutely necessary. Let the Feds use their firepower if needed. You are *all* equipped with alternative protection. Ten minutes and we move out."

Ethan touched the gel on his hair. It had dried. In the next few minutes, he put on his tux, taking care that the tie aligned perfectly. This evening, as emissary for a Russian mafia boss, he pretended to have enough purchasing power in his wallet to buy human lives. There wouldn't be one relaxed feature on him. This mission was strictly business, ruthless, and all in Russian. Gus was a former Russian national who spoke with a perfect Moscow accent. Ethan had learned Russian in school, and on his best day, his American was still detectable. But he and Gus had carved deals in Russian many times before, tossing the negotiations back and forth, achieving the desired results.

He checked himself in the mirror and stared into the emotionless deep-brown eyes of a man far more ruthless than himself. Breathing deep, he tucked the private invitation to the club into his breast pocket. It was showtime.

They slipped into a gleaming black stretch limousine, wordless and focused. Each man peered through his tinted window as the calm green lushness of a suburb morphed into the strident, loud boasting of Philadelphia traffic and neon signs.

The double line of women seeking entrance to the club commenced three blocks before they pulled to a stop. Tickets for the ten o'clock show started at one hundred fifty dollars, while stage-front admission cost three hundred apiece. Their chauffeur parked at the front entrance and opened their door. Women of all ages started screaming, "The strippers are here."

Gus slid out first and gave the ladies a polite nod. Ethan followed and flashed them his most killer smile. A bouncer efficiently checked their tickets and held the door for them. A second bouncer roughly removed a woman clinging to Ethan's side and abruptly shut the door in her face.

They were in. He could only hope it would go as smoothly when they wanted out.

～

IT COULD HAVE BEEN any other nightclub—except this was a front for human trafficking. The Pink Owl was a virtual sea of pub tables and leather chairs, with a large dance floor in the middle. Red velvet roping cordoned off the front VIP area and looming stage. The waitstaff were all men in bow ties. Part of the allure of this place was that a stripper could be any man in attendance, thus the scene at the front door when they'd exited their limo.

A maître d' greeted them in a posh marble-floored lobby laden with nude sculptures. After checking their invitations and recording their names, he summoned security. They were frisked and wanded. Ethan smiled inside—security couldn't detect the full syringes in his hidden pocket and didn't pick up his tiny earpiece.

A stunningly beautiful blonde attendant appeared from the shadows and led them to an opulent private lounge.

"May I fix you gentlemen a drink, yes?" Her Russian accent was warm and seductive.

Ethan gave her a curt nod while Gus monitored her every move from under heavy eyebrows.

"I suggest our smoothest Courvoisier, from Mr. Romanov's home in Jarnac, France."

Ethan dipped his chin. She'd spoken the first of three phrases required for them to know beyond a shadow of a doubt that she was the contact wanting out. "That will be fine." He turned slowly. "Is your kitchen serving food?"

"Certainly, sir. A tidbit plate, perhaps?"

And there was the second code.

Gus cleared his throat. "I'm craving fine caviar."

She smiled. "We have Bemka Crown."

And that was the third. "Very well," Gus agreed. The woman left the room to put in their order.

Ethan drummed his fingers on the shiny mahogany table. So

she was the federal agent who'd been feeding them intel for the past three months and had positioned herself as Romanov's supposed best girl? The woman had balls of steel, riding this assignment that long. Although she'd gotten one word wrong in the code, and that could cost her dearly later.

He glanced at the muted closed-circuit screen provided for their entertainment. While he couldn't hear the music, a steady beat pulsed through the floor. A second monitor panned the bar and the dancing crowd. As per usual, Beck and Mooney had innocuously draped themselves in women at opposite ends of the bar. Ethan knew better than to think they were having fun. They were working.

The same server whisked through the door with their food and set it on the table. Neither he nor Gus had taken a sip of his drink. Likewise with the food. An accidental poisoning was out of the question tonight. Suffice it to say, they both swirled and stirred at proper intervals for anyone who might be watching them on the in-house security screens to think they were partaking.

The frenzied female crowd clapped thunderously on the monitor. Romanov strode onto the main stage with his arms wide open and his hips grinding in time to the music. He was quite the showman in his glittery formal wear. *Enjoy it, man.* Tonight would be the last time Romanov would wear a nice getup. As long as their mission was successful, the trendy orange of an inmate uniform would comprise his attire tomorrow.

"Gentlemen, would you like to watch the show from the hallway behind the stage? I can escort you," their server said. Damn if her throaty Russian accent wasn't a thing of beauty.

Ethan nodded as Mac assured them through their earpieces that the hallway cameras were down. With a gentle twist of his wrist and a shake, a syringe eased from the hidden pocket in the fold of his cuff into his palm. He relaxed a fraction knowing he was armed.

He and Gus followed the woman down the hallway. She was a temptress all right, with her swaying heart-shaped hips. *Hmm ... Tia has better legs though.*

What the hell? He mercilessly fought off any thought of Tia as they rounded a corner to stage left and into the raised-eyebrow glare of Romanov's bodyguards, who motioned for them to stop.

Ethan and Gus spread their arms for the frisking that ensued. The guard assigned to Ethan patted him down with extra concern at the dip of his trousers. When the beast grabbed his nuts, Ethan tapped the guy's neck with the teeny syringe. "Enough. I'm here to conduct business with your boss, not to pleasure you." He took a step back and straightened his lapel.

The bodyguard squinted his black eyes, aiming a thumb at his chest. "I say when I'm done." The contents of the syringe took effect, and he crumpled to the floor with a thud.

Ethan dragged him behind a curtain and left him there.

Gus's bouncer dropped to his knees and fell backward. "Damn, this new stuff is potent shit," Gus noted as he slid the guy behind a row of scaffolding.

Mac chuckled in their ear. "You just gave them the best sleep they've had in years, gentlemen. It's hypoallergenic and won't interact with any medications. The loading-dock cameras are down."

The houselights dimmed as a machine poured theatrical smoke across the stage. Romanov held up his arms. "And now, ladies, for your pleasure, allow me to introduce you to the men of The Pink Owl."

Fire sirens swelled from the speakers, and screams of delight reverberated in the crowded venue. A popular hip-hop song started playing as Ethan peered around the curtain. Several waiters set their trays down, and a dozen strippers filed in from stage right wearing fireman coats. Pull-away cummerbunds, ties, and shirts flew through the air. Ethan snapped his attention back to Romanov, who was heading in their direction. Time to work.

Romanov waved his finger for them to follow him. He wheeled around in the hallway and shut the stage door. "You are here to negotiate, gentlemen?"

"The negotiations are done, Mr. Romanov. We agreed on the terms of sale yesterday. The money has been paid," Gus retorted in Russian.

"I have received much finer merchandise today, but it will cost you. We'll speak in my office." Romanov headed down the hallway but slowed and turned as he shoved a hand into his pocket. His beady eyes searched their faces. "Where are Oleg and Boris?"

Conversation over. Ethan moved like lightning and struck a neck and wrist pressure point, bringing the man to his knees. Gus ripped a piece of duct tape from the inside of his tux and covered Romanov's mouth, and Ethan zip-tied his wrists together. They each slid an arm under the guy's shoulders and dragged him kicking and resisting through the exit where the van waited for them. They handed him over to Derek and Mac and went back inside to extract their server, the Feds' confirmed contact.

Gus muttered, "She got one word wrong in the code."

"I noticed. I'll vet her one more time. Let's try the office," Ethan said.

As they rounded the corner, they came face-to-face with a bouncer holding their server at gunpoint. "You make one move, and I kill her. I found her rifling through the boss's office and loading his personal things into her purse. She's one of you, huh?"

Ethan and Gus glanced at each other. This kind of annoying snafu tossed a mission timeline out the window. Judging by a second glance down the hallway, they would only have to entertain the bouncer for maybe twenty seconds.

Gus rubbed his hands together and raised an eyebrow. "You'll never get a chance to use that gun on her."

"You doubt me? Take one step in this direction, and she's gone."

"Mr. Romanov is waiting. I suggest you hand her over."

"Yeah, right. Looked to me like she's a part of whatever's going down here. Nobody takes Romanov's phone and lives to tell about it." A bead of sweat trickled down the side of his pockmarked face. "What'd you do to the boss? Where is he?" He jammed the nose of his gun into the girl's temple.

"He's waiting for us in the limo. We're business partners."

"I don't believe you. I found Oleg passed out in the backstage area. He always accompanies the boss on outside deals."

Gus held up his hands. "Not this time—our rules."

Ethan smirked. "Hey, buddy. Do you have eyes in the back of your head?"

The guy frowned. "What? You cracking jokes now?"

Beck came up from behind and tapped a syringe into the bouncer's neck as Mooney yanked the man's hand upward and the gun clattered to the ground. The bouncer swung at them before sliding to the floor, clearly out of the conversation.

Gus zip-tied their server's wrists and rushed her down the long hallway to the exit door. "I look forward to finding out who you are, beautiful. Your Russian is impeccable, but you missed a code word."

Ethan grabbed the server's purse and raised an eyebrow at Mooney and Beck. "You guys were right on time."

"Lots of practice, dude." Mooney glanced at his watch. "Nice job sweet-talking the goon while we walked up behind him." He and Beck turned left into Romanov's office.

Ethan flung open the loading-dock door. Mac and Derek had already loaded Romanov into the waiting limo. Gus handed the server to Mac. Mooney and Beck jogged down the hallway, their arms loaded with computers and hard drives. Ethan held the door for them as the erotic pulse of strip music reverberated behind them.

Beck and Mooney quickly filed into the van with Mac, shut the door, and sped off into the night.

Derek reactivated the cameras and the alarm they'd turned off. "Alarm system is active again" echoed in their earpieces.

Ethan and Gus slid into the limo, where Romanov and their server sat strapped to seats opposite each other with black sacks on their heads. The limo rolled smoothly into the night toward a prearranged rural location.

21

———

Once the limo reached its destination, Gus poured a glass of sparkling water and downed a quick sip. He yanked the bag from Romanov's head and ripped the tape off his mouth. He retrieved a Glock from under the seat and set it on the center console. Glaring at the scumbag, Gus spoke in the precise cadence of a Russian mafia boss. "Pavel, my friend, you have the power to right this business deal." He leveled a cold stare at the sweating man, leaned back in his seat, and steepled his fingers. "My boss wants five new playmates, and I will get them for him. I paid you this afternoon. No. More. Money." He yanked the tape from Romanov's mouth and aimed his gun at the server's head. "Where are the girls?"

Romanov squirmed in his seat, pulling at the restraints holding his forearms to the armrests. "I have never been treated so poorly. Let her go, and I will tell you."

An eerie half smile crossed Gus's lips. "You are mistaken. We are not in the negotiation phase. I ask the questions, and you give the answers. It's that simple." He pulled the bag and tape off the server's mouth. "Where are the girls?"

"I—I don't know," she stammered.

Gus waved the gun between the two of them. "At least one of you knows the location of the five women who belong to my boss. I suggest you cough it up before I'm forced to employ more drastic measures."

Romanov dipped his chin. "Let her go. She doesn't know anything."

Gus chuckled. "How can I be sure? Pillow talk tempts a man to betray confidences."

Romanov spat across the aisle, staining Gus's lapel. "I don't discuss business with my women. Ever."

Gus shook his head. "Tsk, tsk. What a shame for her." He handed the gun to Ethan. "Take care of her."

Ethan pulled the server from her seat. He flung open the limo door and hauled her behind him.

Wild-eyed and panicked, she spun around. "Tell them, Pavel. You promised you'd take care of me. Tell them."

The bound man shrugged a shoulder and looked away. "I can't. They will kill me."

"They'll kill you anyway, you son of a bitch. Tell them," she shrieked as Ethan dragged her to the other side of the road. "Tell them, Pavel, please, please, I'm begging you. If you have any feelings for me, tell them."

Ethan guided her toward the woods.

They'd walked maybe ten yards when the server turned and yelled, "I hope you rot in hell, Pavel. I'll tell them everything I know before I'll die for you. I promise." She tripped and fell to her knees.

Ethan pulled her up, nudging her in the back with the gun. "Keep walking." He glanced at the sky. It was partly cloudy with a waxing gibbous moon. Too much light. He'd need more distance between them and the limo.

The server dodged right and ran a few steps back toward the road. "Pavel, I know your wife's address and phone number.

Don't you let me die out here." She gave a chilling scream when her foot caught on a tree root and she face-planted on a bed of wet leaves. She rolled over and stared at Ethan. "I hope you're a gentleman and will help me up. That really hurt."

Amused, he smiled. "Enough of the theatrics. We're on a schedule here." He heaved her upright, aimed her in the right direction, and gave a gentle shove. "Move it. The quicker we get to the clearing, the sooner you'll be free."

She trudged forward. "Right. But I'm marching to my supposed death, so there will be a bit of protest." She paused. "I wonder what you look like in real life."

"Nothing special. That I can guarantee."

She let out another scream for effect, coughed, and spat in the leaves. "The muscles under that tux say otherwise. I like muscles."

The hoot of an owl echoed from a tree on their left. "And I like listening to your accent, but I doubt I'll hear it again."

"What's your real name, big boy? Perhaps we'll get together so I can feel your muscles and you can listen to my Russian."

Ethan gave a wry laugh. "Are you always like this?"

"Always. The direct approach works for me."

"You missed a word in the code. Which word was it?"

"Ah, I'm glad you asked. Otherwise, I'd be expecting a double cross."

"Which word was it?" He really didn't want to use his last syringe on her and turn her over to the authorities.

"We have Bemka Crown, *sir*."

Perfect. He glanced ahead, picked a spot, and cut the zip tie on her hands. "Walk twenty paces and turn around."

"You want me to scream again?"

"If you've got it in you, go for it."

She pulled away from him and stumbled forward with a piercing scream that shattered the forest. The trees rustled, and startled birds took flight. Turning around to face him, she walked backward.

"Pavel's wife's name is Nadia. His kids' names are under her contact in his phone. The access code to his phone is one-three-five-seven-nine-two. Repeat the code to me."

"One-three-five-seven-nine-two." He aimed the gun at her.

"For God's sake, you've got that thing trained on my head."

"I'm aiming slightly to the right. Make sure you fall to your right. They're blanks."

"How good of a shot are you?"

"Number one in my class, lady. On three. One. Two." The crack of the gun sent the forest wildlife into a flurry as the server feigned falling limp to the ground. Ethan shoved the firearm into his pocket. "Don't. Move. Your extraction team will pick you up as soon as we drive away. Have a good life. Maybe take a vacation."

"My name is Lana. We'll meet again, muscle man."

Ethan said nothing, turned, and quietly made his way back to the road. The only woman he wanted noticing his muscles was Tia, and she was still trying to fix him up with one of her friends. Considering his relationship track record, her lack of interest might be wise. But still . . . even he deserved a second chance at least one time.

Slipping the mask of a cold-blooded killer onto his face, he strode to the limo. The real work of rescuing those trafficked women began now.

22

———

Tia shoved aside the lap desk she was using to correct papers on the couch and jumped up. Mo's ringtone chimed close by. She ran for the credenza in the hallway.

Tapping the speakerphone button, she shouted, "Girl, you won't believe what happened today."

"Well, hello to you, too. Sorry it's so late, but the treadmills at the gym were booked, and I took a Pilates class instead."

"No worries. I'm glad to hear your voice."

"Same here. What happened? I hope it was something good."

Tia plopped into a chair and crossed her legs, instantly regretting the move because of the sore spots from Flynn's nails. "A cop stopped me out on Holly Knoll Road, and Flynn decided he didn't like the guy, leaped on top of me in the front seat, and bit the guy's hand. The cop hit Flynn with his baton, and now my sweet dog is back at Bayside for yet another overnight stay. The vet needs to trim his broken claws, x-ray his mouth, and fix any dental damage."

"What? Oh, that poor animal," Mo groaned.

"I know. My heart breaks for him. No dog's life should be this hard. When I got home after the traffic stop, I asked Ethan to get Flynn out of the car because he wasn't listening to my commands."

"That's not good. Why wouldn't Flynn listen to you?"

"Ethan thinks he went into K9 mode to protect me, as if he were working."

"Protect you from a traffic stop?"

"There was something he didn't like about that cop. Ethan said Flynn felt threatened."

There was a long pause. "Wait, who's Ethan? A new neighbor I haven't met?"

"You know, Flynn's other guardian. Detective Kelley."

Mo gasped. "The cop from the ride along?"

Tia grabbed a potato chip from a bag she'd opened earlier and munched. "Yes, him."

"Oh my goodness. The cop who brought you coffee and ordered Thai and bought you that pretty red coffeepot? The kid from the beach bonfire when you were a teenager and the guy you want to fix up with Sarah from your school?"

"He won't let me arrange a blind date so they can meet, but yeah, that's him."

"I never put it all together that he's the guy you're sharing Flynn with. So, Ethan is Detective Kelley and the kid you made out with at the party?"

The chips were just what the salt craving ordered. Tia reached for another. "Uh-huh."

"Last I knew, you couldn't stand him and called him a founding member of the modern patriarchal resurgence."

Tia leaned back against the couch cushions. "Hmm . . . that was harsh. The overbearing men in my life are annoying, but they're just trying to help."

"I can understand Carson's concern after what you've been through the past couple of years."

She sighed. "Me too, I'm just tired of it."

"So when did you and Ethan switch to first names?"

Tia cocked her head and thought for a few seconds. "It's a lot easier to call him Ethan than Detective Kelley. That's two syllables versus five, you know?" She stuffed her hand into the chip bag again.

Mo laughed. "I'm just shocked, that's all. I'm glad you have a friend."

Tia's chip-laden fingers froze midair. *Are Ethan and I friends now?* The first-name thing had happened so organically. Come to think of it, he had called her Tia weeks ago, but when had she started calling him Ethan? Oh, wow, she'd really let her guard down and broken rule number one—stay polite and aloof. When had that happened? It hadn't been the morning he'd brought coffee. She smoothed her forehead with a finger. And it hadn't been the time he'd ordered Thai food. It most certainly hadn't been the day he'd intimated those things about her pajamas in the school office.

Tia bolted upright, planting her feet on the floor. *It'd been the day he'd dropped off the coffeepot.* He'd signed the little gift card "My apologies, Ethan." She shook her head with horror. Man pitfalls were everywhere, and she'd fallen into one of them. She'd even been stupid enough to kiss him.

Mo's alarmed voice shimmered into her thoughts. "Honey, are you still there?"

Huh? She threw the chips into the bag and stammered, "Omigosh Mo, I let Detective Kelley clean Flynn's nail marks on my back with my shirt off."

"You really took off your shirt?"

"Yeah, but I wore a halter swimsuit cover-up on my front."

"I remember you telling me he saw a lot more than your back at that bonfire back in high school."

Tia lowered her voice to a whisper. "Right. But that was

before I had the scar. I was, like, sixteen. My body was perfect back then."

"For heaven's sake, I wear less than a cover-up at the gym. It isn't like you dragged him to the floor and jumped his bones."

Tia paced the main floor. "Well, I did kiss him in the garden just to prove there was nothing between us. Boy, was I wrong."

"What? Seriously?"

"I told him it was like kissing a brother, but I lied. He completely unnerves me, Mo. He's an amazing kisser, kind of takes my breath away. And he's such a nice guy. This is serious. I promised myself I wouldn't get involved with anyone for a long time."

"You're not involved, Tia. You kissed him once and received medical attention from a cop. There's no need to alert the authorities that you're a fallen woman."

"You don't understand. He came with me to the vet earlier, and I let him drive. He cleared my house when we got home because they still haven't found Margie Plante's killer. I look forward to seeing him, and sometimes I find myself gazing at him and wondering . . . things. I don't think I want to fix him up with Sarah anymore."

"Ooh. Well, the first part is all typical cop stuff. It's normal, and considering he's Flynn's other half, you have to deal with him sometimes. He must be something special if he's caught your attention. Maybe don't overthink it."

Hot embarrassment ricocheted from Tia's chest to her cheeks. She set the phone on the kitchen counter and braced herself on her elbows. "And I teased him about his muscles."

Mo sputtered on a laugh. "Really?"

Tia shook her head. "Yeah. He asked me for a description of the cop who stopped me, and I compared his muscles to the other guy's. Ethan is beautiful to look at. I'm not usually so shallow, but he's hot."

"Oh. Wow."

"I told him I wasn't blind, but keeping my distance, and we laughed about it."

"Did it feel good to have a normal conversation, T?"

"That's not important. Ethan is a detective. A. Detective. Mo. What was I thinking? If I were to get involved with someone, I surely wouldn't pick another detective."

"Because of Brent."

"Of course," Tia muttered.

"Sometimes, you can't control who comes into your life. Circumstances tossed you together again, and I see what you're saying about the detective part, but Brent was a dirty cop, and you were one of his victims."

Tia pulled aside the white lace curtain and glanced out the window. There was an unmarked police car in her driveway and two people dusting her Kia hood for fingerprints. She shook her head. "I hate the word victim."

"I don't blame you."

"I refuse to ever be a victim again."

"Good for you. You deserve better than what you got. Don't ever forget that I'm on your side, okay?"

"Thanks. I don't know what I would've done without you these past two years."

"You would've handled it with the same grace and tenacity, my friend. Have you been in touch with my mother's plastic surgeon yet?"

"No. I'm thinking about getting a tattoo instead. Maybe the artist can use the long scar as a flower vine or something. I've been browsing designs online."

"That's an idea. You wouldn't need the grafting surgeries if you made it part of a tattoo."

"My thoughts exactly. It might be a great accessory for my

new badass self. Maybe when I decide to date again in five years, I'll hook up with a biker and get leathers, too."

Mo howled with laughter. "That's a positive mental picture if I ever heard one. But seriously, hon, you've always been a badass."

"No, I haven't. I was sweet and innocent and naïve, and a trusting idiot. And because of that, I'm wearing turtlenecks and button ups every day of my life and have spent months in therapy."

Mo groaned. "Don't go there, T. After the surgery or the tattoo, or even if you decide to do nothing at all, when you're comfortable with your body again, we'll get dressed up and go out for a night on the town like we used to. We should do it soon. Maybe one of those bayside bars with a live band."

Tia sighed. "I like that idea. I'm tired of drinking a glass of wine all by myself."

"You want some company this weekend? I'm free."

"I wish I could, but third-quarter grades are due next week, and I've got a lot to do."

"All right, a rain check, then. And Tia?"

"Yes?"

"Don't freak out when we get off the phone about getting to know Ethan. It's a healthy step in your healing journey, and it's nice to hear you smile again."

"I won't flip out, but I can feel my guard slipping where he's concerned."

"Relax, breathe, do some yoga. Maybe it's time to start mingling again. Enjoy the relationship."

"Yeah, I guess. I'm pretty sure he views me as part of his job."

"Well"—Mo drew in a deep breath—"it's had a positive effect on you. We'll talk soon?"

"You bet. Later this week."

Tia put her phone on the charger and considered the crime-scene duo cleaning the hood of her car. A rather tall woman closed what from a distance appeared to be a metal box. Hopefully, the results would yield a fingerprint for one of Ethan's cases.

Mo was right. She should chill out about Ethan being a detective. It wasn't his fault her ex had been one, too.

23

Ethan slid into the limo, rapping twice on the glass separating their Sanctuary driver from the back. The vehicle eased onto the country road and slowly pulled away. He glanced at Gus and nodded. The second he settled back into his seat, he sensed a stalemate in the negotiations.

Gus waved a finger in admonishment. "That was a terrible waste of a young woman's life." He tossed Romanov's phone to Ethan. "Find me the wife's number. This idiot here is being most uncooperative."

Ethan scrolled Romanov's contacts, most of whom were women. Nadia's name had a little house icon next to it. He opened the contact and handed the phone to Gus. "Her name is Nadia. She's at home with Aleksandr, his son, and Mariya, his daughter. The eldest daughter, Polina, is a junior in college nearby. Shall we pick her up first?"

The panicked flicker in Romanov's eyes told him his information was spot-on.

Gus gave an evil chuckle. "No, we'll save Polina for last and bring her to the boss as a special present. Let's see what Romanov's wife has to say about him." With an exaggerated flair of his fingers, he tapped Nadia's phone number. Romanov remained stoic, but the sweat pouring down his face spoke volumes.

A woman answered the phone in a burst of screaming Russian fury. "Pavel, there are men outside and two waiting in the foyer. What are they doing here? None of our guards are answering their phones."

Ethan shook his head. The last time he'd heard a woman that upset was when he'd had a last-minute Sanctuary rescue on his wedding anniversary. He'd returned home to find a blanket and pillows on the couch. He found out later that that night was only one of the many times he'd disappointed his spouse. She had a list—a really long list—of infractions pertaining to him. Lesson learned. Marriage wasn't for everybody . . . especially his ex.

Pavel leaned as far forward as his tethers would allow and addressed Gus. "You hurt my family, and I will kill you."

Gus shrugged. "Where are the women we purchased?"

"You want a gang war? I'll give you one. I have friends in high places who'll squash you like a dirty cockroach."

Gus raised his eyebrows. "Where are the women?" With the iciness of a chilled summer Chablis, he examined his nails and cracked a tight smile. "Those men won't leave your house until I tell them to. Where are the women?"

"Give me your word you won't touch my daughter Polina."

"You're not in a position to negotiate, Mr. Romanov. Where are my women?"

The phone line had grown quiet, and Nadia started to weep. "Tell them whatever they want to know, Pavel. I don't know what you've done, but tell them what they want so you can come home to me and Polina stays safe. Please."

Gus disconnected the call. "Where are my women?"

Romanov exhaled a deep breath. "At a campground on the west side."

"Address."

"I don't know. It's off I Ninety-Five. Boris does the driving."

Ethan leaned forward in his seat. "You do realize we'll question your family if you lie to us?" Maybe this guy didn't give a crap about anyone. He'd just allowed one of his employees to supposedly die in the woods.

Mac chimed in via their earpiece. "Tell him we have Polina. She's at a friend's house in Fort Lauderdale."

Ethan pretended to scroll on his phone. He held it up for Gus to see. "They found Polina. She's with a friend in Florida."

"No, stop." Romanov sat up straight.

Good call on Mac's part. Polina was obviously Romanov's Achilles' heel. "Address?"

"I only know the place by sight, no address. They're not at the campground but in a blue warehouse at the south end of the airport. It's easy to find. I'll recognize it."

Ethan rapped once on the bulletproof glass, and it slid open. "South end of the airport." The driver picked up speed and swung onto a ramp for 95 South a few minutes later.

With Romanov stammering directions, the limo wound through the myriad of buildings, cruising to a stop at a dark-blue warehouse. Mac's crew and the Feds had followed their vehicle from a safe distance.

His heavy eyebrows raised, Gus inquired, "This is it?"

"Yes. Your five women are in a produce truck inside. They have red numbers on their backs. Leave the rest of my pretty merchandise alone. Someone comes to take care of them twice a day."

Ethan's stomach clenched at Romanov's words. Women and children weren't merchandise to be stored in a dank truck in a warehouse. What kind of human being did such things to people, women no less? He glanced at Romanov's face and it was a mask of stone.

Gus tapped Ethan's arm. "Go get our women. I'll watch him."

He stepped into the cool night air laced with fumes and breathed deeply. Mac's van hurried from the access road to the warehouse door. It only took a minute and a pair of bolt cutters to gain access to the building and the fruit truck. Mac notified the barrage of Feds, local law enforcement, and medical personnel waiting nearby to take control of the scene.

A few minutes later, Gus stepped out of the limo, turning Romanov over to the FBI.

Romanov's mouth started hurling accusations. "You killed my employee, you bastard. I'll tell them everything."

Ethan snickered. "Go right ahead." Of course, the Feds already knew that he had staged Lana's supposed execution to extract her from Romanov's organization.

Several ambulances pulled in. Two doctors jogged by with medical bags. One of them yelled for stretchers and pointed at the building. "The FBI says there are twenty-one women in there, ages twelve to late twenties. We need more ambulances and a chopper. One of them has lower abdominal pain. She needs immediate evacuation."

Ethan bent over, bracing his hands on his knees. *Twenty-one women.* Maybe he should go inside and help?

No. He wasn't what they needed now. They needed medical attention. And experience had taught him not to look at their faces. Their terrorized expressions stayed with him. It was enough knowing each of them would have the opportunity to go back to their life or build a new one. He'd done his job.

Mac's voice crackled in his earpiece. "This scene belongs to the Feds now. Let's go, gentlemen. A black limo waits across the parking lot to take us to the airport. I, for one, could really use a strong coffee. Move it."

Ethan peered beyond the chaotic bustle of the medics and caught Mac's wave. A gurney rumbled past, transporting a crying woman with red hair. His mind instantly switched to Tia. *Naw, she's fine.* The guys watching her house would make sure of that. He glanced at his watch. 3:37 a.m. One of the things he missed about being in a relationship was talk time after a night like this. Someone to unwind with.

This was one hell of a second job. *Twenty-one women.* One would've made it worth it.

24

—————

*T*ia wrapped the royal-blue cashmere sweater tight like a hug and turned her face to the warm sun. Who were those men waiting by her car? Was her uncle all right? They had to speak with her down at the station. She should leave her car here. She floated into the back seat of the police cruiser.

The precinct loomed like a dark castle, the inside full of somber faces and quiet whispers. No, she didn't want coffee or a lawyer. Was Carson all right? How could she not know? What had she seen?

That interrogator in a room. Yes, she wanted a lawyer. Where were her car keys? And Brent was so angry, waiting for her at home, and screaming at her. She had to go with him. No, no, she didn't. Where was he on Saturday the seventh between 7:00 p.m. and 11:00 p.m.? Was he in trouble?

Brent dragging her to his car. He'd drive. His ranting and raving on Route 301, careening around slow-moving farm equipment. The blur of closed fruit and vegetable stands waiting for summer. His eyes in the rearview mirror pleading with her to understand.

Tia bolted upright on a gasp with her chest fluttering like frightened prey. Grabbing a rosebud-covered pillow, she rocked back and forth on the bed. It was just the dream. She'd survive. It wasn't real. Not this time.

Would her subconscious never forget the vivid details? Tia ran both hands through her hair. Dammit. She hadn't had the nightmare in six months. Why did her subconscious insist on reliving that horrible event at night?

It would fade with time. But right now? She remembered everything. The red light. The black semi swerving into a jack-knife, always in slow motion. Their car spinning out of control, flipping, bouncing, and the thud of glass and metal. How her head had hit the roof and the floor over and over again. There was that hideous scraping when it had screeched to a stop, and she couldn't move. She'd slept and had woken searching for air, as if swimming to the surface of a pond.

She'd never forget how the firefighters had apologized for hurting her, and the other firefighter asking her to stay with him. They'd get her out. They promised. And then, there was the unbearable burning in her chest, and equipment resembling oversize garden shears.

Oh, how the sleep had tugged at her eyelids. There were people yelling and running and a ferocious wind that morphed into a helicopter.

She still couldn't process that Brent had turned out to be a dirty cop. How was she supposed to know? They'd dated for several years but in reality only spent weekends together, and she had no idea where he'd been on such and such a date at a particular time. All she knew was he always showed up with a smile and flowers, every week without fail. And she'd believed everything he'd said until that day.

Tia choked out a bitter laugh. It still hurt that during the interrogation, she'd just known that Carson was behind the two-way glass. He'd had to be there that night because Brent was a dirty cop in his precinct, and his niece's betrothed.

They'd promised not to prosecute her if she told them what she knew, but she didn't know a damn thing. That was the kicker. How gullible was she to not know anything? How many times had Brent lied to her? She'd never know the answer.

There were no feelings left for her former fiancé. They'd died the minute he'd thrown her into his car, forever changing her life. The selfish bastard hadn't been there to help her handle the police interviews, the surgeries, the trauma, the scar that ran the length of her torso, and the relentless questions from the press. Thank goodness for her mother and Yolanda and Mo.

Tia glanced at the self-defense certificates on her wall. She was prepared if there was a next time.

She and Mo had briefly discussed Brent earlier. Maybe that was why the memories had resurfaced in a dream? She'd worked so hard with this new kick-ass therapist and had gotten very good at replacing negative thoughts with positive, powerful affirmations. Tia grabbed her phone and texted Mo.

We can't discuss the B person ever again. Had the nightmare. xo

Mo texted back a minute later.

I'm so sorry. I'm up now and packing. I'll be there in a few hours.

Tia shook her head and forced her trembling fingers to move.

No. I can handle it. Stay there. If I need you, I'll call. Go back to sleep.

Tia crawled out of bed, forcing herself to stand on shaky knees. Still holding the pillow for comfort, she let the night-light guide her as she hobbled to the bathroom and started the shower. The crash injuries hurt like hell after every nightmare, almost as if the event had just happened. But experience had taught her that the aches would subside as she moved. The hardest part was shaking off the aura of foreboding, but light always helped.

Lamp by lamp, she illuminated the house, flooding it with

brightness. She glanced out the kitchen window and flipped the outdoor lights on, including the front porch duo. It was three forty-five a.m. for heaven's sake. But after trembling in a steaming hot twenty-minute shower to warm up and then brewing a pot of coffee, Tia sat down at the kitchen table to read.

There'd be no going back to bed. Not after that.

25

———

Ethan took several boxes of doughnuts from the lady with dark circles under her eyes and smiled. "Thanks for being open all night." He forked over a twenty-dollar bill as a tip, and her face brightened. He handed all but one marked box to Mac in the back of the limo, then bit into a doughnut from his box, savored, and closed his eyes. *So good.* Holding up the jelly stick, he admired its slightly crunchy outside and tender inside with strawberry filling.

Mac tapped him on the shoulder. "What is it with you and these doughnuts? You want to come here every time we're in the area."

Ethan chugged some of his black coffee. "This, my friends, is the best damn doughnut on the east coast. I can't get them at the shore. Jelly sticks are unique to the Philly area. Down where I live, all they have are three kinds of doughnut holes and a couple of way-too-sweet glazed doughnut things. They're not even worth the calories. But these"—he held up a second one —"these are a slightly crusty, fruit-filled treat made for connoisseurs."

Snorts of laughter and comments erupted from the back of

the limo.

Mac tossed out, "That's the same way you like your women, man."

Ethan chuckled as he bit into a raspberry jelly stick. Though not disappointed by the flavor, he'd been hoping for a lemon. And his best friend wasn't far from the truth. He'd always enjoyed women who swam against the tide and mouthed off a little. It kept things . . . fun. Tia was kind of like that, a little bit crusty, but without her bravado? He'd bet she was all jelly inside.

He'd seen glimpses of her softer side the past two weeks with Flynn. Only Flynn. They'd been late for the dog's vet appointment because Flynn hadn't eaten his food one day. *He doesn't like the flavor of the premade meals. It'll only take me a few minutes to fix him some ground lamb, and the rice is already cooked.* And damn if the woman hadn't pulled ground lamb out of the fridge and started browning it. But when he looked in the fridge, the only human food in there was a shriveled-up English muffin and a jar of horseradish. Did she ever really eat?

Eh, he had to stop thinking about her. She had a *No Trespassing* sign wrapped around her psyche, although he was pretty sure Tia had lied about their kiss. But their relationship had evolved into easy conversations and kind gestures. Maybe she was more interested than she let on? They'd both had horrible previous relationships that had ended quite a while ago. Perhaps it was time to let go of past mistakes and move on? He'd hate to miss the woman in front of him because he was so busy scrutinizing the past. And right now? He wanted to be with Tia and couldn't deny the attraction any longer.

Mac leaned forward and handed him his burner phone. "The Feds watching your witness say her house is lit up like the Fourth of July. She's got lights on in every room, the driveway, the backyard, and even the Christmas lights on her deck rails are fired up. Do you want them to go in there and see what's going on?"

Ethan took the phone from Mac and thought a minute. Tia didn't know the Feds were sitting on her house. If they went to the front door, they'd freak her out big-time. He replied by text.

Stay put. Will call her and report back to you.

He tapped Tia's number, hoping she'd answer without recognizing the number. She picked up on the third ring.

"E—Detective, do you know what time it is?"

There was his crusty girl. He glanced at the time and grimaced. 4:20 a.m. "Uh, sorry. I'm just getting off work. Did you ever hear back from Mike about Flynn? Is he all right?"

"Well, aren't you the devoted dog daddy? I heard from Mike around ten p.m. Flynn'll be fine. He had four chipped teeth, which they smoothed out; nothing's broken, and they trimmed his nails. Casey even did a full groom on him since he was asleep, which is pretty cool. When Flynn comes to, he will have had a full mani-pedi and all his dental work completed. I'm a smidge jealous," she laughed.

He nodded with a smile. "Good, good. You sound like you're wide awake."

She hesitated a couple of seconds before answering. "Yeah, well, I couldn't sleep. It was one of those off nights, you know?"

"Is everything okay?"

"Yup. Just fine. Getting an early start to the day."

He glanced at his box of doughnuts. "How would you like to try one of the best doughnuts in the world?"

"Excuse me?"

"I stopped after work and bought some. I've got plenty to share."

"What flavor are they?"

"Assorted, and they're delicious."

"You're tempting me, Detective. And I was thinking about making eggs and bacon."

Now we're talking. "You're kidding me. You shopped?"

She laughed richly. "Sort of. Got a late delivery. I was out of fresh meat for Flynn and added a few things for me into the order. You'll be here in a few minutes?"

He sat up straight. "Um, no. More like an hour."

"An hour?"

"I'm sure of it." He still had a forty-minute chopper ride back to the Eastern Shore.

"All right. I'll trade you one of your special doughnuts for some eggs and bacon. I'll start the bacon in a few minutes."

"I'll be there, T." He could hardly wait to see her.

ETHAN TOOK A FAST SHOWER, and by the time he got to her house, only the main-floor lights were on. They looked kind of pretty against the pastel palette of the upcoming sunrise. She swung the door open wearing pajama bottoms, a blue turtleneck, curly hair, and a spatula. He hadn't known she had curly hair. She must use one of those things to straighten it.

Tia clasped a hand across her mouth. "Oh my goodness, you shaved?"

Oh yeah. He'd forgotten all about it. "I clean up once in a while. It'll grow back soon enough." He'd shaved many times for missions and was used to the abrupt change. But judging by the appraising look on her face, he'd taken her completely off guard. He handed her the box of doughnuts.

She waved him in and hurriedly placed the sweets on an end table. Scrutinizing his face, she pointed her spatula. "I like it."

Her words warmed him on the inside. "Thanks, but I'll grow it back. It helps to have facial hair when I work undercover."

"Suit yourself, but I'm not a fan of the scruff trend. You look good without it." She set the spatula down near the stove and waved her hands around apologetically. "But I understand you'd need it for work. And really, it's none of my business, so just ignore me. Too much coffee, I guess."

Okay. She'd noticed more than his muscles and liked a smooth face. Filing that information away for a later date, he kicked his shoes off by the door. "Everything quiet around here last night?"

A troubled expression flitted across her face. "Yes. It was fine. Missed having Flynn for company, but I'll pick him up later. How'd work go?"

"Great." It wasn't every night he fake assassinated a federal operative and rescued a truckful of young people in the process of being trafficked. "I really like my second job."

She glanced at him while pulling out a frying pan. "I don't know how you do it. Are you saving to buy a boat or something?"

Hardly. "No. My police job is my bread and butter, and pension. My second job is more like my calling, if that makes sense."

"You mean your job with the kids?"

"Yeah." Information about his second job was on a need-to-know basis. Carson and Earl were the only contacts in the department who knew about his work with Sanctuary. But maybe he should add her to the list.

Tia pulled a few things out of the fridge. "That's nice. Working with kids really does it for me, too."

Ethan tapped a finger on the countertop. "Hey, um, I was wondering, why do you refer to Chief Carson by his last name? He's your uncle."

A flash of humor darted across her face. "Yeah, it is unusual. My father and Carson were brothers with the same mother. But they each kept their father's surname. As long as I can remember, they addressed one another as O'Rourke and Carson, and I grew up calling him Uncle Carson. I think it started as some kind of inside joke between brothers." She sighed deeply. "They were best friends until my dad passed away. Carson lost his wife and my dad all in the same year. It was really hard on him, which also explains why he's so fiercely protective of me. He and my aunt never had any children. I'm the kid he never had."

Yeah, that explained a lot of things. "I'm sorry. Maybe I shouldn't have asked, but it struck me as odd."

She waved his apology aside with a quick smile. "No biggie. You had an honest question."

Honest or not, it was time to change the subject. "Looks like you're ready to cook up a storm. How can I help?"

"You can let me taste one of those doughnuts you were bragging on. Is a western omelet okay?"

"Sounds great." He grabbed the box of doughnuts and brought them to the kitchen counter, where she was chopping peppers and onions. "Here, pick one."

"You pick for me. I'm cooking."

He lifted one from the box and held it out to her. "I got an assortment. The filling is always a surprise."

She offered him a timid smile and leaned in for a bite. A little smudge of powdered sugar stuck to her lips as she closed her eyes and chewed. "That is a great doughnut." She pulled his hand in and took a second bite as she poured eggs into a large frying pan. "Lemon, my favorite."

Dragging his eyes away from the powdered sugar on her lips, he turned the jelly stick around. "You got the lemon one?"

"Sure did," she mumbled with her mouth half full. "Why? You like lemon?"

"Affirmative. I ate two jelly sticks looking for a lemon."

"Well, share it with me, Detective. I usually like one bite

from the middle and the crusty end." She loosened the edge of the omelet and raised her eyebrows at him. "Go on. I don't mind. If you eat some of it, then I'll try another one. That's how I get to taste *all* the doughnuts."

He eyed the treat, considering her proposition.

She waggled her eyebrows and gave a throaty chuckle. "C'mon . . . you know you want to."

"You're a schemer, T." He bit into the prized lemon doughnut and sighed with satisfaction.

26

Tia leaned back in her chair and took a deep breath because her stomach hurt from laughing. "The stories of you and Sergeant Thompson during those hell workouts are priceless. Earl has always played it straight around me. I had no idea he was such a prankster."

Ethan nodded. "Oh yeah, Earl is a master at maintaining his poker face. He pulled a prank on my ex a few years ago—" He paused and shook his head. "I don't need to be talking about that right now."

The turmoil rolling across his face was almost palpable whenever he referenced his ex-wife. "Tell me something, Ethan. You don't seem to have any obvious flaws. What happened?" She reached into the box of doughnuts and pulled out another one.

He put his fork down. "You go straight to the heart of the matter, huh?"

She made an offhanded gesture. "It's just that the subject makes you so sad. I've spent some time with a really great therapist, and one thing I've learned is that I've got to get over the fact that I messed up."

He looked straight into her eyes. "Well, I wouldn't leave my career for my ex. That was her final straw. I don't blame her." He picked up a piece of bacon and took a bite. "I worked too much and didn't take care of her social needs."

Tia narrowed her eyes. "Why were you responsible for her social needs?"

"I guess she wanted our life to be like it was when we were dating."

"When did you start dating?"

"We dated on and off through college and then lost touch after graduation until our late twenties, when we got together again."

Tia bit into the side of a doughnut so she could get to the filling faster. "I don't know any adults whose social life is the same as it was in college. I drank and partied all weekend back then." She raised her eyebrows and gave a short laugh. "My third graders would eat me alive if I tried to do that now." Leaning across the table, she held the doughnut to his mouth. "It's peach. You can't say no to peach."

He smirked and took a bite. "I'm not quite sure how my ex and I ended up together. Maybe it was convenience and the desire to settle down. We thought we knew each other pretty well, but as soon as we married, I wasn't what she wanted, or needed. It felt like I was always doing something wrong."

"Like how?"

"Like I detest yard work, so I hired a neighbor kid to mow the lawn and clean up the leaves. It irritated her that I'd waste money hiring the work out. But with my work schedule, I thought it was the most efficient way to get it done."

Tia set her head in her hands. "I'd love to have the money to hire someone to do my lawn so I could have time to fuss with my flowers."

"Yeah, maybe we're alike that way." He forked a bite of omelet. "I disappointed her a lot, and I'm sorry for that. I missed our second anniversary because I was on a work assignment. I certainly didn't go into marriage thinking it would end. There was this one time when I'd just come off an eighteen-hour shift and we met for breakfast. She swore the waitress was flirting with me, and I didn't pick up on it. We argued all weekend over something I didn't even see."

Tia waved her fork at him. "You definitely should've put that waitress in a choke hold before she had a chance to toy with you."

He leaned back and laughed. "I doubt you can make light of the fact that one time, I unknowingly used the last of the coffee. The whole week was ruined after that."

Her eyes grew huge on a gasp. "I agree with her on that one because, as you know, I have to have my caffeine in the morning. Using up the coffee is definitely grounds for divorce. No pun intended." She tapped her finger on the table for emphasis. "Maybe you should've driven tired and let Jesus take the wheel, you insufferable oaf."

His laugh was deep and warm. "It gets worse. I got hurt on the job and needed months to recover. I kept secrets from her. Then I spent my days gaming and drinking. I'm flawed, T. When she left, I was relieved. We were never meant to be together."

Her head popped up. "What kind of secrets?"

He ran a hand through his hair. "She didn't like that I was in law enforcement to begin with, and my second job involves rescuing young people at risk. Both jobs can be dangerous. I stopped telling her anything about my work and basically lied by omission."

His expression grew tight and strained. "My degrees are in forensic accounting, and it was no secret she wanted me behind a desk somewhere, safe and sound." He shrugged. "But I'd wither on the vine with a desk job. I need to be with someone who doesn't object to and can handle my career. It's a part of me.

I was one of those kids who played with his Superman cape and action figures until I was eleven or twelve."

Tia nodded slowly and fought the overwhelming urge to wrap her arms around him. *Whoa, girl.* She had to think before leaping this time. How many divorces had she seen in the police department over the years? Her father was a civilian who had run the 911 call center for decades, and her uncle was a cop. As a kid, she'd heard plenty of discussions over Sunday dinner.

Ethan rested a hand over hers. "The long and short of it is that my ex told me I was a lousy husband, and that crushed me. But it wasn't all her fault. I'd be a tool to say that, and I don't like to criticize her for opting out. That was her choice. It doesn't matter anymore. She remarried a few months after the divorce was final."

Tia's chest squeezed. She hadn't expected him to open up with such candor.

Ethan lifted their plates, set them in the sink, and filled it with hot, sudsy water. He flipped open the box of doughnuts. There were four left. "I'm glad today isn't a hell workout. We polished off six doughnuts. That's impressive."

"It's Saturday morning, and I won't be hungry until tomorrow," she retorted. "We not only ate six doughnuts but also one four-egg omelet apiece and almost a whole pound of bacon." She flung open the dishwasher and started loading.

Ethan reached around and grabbed a soapy sponge to clean the countertops. She held her breath for the few seconds their bodies brushed against each other. When he pulled away, his arm grazed hers. Her skin warmed and tingled.

Tia gazed out her pretty kitchen window with the graceful lace swags. Was she wrong to allow herself the luxury of a man's company after all this time alone? She'd grown a lot in the past couple of years. And acting like she wasn't attracted to Ethan wasn't working anymore. She loved sharing time together, especially after the nightmare. Breakfast was just an excuse to get him here. The heart sharing was a bonus.

She could watch her emotions and keep her guard up for the time being. Right? Maybe he had similar feelings? That would be a scary but good thing. After all, he was the one who'd offered to bring doughnuts over at five thirty in the morning.

The sponge plopped into the suds, and Ethan kissed her cheek. "Thanks for breakfast, T. My grandmother always taught me to kiss the cook." He crossed his arms and leaned against the counter. "You're a million miles away. Whatcha thinking?"

Telling him would make her vulnerable, a feeling she'd avoided at all costs. This was one of those defining moments when sheer timing demanded an answer. She needed to get in or get out. After staring at his mouth for an entire breakfast, she wanted to kiss him again. And one more kiss would be all right. She'd been thinking about it since he'd arrived with that shaved face.

Tia reached over, fisted his shirt with a wet hand, and held her breath. Fear singed the edges of her mind. Did she dare? *Oh, to hell with it.* She just had to know if the kiss in the garden had been a fluke.

She rose up on her toes and kissed his chin. Of course, she'd aimed higher, but he'd moved at the last second, and she'd missed. Even so, he groaned. She was all in now and rested her lips against his. What was she waiting for? Well, close up, his green eyes fascinated. Meadow green. Was there a crayon in the box with that name? As a third-grade teacher, she should know. But she couldn't remember. Anything. At. All. Except three *a*'s in a row was an alliteration. Yeah, she'd covered that in class last week.

Thank goodness he took control.

Brushing the curls from her face, he set his lips on hers and nudged them apart, pulling her into his huge arms. One hand guided her head while the other slid to her waist, sensuously stroking the side of her body. She didn't know which sensation was more erotic, his hands in motion or his mouth coaxing her into a feverish dance of firm lips and gently probing tongues.

Her body simply couldn't remain idle. It had a mind all its own as she pulled him closer and her palms smoothed up his abs and over his chest. And she had to admit, for reasons beyond her, she felt perfectly safe with him. He pulled from her moist lips and kissed a trail of little love bites across her jaw to her ear.

Swooping her up, he sat her ass on the countertop while muttering, "No more height difference, I can touch everything now."

Oh glorious day, don't stop. The sensory overload awakened her soul. Her hands slid up his arms to his hair. His lips returned to her mouth, and she matched him kiss for kiss, the urgency of exploring each other so enticing. The crisp cotton of his shirt smelled like a fresh ocean breeze layered with raw man. The corded muscles in his arms jumped under her touch, and their exquisitely charged passion sent her pulse soaring. *More . . . please.*

Teenage Ethan had been hot, but here and now? This Ethan was powerful enough to bring her to her knees.

His kisses were an art form, an explosive pull and release, a sway and a sigh turned tender. This man was an experience. It had been so long and never this good. Softly breaking the kiss, she inhaled a quick breath.

His lips smiling against hers, he whispered, "I never imagined you tasting like doughnuts."

So he had been thinking about her? Well, then, her turn to take over the kiss. She nipped an earlobe, and his whimper rewarded her. But whoa—what was she doing? Her chest was a road map of violent scars she'd never let him see.

Tipping her chin up, he searched her eyes. His gaze was as

soft as a caress. "If you tell me that what just happened between us was like kissing a brother, I'm going to take you right here on the floor."

Tia gazed at him with amused wonder as she kissed his pecs. "I have a few flaws of my own, you know. I rarely grocery shop and got hurt off the job and needed over a year to recover."

His lips grazed hers, his teeth nipping them this time, leaving a slight sting.

"I have a secret," she whispered, "but no gaming or day drinking. I'm flawed. Like really, really flawed."

He trailed kisses across her cheek. "You're alive and talking to me. It can't be that bad."

She dipped her chin. "Some days, I can't even look in the mirror. It's bad. Like right now, I'd love nothing more than to take this between us to my bedroom. I really want to, but I won't take my shirt off. I can't. Not yet."

Nodding, he framed her face with his hands. "What's your shirt got to do with it?"

She smacked her lips together and winced. "That's my worst flaw. Scars from an auto accident. They're tragic—disfiguring."

He raised her chin with a finger and peered into her eyes. "Scars are just that. Scars. The most unattractive qualities are attitudes." He pulled her in for a hug.

She relaxed into the expanse of his chest, wrapping her arms around him. "I haven't wanted anyone in, like, forever, and I want you in the worst way right now. But I'm not prepared to share my scars—not yet."

He held the embrace and massaged her back. "You can have your way with me when you're ready. It's a trust thing. I get it."

Tia leaned back, peering deep into his eyes. "Haven't you read about me at work or had somebody tell you? Believe me, my bad decision was worse than any of yours."

He held up a finger. "No. I haven't read about your life at

work. I could, but I'd rather hear it from you when you're ready —*if* you ever want to talk about it. That's up to you, your decision." His expression stilled and grew serious. "Where's the guy now?"

"What makes you think a man was involved?"

"Tia, please."

"He's dead. The same auto accident that kept me out of work for over a year and gave me the scars I want to hide. He was a detective and, I found out that night, a dirty cop, too. I think he made a mistake and was blackmailed, because he was crazy with remorse the night he died. I had no idea even though we were engaged."

She startled when his phone vibrated in his pocket.

His big hands kneaded her shoulders as he glanced at the number. "I'm really sorry. I have to get this." Slipping his hand through hers, he traced the sensitive underside of her wrists as he answered the call. "It's Ethan." He kissed Tia's forehead and mumbled, "Uh-huh. Is she all right?"

The voice on the other end sounded rushed, urgent.

"Okay, tell her I'll be there shortly." He disconnected the call, returned to her bottom lip, and savored like she was a delicacy he meant to enjoy. Painstakingly slow. Shaking off the moment, he straightened and cleared his throat. "I gotta go. My grandmother tripped on the stairs."

Tia hopped off the countertop. "Nan?"

He nodded. "Yeah, they think she's okay, but they're taking her to the emergency room to make sure nothing's broken. I want to be there with her."

"Yes, of course. Do you want me to go with you?"

He gave her a quick kiss. "No, thanks for offering, but you're scheduled to pick up Flynn, our other patient."

"Oh yes, right."

Tia swatted his butt. "Then get out of here before I rip off your clothes, climb on top, and ride you like a rodeo queen. I need to think about all this. Please take the sweets. It's harder to think when I feel fat." She shoved his jacket and the leftover doughnuts into his arms.

Halfway out the door, he leaned his head on the frame and whispered, "Tell me you'll do that rodeo-queen thing sometime, T. I'll live for it."

She was barely able to keep the laughter from her voice and gave him a gentle shove onto the porch. "Text me later and let me know how Nan is doing or if either of you need anything."

"Will do." He headed down her walkway.

Tia shut the door and grinned. Whoever said that breakfast was the most important meal of the day was right.

27

Two days later, Tia stopped to admire her new garden. The blend of colors was almost magical, a real stunner. She could just imagine how vibrant it would be in late July and August when the perennials in the back of the bed had matured and the annuals in the front had grown to their full width and height. Oh, she could hardly wait. Planting had been a fabulous investment of her time on what would've otherwise been a wasted afternoon.

And wasn't she the lucky one when Ethan had trenched and removed the sod on the new section? His generosity never failed to get her attention. Most people would've said goodbye and gone on with their day. Not him. Much to her recent delight, he almost always stopped to help. She'd seen it with complete strangers several times. And that kiss over there? Her insides tingled every time she thought about it.

Maybe she should trench the big sugar maple and plant variegated hosta or even liriope underneath? She ambled closer to the tree and crossed her arms as she imagined the fresh plantings. Well, the hostas would be showier, what with their purple-stemmed flowers. On the other hand, liriope would require less maintenance, and the debris in the late fall would be far less to manage.

Hmm. She walked the circumference of the tree, considering her view from every angle. The size of the tree simply begged for the hostas. Decision made, she stood back to double-check.

Her heart stuttered. Was that a camera winking at her from about ten feet up? *Omigod.* It was aimed directly at the front of her house. What pervert would mount a camera on her tree? Could they see in her windows? *Holy crap.*

She marched to the garage, grabbed her ladder, and climbed up to remove the damn thing, but it was mounted in such a way that it wouldn't come off. *What the hell?*

Maybe it was time to call her uncle? He'd shoot it down. And although Carson had worked very hard to keep an eye on her and was overprotective, he simply wouldn't stoop low enough to install a secret camera and watch her day and night. The goose bumps on her arms agreed.

Which left her with the same question: Who had put a camera on the tree?

With her nerves jumping and temper flaring, she checked to see where Carson was now. Calling him while he was at work wasn't cool. Wait—she was sharing locations with Ethan? How? She remembered verbally agreeing to it on a temporary basis until the lieutenant's killer was caught. *But . . . hold on.* She hadn't actually *set up* location sharing with Ethan on her phone.

She closed her eyes and thought a minute. The only time she locked her phone was when she traveled. Tia worried her bottom lip. Had Ethan gone ahead and set it up for her? Without saying anything? Without asking?

What the hell? Phones were personal spaces. She'd never touch anyone's phone without permission. Maybe the good detective wasn't as honest as he appeared on the surface?

Oh lordy. What if he was a control freak like Brent had been?

No freaking way would she tolerate another man with sneaky habits. Her fist clenched as indignation surged.

Returning to the short list of people who shared her location, she pondered Ethan's name. Had he gone behind her back and done this? Her spine tickled with unease. He didn't seem the type, but if she'd learned anything in the past few years . . . looks could be deceiving.

Nah. She tried to shake it off. If Ethan did this, he wanted to protect her, even if his methods were highly questionable.

More than highly questionable. He should've asked to access her phone. Or at the very least, reminded her a time or two to handle it herself.

Tia spun around, facing the tree. And where the hell had that camera come from? Who was casing her house and watching the video feed? Were they planning a robbery, or posting videos of her in her house on social media? She had to find out. Now.

She hurried Flynn into the car, checked Ethan's location, and managed a choking laugh. This side trip would either be a disaster or a bit of fun. Either way, she'd get an answer.

TIA FOUND him in the big grocery store on 90th street. After she checked with the office and courteously identified Flynn as a K9, the manager waved her the go-ahead. She grabbed one of those coveted small carts, turned a wide corner, and located her suspect perusing the meat cases at the far end.

She squared her shoulders. The temptation to let go of Flynn's leash and give the attack command was damn near overpowering. *Fass, Flynn, fass.* How priceless would it be to watch Ethan anticipate the hit and go down with a twelve-pound spiral-sliced honey ham in his beefy hands? But there were several people with carts in the aisle, and seeing as this was her favorite grocery store, she couldn't let that happen.

Flynn's tail thumped in time to the store music, which meant he'd already spied Ethan. Or scented him. One could never be sure which it was with this dog. A few feet at a time, Tia browsed the meat cases, tossing several packages of sale-priced ground lamb into the cart. And because it was a healthy craving, she grabbed a bag of fresh sauerkraut. But wait, organic extra-firm tofu was on sale. She stacked several in her cart.

Flynn's happy wag was starting to produce a breeze. His whole body shimmied as his head swiveled back and forth between Ethan and Tia. He peered at Tia and whined the softest plea.

Okay, okay. I know you like him. She, however, was on the fence since discovering he might have touched her phone, not to mention the hell there'd be if he was responsible for the camera on her tree.

Nonchalantly, she pretended to eyeball the chicken thighs versus the bone-in breasts while inching her cart closer to his. He was holding an entire beef tenderloin and inspecting it for— she assumed—gristle and fat.

Flynn expectantly stared her down, willing her to acknowledge Ethan's presence.

She rolled her cart one final time and bumped into the detective's. Glancing in his direction, she said, "Oh, sorry about that."

Ethan looked up. His eyes immediately softened when he saw her. "Hey, T, what are you two doing here?" He got down on one knee, giving Flynn the praise and attention he'd been craving.

She ran a hand through her hair. "We were in the neighborhood. I figured it was a good time to stock up for the week."

He casually scanned the contents of her cart. "You like tofu?"

"Yeah, I prep it ahead of time for lunches."

"Sauerkraut, huh? I already know who's going to eat the ground lamb," he murmured with a raised eyebrow glance in Flynn's direction.

Tia peered into his cart. "Are you planning on devouring that whole tenderloin?"

A small smile tugged at his lips. "Uh, no, I've got a friend flying in from Baltimore in the next day or two."

Her eyes widened. "Flying from Baltimore?"

"Yeah. This guy has his pilot's license." He gave a good-natured shrug. "Maybe you and Flynn would like to join us for dinner?"

She smiled politely. "No, but thank you."

He leaned back against the meat case. "Is this your usual grocery store?"

"It's the store closest to my house. You and I probably shop at different times of the day."

"Yeah, maybe." He leaned slightly closer. "I would've noticed you."

"Is that so, Detective?"

"Definitely."

Tia folded her arms across her chest. "I *noticed* the oddest thing on my phone a little while ago." She pulled it out and tapped the screen. "I don't remember actually setting up location sharing with you. Do you know anything about that?"

He closed his eyes and nodded. "I did that while you were putting your pizza in the oven a couple of days ago. You agreed to do it temporarily, and I was concerned about your safety overnight because you were alone."

Her voice rose half an octave. "So you touched my phone? You enabled it for me?"

Ethan smiled agreeably. "I didn't want to forget."

"Ooh, is that all?" She rubbed her forehead and summoned her most reprimanding schoolteacher voice. "I thought you might be creeping on me or something weird like that."

Shock darted across his face as he held up his hands. "Hell, no. But I was in a hurry and didn't have time for the conversation we're having now. I wanted you safe."

Tia held up a picture of the tree camera and enlarged it. "Do you know anything about this on my sugar maple in the front yard?"

He stiffened at the question. "Yes, I need to talk to you about that, but not here. Somewhere private."

"I'm not going anywhere private with you until I have an explanation for this," she quipped, pointing at the phone.

He lowered his voice, leaned closer, and raised his eyebrows. "Your traffic stop? Flynn was at the vet, and I was working that night. I was concerned for you."

She tapped her foot insistently. "I was perfectly safe, and I know how to take care of myself."

"I get that. I should've asked. I apologize."

She pursed her lips. "You should never touch someone's phone without permission. I spent two years with a man who did things behind my back. My tolerance for shifty practices is nonexistent."

His eyes turned sharp and assessing. "Understood."

She held her phone up. "I have half a mind to remove you from my location sharing."

He stepped closer and touched her arm. "Think about it, T. If you needed help, wouldn't it be easier for me to find you with location sharing on?"

"If I needed help, I would simply call you and you wouldn't have to know where I am twenty-four seven. It is invasive, Ethan, no matter how you justify it."

He shook his head. "My bad. I apologize."

"I have Flynn now. Rest assured he'll take good care of me." She pulled her cart away so other shoppers had access to the meat case and pointed an index finger at Ethan. "You don't think I can take care of myself, do you?"

His expression tightened. "Of course you can."

"Then what's got you in a dither about my safety?"

He raked a hand through his hair and whispered, "Look at the difference in our sizes, Tia. I'm a foot taller than you and at least a hundred pounds heavier. You said the guy at the traffic stop was tall. He already has that advantage over you."

"You're forgetting that I know how to defend myself and own a legal firearm."

"I haven't forgotten. But I'd prefer to nab an intruder ahead of time."

"You're completely ignoring the fact that I know Krav Maga. I asked you to fight me once before, and you wouldn't." She glanced at the shoppers eavesdropping on their conversation and lowered her voice. "My house, front lawn, in a half hour. If you win, I'll keep sharing my location with you. If I win, you back off and stop trying to protect me."

Stepping away, she crossed her arms and raised an eyebrow. A female shopper swerved around Tia's cart and muttered, "You tell him, honey."

Ethan's eyes widened. "Are you freaking kidding me? I'd hurt you."

She laughed, grabbed a Cornish hen from the case, and lobbed it at him as she clucked like a chicken.

An older man wearing an Orioles ball cap elbowed Ethan in the side. "You can't let her get away with that, you know."

Tia lifted her chin and stood her ground. She couldn't back down now, but the befuddled look on Ethan's face was victory enough. Besides which, the people gathering between the poultry and beef sections were craning their necks to hear his reply.

"You want to compete . . . against me?"

"I most certainly do. Let's settle the question of whether I can take care of myself or not."

He held out his hands. "You've got me at a distinct disadvantage here, Miss O'Rourke. If I sound the least bit threatening, these good folks will call the cops. But if I back down, your safety is in jeopardy and you'll think you've won."

Tia shrugged one shoulder and pointed at him. "You're chicken." She peered straight into his eyes, where the green was stormier now.

A frazzled-looking woman forced her cart through the crowd. "For crying out loud, I came here to get away from my bickering teenagers, and there's drama in the meat aisle. Get it together, people. The grocery store is a hallowed zone for weary parents." She grabbed several large packages of hot dogs and a family-size tray of pork chops and tossed them into the belly of her cart.

Ethan's lips flattened into a grim line. "All right. You can show me your moves in a half hour. But I'm not fighting you."

A pissed-off heat rose through her neck to her scalp. *The patronizing ass,* as if she were a five-year-old showing off a new karate move. "You're a chicken." Without another word, she broke free of the carts in the meat section, zoomed into frozen foods, tossed a few necessaries into the basket, and made a beeline for the cash register.

Ethan was already paying for his tenderloin, so she hurriedly backed up and began checking out at a self-service, but the tofu wouldn't scan. *Dammit. Dammit.*

Glancing over, Ethan headed toward the door with a large bag and a bouquet of flowers in one hand.

Tia held up a bag of frozen vegetables and called after him, "I got some frozen peas. You'll need them later."

He waved goodbye without turning around.

Yeah, she'd show him her moves, all right.

28

Ethan slow jogged to his truck. The only thing he'd been able to do in that store was own it and apologize. What the hell had she been thinking confronting him like that? There was no way he could argue with her in a public place without repercussions. The humiliation didn't bother him. Much. As a policeman, he put up with all kinds of verbal abuse. But his ex-wife had been a pro at making him feel small, especially in public. That was probably why he was fuming and furious inside.

But if Tia thought for one minute that he was going to let her function without any security with a murderous madman at large, she had another thing coming. He dropped the tailgate, opened his toolbox, and rummaged. He always kept extra supplies, just in case. He couldn't let her leave the lot without a layer of protection.

Shit. He'd blown it but good.

There it is. He pulled a small box from the lower shelf and opened it. It was brand-new, a fifty-dollar investment he was damn glad he'd purchased right about now. He inserted fresh batteries while glancing at the store's exit doors. She was still in there. Good.

Ethan tapped an app on his phone and synced the tracker with the app. A green check mark appeared thirty seconds later. The tracker and app were communicating. *Hallelujah.* He closed the toolbox and tailgate. Where was her car?

After sliding on a pair of sunglasses, he scanned the lot patiently—one row at a time. There was no margin for error. If she stayed upset, he wouldn't be able to get near her for a while without it feeling weird.

He never meant to infringe on her personal decisions, but he couldn't leave her unprotected. And while the tracker was only one level of security, at least it was something.

Ah, that's it. He casually walked three rows over and five cars up while keeping an eye on the store's exit. She hadn't come out.

He sauntered to her car, bent down, and stuck the GPS tracking device on the back underside of the vehicle. His phone pinged. *Success.* He could just imagine telling her about this.

Maybe he'd let her win their lawn games today. *Nah. That would only insult her intelligence.*

Or maybe she'd take him down for real and he'd need the frozen peas. *Possible . . . not probable.*

But all he really wanted to do was take her down on a nice firm bed and love her until she breathlessly whispered his name.

TIA PARKED, grabbed the groceries, and hustled Flynn into the house. Would Ethan even show up for the takedown?

She changed into yoga pants and made certain Flynn was behind closed doors in her bedroom, unable to observe his two people sparring on the lawn. The poor animal didn't need any more trauma. But no sooner had she walked away than his barking and whining started.

Tia stuck her head in the bedroom. Oh geez, she'd left the closet open and the offending laundry chute exposed. She shut the closet door, and Flynn hopped on the bed for a nap. Yeah, Flynn sleeping on the bed needed addressing, but not now.

Ethan pulled into the driveway as she corralled her hair into a ponytail.

Jogging out the front door, she yelled, "I'm surprised you showed up, Detective, what with being chicken and all. I hope you're not planning on doing this in those nice pants and shirt. It's bound to get messy."

The piercing look he shot her should've had her reconsidering their competition, but it was too late to turn back. She'd thrown down the gauntlet and had to convince him she could take care of herself.

Ethan dug through the ever-present duffel bag in the back of his truck, snapped a pair of shorts over a shoulder, and headed for the front porch. "I'm putting my tenderloin in your refrigerator and changing my clothes. Give me two minutes."

"Uh-huh. I'll use the time to warm up. Don't let Flynn out of the bedroom. He doesn't need to see me take you down."

Ethan threw his head back and laughed out loud before going in the house.

Ooh, maybe she was pushing him a little too hard, but he'd remember this day. Next time, he'd ask before assuming he had the right to take over her life. She stretched and slid into a full split. After today, she probably wouldn't be able to do this move for a while due to sore muscles. Sparring with a man Ethan's size had consequences.

She glanced at the camera on her maple tree. A wave of fresh irritation fueled her resolve. Sparring with her had consequences, too.

~

ETHAN FOLDED HIS ARMS, watching Tia ease into that perfect split. He could think of a whole lot of fun things to do with a woman with that kind of flexibility, but this was not among them. Shutting the door behind him, he called out, "All right, show me what you've got."

Tia rolled her shoulders. "We're not here to audition for each other. You want to attack me first, or shall I come for you?"

Oh, when he finally got his hands on her, she'd come for him. He was looking forward to it. Lifting his eyes to the tree-tops, he refocused. Fighting with any woman was distasteful unless said woman threatened those he'd sworn to protect.

Now, with Tia, it wouldn't be a fair fight if she attacked him. He'd have advance warning, and the element of surprise would be gone. "I'll attack you first. Turn around."

Distract, disarm, and disable. He tossed a ball Flynn often played with past her as distraction as he moved in and grabbed her from behind. She clawed like a feral cat, bit his arm—drawing blood—broke free of his choke hold, and spun around with a groin blow he could only describe as lethally quick.

He sank to his knees, retching. Competitors in his various trainings had landed the same move before, but not a one of them had hit the bull's-eye like she just had. He groaned in pain, and his watering eyes burned.

Tia stood over him. "Now do you believe I know how to take care of myself?" She turned to walk away.

Still wheezing, he recovered his presence of mind. *Not so fast, O'Rourke.* He wasn't a one-and-done kind of guy. He reached out, wrapped his hand around her ankle, and yanked hard, landing her on the ground. This time, he was ready for the shoulder blow from her other foot and dodged left, then threw his full weight on top of her, pinning her face-down.

He coughed, summoning his voice. "I'm the bad guy, all two hundred sixty pounds of me, and you've really pissed me off now." Driving her face into the grass, he asked, "Should I kill you first or rape you? You're helpless and pinned underneath me. What are you going to do, T?"

Ethan held her in the tightest controlled vise grip he'd ever used on a woman. She couldn't budge even an inch. "You've got to get out of this before I kill you, all right?"

While he'd never considered that she'd do it twice, she sank her teeth into the flesh of his hand, biting so hard he cried out in pain. The second he jerked away, she reared her head back and nailed his right eye with the precision of a surgeon. He literally saw stars. The woman was Godzilla in a five-five frame.

Ethan shifted his weight. He had to. Self-preservation kicked in, and too many body parts throbbed at the same time. He moved for only a second, but she drove her pointy elbow straight into the middle of his diaphragm. The air whooshed from his lungs as it hit with the speed of a bullet.

Tia scrambled from beneath him and crawled out of reach. There was grass and mud in her hair and dirt on her face. She was trembling. "I hope you're convinced I can protect myself?" Groaning, she cradled his cheek with a hand. "You're going to have a shiner."

Ethan gasped. "Biting is not Krav Maga."

"No shit, Sherlock. But if there's a huge man trying to hurt me, I'll use whatever tactics I deem necessary to free myself. Satisfied?"

He gaped at the blood running down his arm.

Tia squatted down. "You already know that my fiancé picked me up and threw me into the back seat of his car. I live with the scars from that accident every day. I had to learn how to defend myself."

Wiping the grass from her face, she continued. "No one will

take me against my will ever again. This out here today wasn't personal, but you had to see for yourself."

Tia rose. "I'm half in love with you, Ethan. But you must understand my boundaries. You need to ask permission instead of assuming control over my life, and that includes touching my phone and installing cameras in my yard."

Ethan took a ragged breath. "Full disclosure, there's a second camera in the backyard, and I put a tracker on your car, too."

"What? Why?" She stared down at him, one hand on a hip, utterly confused.

He sat back on his haunches. "Because I care, T. Probably too much." He swiped at the blood on his hand. "I want you safe, and you act all nonchalant about your security. I don't want to lose you. I've lost so many people I care about. I couldn't handle losing you, too."

His balls hurt so bad he sat on the lawn and slowly stretched his legs out. "By a stroke of pure providence, we came back into each other's lives. You saw what that madman did to Lieutenant Plante. I'll be damned if I give him a chance to do that to you. He's got your address, T."

Shaking his head, he said, "I think I love you more than halfway. My whole world righted itself when you walked back into it. I'd swear the sun shines brighter when you smile."

Tia dropped to her knees facing him. Pressing her lips to his, she murmured, "Come in the house, Detective. I'll get you an ice bag for your face and those peas for your balls."

29

Vince flinched in the front seat of his car as the red-haired lady cop disabled the detective. *Oof*, that had to hurt. *Who's the big man now, Mr. Detective?* Vince was in his car, one street over from Tia's, with a clear view through the yards. Binoculars were a handy way to watch the goings-on in the neighborhood from a distance.

Well, hell. Today wouldn't be the day he'd get that dog. He'd scratch all of his neatly laid plans and start over, which was damn inconvenient considering he'd hoped to move to a new town sometime this week.

He'd need more equipment to deal with the redhead. Just because he recognized her self-defense moves didn't mean he had the skill to fight her. Look at the massive dude lying on the grass. The man still hadn't gotten up.

It was a damn shame he had to wait and plan some more. Sometimes the itch to strike again was unbearable. However, he'd been patient with Margie and had waited until she was her most vulnerable.

How would he disable the redhead? Shooting her wouldn't be any fun. He wanted to play with her first.

~

ETHAN EASED down gingerly onto a kitchen chair. He would've preferred a softer seat, but he was covered in dirt and grass stains just like Tia. The woman could kick some serious ass, and as soon as his body stopped screaming in pain, he'd be proud of her.

Tia grabbed an ice bag and peas from the freezer and straddled his lap. "Here. Put these peas where you want, and I'll hold the ice pack on your face." She chuckled. "I kind of wondered if I'd be the one needing these today."

Ethan swung the peas under his leg and sighed with relief. He let her perch on his legs again. "I can hold the bag myself," he said, pressing it on his cheek. "Your hits are extremely accurate."

"Thank you. I've worked at it. Do you want a beer or a cup of tea?"

"I wouldn't mind a bottle of water and a few ibuprofen, if you have them."

"Coming right up." After placing both requests on the table, she straddled his legs again. "I'm so sorry you're in pain. If it's any consolation, you can keep the cameras up and the car locator in place. It isn't that I don't take security seriously, but I have Flynn and a gun. I handle myself pretty well. I was just madder than hell because you went into my phone and installed the camera without my permission."

He laughed wryly. "When I looked at the situation from your point of view, you had a right to get upset. When is your security system being installed?"

She bit her lip and thought a second. "Ten days from now."

Ethan glanced around. "Where's Flynn?"

Tia cocked her head and smiled. "Remember? He's upstairs in my room so he couldn't watch us sparring. I'll get him."

She went to move, but he tugged her back. "Wait a minute. I like you here. Let's talk about the things we said outside." He pulled the ponytail holder from her hair and watched in fascination as the curls tumbled. And then it hit him. He didn't want to talk at all.

Tia ran her hands up his chest and looped them around his neck. "You're looking at me like I'm a box of lemon doughnuts, Detective."

He ran his thumb along her bottom lip and remembered the clinging powdered sugar. She was like his very own lemon doughnut, a little bit tart and a whole lot of sweet. His resolve snapped, and he pulled her flat against his chest, taking her mouth with greedy kisses and little nips.

She eased back, bathing his bruised face with angel kisses, whispering, "I'm sorry about the shiner."

"Don't be. I asked for it." His voice had turned to gravel, and they were right back into devouring each other. He couldn't kiss her deep enough. He couldn't feel enough skin. At some point, it dawned on him that his equipment was working just fine, and he removed the bag of peas, tossing it onto the table.

Her soft squeals and little noises drove him onward. He wanted to please her. He hadn't wanted to please any woman in a long time, but Tia—she urged him higher and higher with her barely audible sighs and the way she traced his ear with her tongue. It was maddening.

She was freaking hot—he was on fire. Together, they were combustible. He nudged her back an inch, dragged his T-shirt over his head, and tossed it somewhere. He waited for her to take hers off, but she kept it. *No problem. Keep the shirt.* He eased right back into taking her sassy mouth over and again.

He had no idea how long they feasted on each other, but he strained for control when she began rocking against his boner. His hand found the seam of her yoga pants and stroked. It was her moan that forced him into action. He stood with her legs tightly wrapped around his hips. "Couch … "

"Bed. Upstairs. Please."

Her wish was his command. At the top of the stairs, he set her on her feet. He'd think the stairs would've cooled them down, but she pushed a door open, jumped into his arms, and kissed his chest with ravenous desire.

It was surreal. Ethan hardly recognized himself, addressing the dog like a drill sergeant. "Get off the bed, Flynn. Now." The dog scrambled to the edge and leaped only seconds before they tumbled headlong into the middle.

He wanted sheets. Ethan tugged her back into his arms, yanked the coverlet down, and set her head on a white pillow with pink rosebuds. After removing the gun from under the pillow, he tossed his shorts and seconds later draped her yoga pants over the bedside table.

She was soft and sweet as whipped cream in his mouth, and a natural redhead. But the thing that slayed him was how she crooned with desire in his ear. *Don't stop. More. Oh yes.* He could live his life as her love slave for nights like this.

Their passion crescendoed in the fading dusk with a moment of keening and murmurs, panting and pleading, and one final shout of ever-loving freaking joyful bliss.

Flynn barked twice, lifted his snout, and howled at the rising moon.

SOMETIME DURING THE NIGHT, he awoke with the pictures from Margie Plante's bookshelf on his mind. He stroked Tia's back and hair, half resting and half thinking about Guy Evans's fingerprints on the white keys of the piano.

Tia snuggled closer, traced the outline of his face with a finger and whispered, "Whatcha thinking?"

"Did you ever take piano lessons?"

"Yeah. For about four years when I was in elementary school. I wasn't very good and dropped it. But my mother still has the piano in her living room." She sighed. "Is this what you think about in between rounds of mind-blowing sex?"

He chuckled. "I do my best thinking when I'm relaxed and dozy. Go figure."

She rose up on one elbow. "Are you thinking about Margie's case?"

"Uh-huh. Someone's fingerprints are on the white keys of her piano, but not on the black ones. I don't get it, but I don't play piano. And I can't chalk it up to coincidence."

"Hmm . . . there are finger exercises that only use the white keys. I remember doing some of them."

He thought a minute. "I don't think this person was doing finger exercises that day."

Tia bolted upright. "There is this one song—Heart and Soul."

Ethan's eyes drifted lazily from her shoulders to the small of her back. She was exquisite as the light from a streetlamp illuminated her hair and creamy skin. "What's heart and soul?"

"It's a piece for piano, I think. I used to play it with my dad. I banged out the melody, and he played the chords on the bottom. It's very easy to memorize and makes even the worst piano student feel like a pro when done as a duet."

Ethan folded his arms under his head. "Okay."

She waved her arms around excitedly. "You don't get it. It's only played on the white keys. That's part of what makes it easy for a novice piano player to have fun."

Huh. He reached for his cell phone, opened the picture library, and started enlarging the photos he'd taken of Margie's pictures. Two of them had Margie and Guy Evans holding trophies. But what were the trophies for?

Ethan took a screenshot of the inscription on the trophy. He handed the phone to Tia. "Can you read the writing on that thing? I took my contacts out before your ass kicking."

"No," she murmured. "Let me get the magnifier from my desk." She hurried over, turned on the light, and rummaged through the top drawer. "Here it is. The engraving says First Place Amateur Piano Duet, but I can't make out the year. Does that help?" She glanced at him expectantly.

Oh, hell yes. That meant there was nothing nefarious about Guy Evans touching the white keys on Margie's piano. They had played their duet when they were together. Maybe they'd been reminiscing. Ethan scrubbed his face with a hand. It would've been much easier to ask Guy Evans about the white keys, but he'd lawyered up and clammed shut after his first interview with NYPD detectives.

Ethan held out his hand. "You're brilliant, Tia O'Rourke. Get your sweet ass back in this bed, please."

"Ooh, I love it when you say please, Detective. Is there a reward for helping with your case?"

He patted his lap as his cock twitched and raised the sheet. "Sit down right here, and I'll explain my incentive program."

Tia laughed lightheartedly, turned out the light and crawled across the bed. "I can hardly wait to see what I won."

"It's better if I show you." He fluttered the rosebud sheet over her and slid underneath.

30

———

Ethan swung a towel low on his hips and headed for the guest room, where he'd stowed clean clothes from his duffel. Stepping over Flynn at the entrance to the hall bath, he locked eyes with Tia in the bathroom mirror. Even now she was breathtaking, with her hair wet from the shower . . . wearing a fuzzy pink bathrobe. Her pretty blues glistened back at him like pools of rain as she dabbed ointment on her chest with a finger. An open jar sat on the counter.

The scar. He'd felt it during their heated moments when she'd abandoned her inhibitions and let go. It was like a road map down her front, with little detours left and right all the way past her navel. It'd been hard for his fingers to avoid grazing it due to its sheer size. He'd been so relieved when she'd stopped pulling away from his touch and allowed herself to enjoy the sensations and pleasure.

Ethan pushed the door open a few more inches and stepped inside. He picked up the jar of ointment and dipped a finger in. "May I?"

Her face flashed with alarm and then a quiet determination

183

as her shoulders squared. She answered with a barely perceptible nod.

Standing behind her, he slid the bathrobe farther down her shoulders, exposing her chest. "Look at me, T." She lifted her eyes to his in the still-steamy mirror. With an index finger, he stroked the scar with salve and kissed the side of her face, then her neck. She couldn't warn him away anymore with her bravado and toughness. Somehow she'd gotten to him, had touched the lonely depths of his soul. Her friendship had given him the confidence to love again.

He swiped at the jar of cream and stroked the scar just below her collarbone. "This scar is the part of you that tells a story of love and loss but, most importantly, survival."

She leaned back against his bare chest, closing her eyes.

His finger zigzagged slowly down her body as he nibbled her ear. "It's a banner to be proud of because you healed and started over. But most of all—and I mean this with my whole heart—this scar is the road that brought you back to me."

Tears streamed down Tia's face, and her voice trembled. "That's sweet. But I know I can't hide it forever and I don't want people to gawk. It's obvious enough to call attention to itself."

He kept his eyes glued to hers in the mirror. "You can only be who you are. You're not responsible for people's reactions. You're amazingly strong, someone who endured an extensive recovery."

She drew in a shuddering breath. "A piece of the sunroof lodged into the length of my chest. I was flown to Shock Trauma with it sticking out of me. Almost every muscle in my torso had stitches, and I had no strength in my arms. Today, I can do one hundred push-ups and finally, finally crank out twenty-five pull-ups, and I can bench-press almost eighty percent of my weight."

She sniffled and reached for a tissue. "I've decided to get a tattoo that camouflages the longest scar. Something colorful and pretty, like the flowers I use in my garden."

He smiled at her. "You're right. Something delicate and lovely like you is good."

"I'm not lovely, Ethan. I used to be, before everything happened."

"I beg to differ. You're more gorgeous now. There's nothing more attractive than the beauty of a triumphant survivor."

31

———

Ethan smacked a breakfast sandwich onto the table next to an engrossed Earl and poured himself a cup of coffee. "Whatever you're reading must be good."

Earl reached for the sandwich, took a bite, and started talking with his mouth full. "It's the report from NYPD about Sergeant Guy Evans." He glanced at Ethan and stood up. "Holy crap. I can't believe it. You couldn't leave it alone and tangled with Tia, didn't you?"

Ethan joined him at the table, sipping his coffee. "Why would you think that?"

Earl peered at the shiner surrounding Ethan's eye. "She destroyed one of the recruits the same way. Her nickname at the training gym is the Terminator."

Ethan barked a laugh and opened his sandwich with his unbandaged hand. "Why is now the first time I'm hearing about this, Earl?"

The older man's eyes widened. "Not my story to tell, Son."

Ah, yes, that again. "You know, Earl, the next time you hear a tidbit of information about Tia O'Rourke, would you mind giving the other detective on the case a heads-up? That would be me, in case you're wondering."

Earl threw an arm into the air. "I tried to warn you off. Told you to go sniff somewhere else, but you got offended and didn't listen to me."

Ethan picked at his egg sandwich, taking very small bites because chewing made his eye hurt. Not only that, but his achy balls throbbed in unison with the bruise on his chest when he swallowed. It was weird how injuries hurt twice as bad the next day. But he'd go through it all again to have another night with Tia.

However, the worst had been running into Chief Carson this morning in the hallway. The usually placid and dignified Carson had broken into a wide grin, shaken his head, and walked away.

His pity party over, Ethan turned his attention to Earl and whatever he was reading. "Good news?"

Earl frowned. "It certainly is enlightening and a whole lot more interesting than the back of a cereal box. I sent it to your email."

"I'll be caught up in a minute." Ethan woke his laptop and opened the document. The room was quiet except for the occasional rustle of their sandwich wrappers.

Earl piped up. "You reading it?"

"Oh yeah. Sergeant Evans visited Margie Plante the day before her murder."

"Not only that, Son, but he and Margie had an ongoing romance for the past fifteen years. They toyed with the idea of getting hitched for years, but she ended their relationship when he visited her that final time."

Ethan's eyebrows drew together. "Why would she do that?"

"Beats me. Maybe their retirement goals didn't mesh or she liked being single, or he's a needy dude and she didn't feel like dealing with him permanently. It's too late to ask her."

"Yeah, but it says Evans was inconsolable when he found out she'd passed away."

Earl tapped his finger on the table. "Maybe he *acted* like he was devastated. I'll play devil's advocate here; he stayed in the area overnight and killed her the next day. Premeditated at that point, not a crime of passion."

Ethan shook his head. "Doesn't make sense. He retired last month with a boatload of honors. Why risk his freedom, his reputation, his pension, and his retirement? He'd already done the tough stuff. Why blow it all with a senseless act?"

"Maybe when Margie ended their relationship, it took him off guard and he lost his mind?"

"No way, Earl. I don't buy it. We don't have enough evidence to bring a case against Evans although he may have been the last person we know of to see Margie alive."

"You might have to consider it, because Guy Evans has no alibi for the period of time between when he left Margie's after they broke up and when she was found dead. He says he drove home, took a sleeping pill, and crashed."

"Is there any record of his whereabouts on an E-ZPass? There are a lot of tolls between here and the Bronx."

"He says he left his E-ZPass at home and paid the tolls in cash."

Ethan shook his head. It wouldn't be the first time a man took a sleeping pill and went to bed after an emotionally draining day. He remembered doing it twice during his divorce. "I don't think Guy Evans is our man. If Evans did it, why would he tell people that Margie ended their relationship if that prompted him to murder her? For that matter, why admit he'd visited her the day before her murder, especially if there are no E-ZPass records? There isn't a hint of excessive force or violent tendencies during his long career. Oh, and I figured out why his fingerprints were found on the white keys of the piano."

Earl's head snapped up. "Why?"

Ethan explained the "Heart and Soul" pictures and trophies.

Earl poured another cup of coffee. "Okay. So I agree with you about Evans. I wish we could eliminate him from our suspect list. But you know what else? There are no usable fingerprints on that lock pick set we found under the stove in Margie's kitchen. Not even a partial, and the engraved initials on the front are VMM. For all we know, that set has been there for years. Maybe we didn't find what Tia kicked across the floor. Or maybe whatever she kicked had nothing to do with the murder."

"What about the security footage from the funeral and the repast? Are all the faces accounted for?"

Earl inhaled a slug of coffee while opening another document on his laptop. "Every person had a reason for being there. We identified the caterers and all their staff." He peered over the rim of his cheaters. "How's Tia managing after the cop-impersonation incident?"

Ethan kept his eyes focused on the computer screen. "She seems fine. Flynn will take care of her."

"I wish she'd stay with her mom until this case is solved."

But then she'd be living with her uncle, too. "I feel the same way, but thirtysomethings don't relish trading their independent lifestyle for a teenage bedroom in their parent's house." And Tia had her own feelings about her mom and Carson living together. No way was he discussing the chief's living situation with Earl.

"You know, Earl, we need to remain open to the possibility that the police impersonator is also the person who killed Margie. Flynn reacted the way he did during the traffic stop to protect Tia."

Decisively, Earl planted his palms on the table and rose. "We need the public's help with this case. It'll cost some taxpayer money to weed through a tip line, but *someone* has to have seen *something* on the day of the murder. We're missing a chunk of the puzzle." He paced the room. "We'll get a sketch artist to make a composite drawing with a description from Arnie and Mabel Hawkins. Their traffic stop lasted for several minutes, and they got a good look at the man who stopped them. I need to talk to the chief. Let's touch base in an hour, and I'll let you know what he says."

With Earl gone, Ethan took a minute and scrolled the security footage from the cameras around Tia's house. There were several squirrels, a fox, and that damn cat in the bushes again. It was a quiet Monday afternoon, and he'd finally reunited with the beautiful beach girl from his past. But he felt edgy —unsettled.

Why did he feel like this was the calm before the storm?

32

———

Tia was *so* late. *Poor Flynn.* He'd been alone since early this morning, and although her usual schedule allowed time to run home during lunch to let him out, that hadn't happened today. She'd ended up watching another teacher's class during her lunch break, and then the staff meeting had run later than usual.

Guilt swarmed her thoughts. *I am a terrible dog mom.* Flynn deserved better. Why hadn't she just left school and run home anyway? She should've hired a dog walker so he could get out and do his midday business. Maybe Mike and Casey would let him stay at their office during the long days? She'd ask. He deserved extra time at the dog park or Harlan's farm this weekend. Definitely. Yeah, she'd do that and give him an extra bone.

Bolting from the car with the keys jangling in her hand, she ran to the front door. *He's such a good boy. I can never let this happen again.* She shoved the wrong key into the lock and jimmied it out. *C'mon.*

Tia flung the door open, tossed her school tote onto the kitchen counter, and wheeled around. "I promise I'll never let this happen again." *Wait*. He always greeted her at the front door. Where was he?

"Flynn? Flynn?" She raced into the living room and came to an abrupt halt.

Her hands flew to her face. "Oh my goodness." He was stuck in the old doggie door. The back two-thirds of his body were in the room, while his head and upper torso faced the screened porch. She could barely hear his muffled whine.

Tia fell to her knees behind him and stroked his coat. "You poor thing, I'm so sorry. Let me help you out of there." But her hand didn't fit in the opening where he was stuck. The dog door accommodated an animal of twenty pounds or less, not a sixty-five pound muscular beast. His hind feet were sliding all over the tile, and he was getting nowhere.

The door hinges creaked, and with a crack, the frame began pulling away from the wall. *No, oh no.* Flynn was still stuck, and his every movement pulled another nail free.

Racing into the kitchen, Tia grabbed her phone from the tote and tapped Ethan's number. She set the phone on a nearby bookshelf and braced the doorframe with her hands and body weight.

"Hey, you, what's up?"

"Ethan, I need help," she yelled. "Flynn's got himself stuck in the dog door, and the doorframe is pulling away from the wall. I'm holding it up."

"What? How'd he get in there? No, never mind. I'm on my way."

Tia heard him running with the sound of honking horns and engines in the background.

"Hurry. Every time Flynn moves, the door sways." Her arm muscles already burned from holding the frame. The sound of a siren blasted, and the line went dead. He must've disconnected the call. Tia kicked off a sneaker and stroked Flynn's fur with her sock-clad foot. "You hear that, buddy? Your daddy's using his lights and siren for you."

How in the world had he gotten himself caught in the dog door? She'd kept it locked ever since a stray tabby had sauntered into her kitchen like he owned the place six months ago and scared the bejesus out of her. This didn't make sense. Flynn had never paid any attention to the dog door before today. Maybe that stray cat or a squirrel had somehow gotten onto her screened porch? Even so, Flynn was disciplined . . . he'd never take off after an animal without a command.

Maybe the tabby had come in the house and Flynn had gotten stuck chasing it out? Or he had desperately needed to whiz and tried to get outside? Lord knew he hadn't peed in the house since she'd known him. And he'd only woken her from sleep so he could relieve himself once.

Ethan had warned her that the door wasn't secure, and she'd avoided using it. Damn supply-chain issues. She'd ordered the new custom door almost four months ago. When the contractor who would install it had stopped by two days ago, he'd taken measurements for the decorative wood molding she'd asked for, but the actual installation was still a week away.

None of this mattered right now. As long as Flynn wasn't hurt *again*, she'd count her blessings and slide the huge antique hutch against the frame until the new door arrived.

The front door opened, and Ethan barreled in with another guy. "Tia, this is Mac."

She craned her neck. "Hey, thanks for coming."

Mac immediately took over holding the door and frame in place. "I got this. You two figure out how you're going to get the dog out of there."

Tia stepped back, shaking her arms. Her hands were almost numb. She gave Mac the once-over. He was slightly taller than Ethan but with a slimmer build and the deepest, most serious brown eyes she'd ever seen. The guys were already engrossed in the project at hand, murmuring to one another with grunts and nods. "I'll head to the screened porch where Flynn can see me."

Ethan nodded. "Good idea. He needs you. Take your phone so we're not yelling through the door."

She dashed around the house to the porch. *You poor dog.* He had one paw on the floor, and the other was stuck with his torso in the dog door. He had to be exhausted, standing on one paw like that. Why in the heck had he done this to himself? She got on her knees in front of his face and soothed him with soft words and loving strokes. Her phone rang. *Ethan.*

"T, I'm sending you a link to a YouTube video of some guys helping a large dog back out of one of these contraptions. There's no way Flynn's gonna fit the rest of his body through the opening. We have to help him back out. Give the video a look, and let me know what you think?"

Tia continued to pet Flynn's face and tapped the video. *Omigod.* The dog in the video was really fat and stuck like a hog in the opening. She turned her phone sideways and watched the video again, noting where the emergency workers had placed their hands. She took a deep breath. "Yeah, we can do this. Watch the clip again, Ethan. First, we need to free up the paw that's stuck next to his body, and we've got to be careful that the harness doesn't get hung up."

She set the phone down next to her and held Flynn's face in her hands. Searching for any kind of gap to free his paw, Tia tried sliding a couple of fingers in several places and found nothing. She couldn't even get her index finger in there. "See if you have a gap where you can slide a finger in and free his left paw, Ethan. But be gentle."

"Okay."

He must have found an entry point, because Flynn whined.

Tia stroked his face and praised him. "You're so brave, Flynn, just so brave."

"I found his paw. His back end is squirming, so I know he's uncomfortable. I'm lifting his paw with my finger now and tugging toward me. I really can't tell where his harness is. You'll have to watch him."

Flynn started whining in earnest but stopped seconds later.

"The paw is free, and I've lifted his back end onto my knees so he doesn't keep sliding on the tile floor. He might be able to help us now because he's got traction."

Tia sighed with relief. *Only one shoulder and a front leg to go.* She squeezed a finger in through the side and found his harness. The metal buckle had caught on an inside gap of the little door. Try as hard as she might, the buckle wouldn't budge. "Ethan, unbuckle the harness under his belly so it has room to move."

"Gotcha, doing it now." He started laughing.

"What's going on?"

"I've got a face full of dog butt and wiggling haunches, but the harness is unbuckled."

Tia kissed Flynn's forehead and praised him again. Leaning back on her legs, she tried to figure out how to get the rest of him freed. If she pushed—no, she didn't want to hurt him. "Got any ideas on how to proceed?"

Ethan was quiet for a few seconds. "If I lift his torso a couple of inches and we turn him toward your right, it'll take the pressure off his shoulder and you can try feeding him through. Maybe we try one time. If it doesn't work, we should probably call Mike at the vet to help us."

"All right." She could picture what Ethan wanted to do but worried about Flynn's bulky shoulder and especially his front leg getting through unscathed. Maybe she could bend his leg naturally and guide it once the shoulder got free? Yeah, she could try that. One thing was for sure—she never wanted another pet door to contend with.

"I've got a plan for this side, Ethan. Give me a three count so I know when you're lifting and turning him."

"Roger that. Remember I'm turning him toward your right."

"Okay."

"Three, two, one."

Flynn's eyes widened. Tia squeezed her hand into a tiny fur gap and freed the harness buckle. Using her other hand, she folded his paw and leg. "I've got his leg protected. Give him a tug."

Things got loud for the next thirty seconds. Flynn whined like a puppy as his shoulder squeezed through to the other side. Using both hands, she fed his leg and paw toward Ethan.

"He's out, T. I think he's okay. He's shaking himself and licking my face. We did it."

Oh, thank God. Hearing her dog cry wasn't easy. Tia fell backward onto the porch rug and brushed the tears off her face.

Ethan shoved his hand through the flap opening. "Shake my hand, girl. We did it." Upbeat enthusiasm filled his voice.

Tia placed her hand in his. A few weeks ago, she'd hesitated to touch him because he was large and intimidating. But now? His hand represented strength, warmth, and safety. She kissed his callused palm in gratitude for helping her with Flynn. What was happening to her? How had he worked his way into her trust with coffee and Thai food and doughnuts and those deep-green eyes she'd never get enough of? She let go of his hand.

His concerned face poked through the dog flap. "Hey . . . you're bleeding."

What? She glanced at her hand. *Oh.* "I slid my fingers under Flynn's shoulder so he didn't get scraped up. No worries, I'm fine. Is he okay?"

"He's good and doing the *I gotta go outside* dance."

She dashed out of the screened porch and paused at the side of the house. Why was the pachysandra trampled? How had that happened? Maybe the cat was back? Nah, the cat couldn't flatten a hardy plant like that. *Huh.*

Ethan handed Flynn's leash over at the front door. "Mac and I will secure that back door. You wouldn't happen to have any plywood, would you?"

"Yes, in the shed by the back fence. A contractor forgot it and never came to pick it up. I've got nails, too, and an electric screwdriver."

He gave her a raised-eyebrow look. "I'm impressed."

"Why? Because I've got power tools?"

Flynn finished relieving himself on a tree and pulled his leash toward the backyard.

Ethan cocked his head. "I kind of expected you to have power tools because you're prepared. But the plywood? Not so much. Where's the key to your shed?"

"My key ring, kitchen counter." She let the dog lead her wherever he wanted. He didn't seem any worse off from the experience of getting stuck and then unstuck from the doggie door. For that, she was grateful. Seriously, how long had he endured that position? It would've been awful to parade into the vet again with an injured dog.

Flynn sniffed at the pachysandra, growled, and pulled her toward the screened porch with his nose to the ground. He sat down next to a piece of fabric. It was probably a loose piece of garbage. She bent down to grab it.

"Don't touch it," Ethan yelled. He jogged over, pulled a plastic bag from his pocket, and lifted the fabric with his pen to slide it into the bag. "When a trained K9 alerts next to an item, they're telling you something." Ethan got down on one knee and praised Flynn. Turning the bag over, he inspected the material. "This is blood, and these might be teeth marks on this denim."

Tia gave her small backyard a slow perusal as anxiety tiptoed through her chest. "What do you think happened out here?"

Ethan got up. "I don't know, but this little piece of fabric may give us some insight. And you've got cameras. We'll check the footage."

She straightened. "I'm creeped out, Ethan. I've always loved this yard." Giving the place one last look, she tugged on Flynn's leash. Maybe it was the evening chill in the air or that Flynn had found a piece of bloody fabric that didn't belong back here, but the hairs on the back of her neck prickled, adding to her growing sense of unease.

33

Once inside, they crowded together to watch the recordings from the backyard camera on Ethan's phone. There was a lot of footage of Flynn and Tia, Ethan himself, and Mac. He scrolled to the beginning.

Tia gasped. "Look at that. That guy checked out the windows on the side of the house and got into the screened porch. No wonder Flynn lost his cool." She glanced over to where the dog eagerly licked the remnants from his food bowl. "He's such a good boy."

Mac was standing behind Ethan and Tia. "Oh, wow, did that idiot just stick his face in the dog door? There's Flynn. Aw, dude, he bit his face and hands."

Ethan groaned. "There comes Flynn out the door—well, partially, anyway. It looks like he may have gotten the man's leg and ankle, too."

Mac shook his head. "That fella is hurting tonight."

Ethan scrolled back a ways. "There aren't any good face shots of him on the porch. Let me switch to the front camera. Maybe there's a clear shot as he approaches the house."

Mac peered closer. "Do you see his car?"

"No, if he drove, he parked somewhere else. There. He's walking up the street with some sort of backpack, goes right up and rings the front door. I can't see his face because of the hoodie," Ethan noted.

Tia enlarged the picture. "All that footage and not one clear image of his face?"

"No. See if your doorbell cam has a better picture of it."

She grabbed her phone and scrolled, then offered it to Ethan. "There he is at the front door."

He flipped through the surveillance footage. "Yes, there's his face. It's not crystal clear, but an artist might be able to do a sketch from the video. Would you mind sending me that clip?"

She nodded. "Sure."

TIA SIPPED her tea leaning against the kitchen counter while Mac and Ethan finished their beers, ribbing each other like lifelong friends. "So how long have you two known each other?"

Mac ran a hand through his hair and smiled. "Since eighth grade—military school. We were roommates. Ethan didn't like the whole boarding-school experience. I, however, loved the freedom of being on my own."

Ethan caught Tia's eye. "Boarding school was a lot to absorb after losing my parents. I wanted to stay at the beach and live with my grandmother, but she chose to abide by the plans my parents had already made."

"That's a lot to take in. How old were you?"

"Fourteen," Ethan and Mac said in unison.

Mac offered her a sudden arresting smile. "I taught Ethan the social ropes and pulled his head out of the textbooks."

"And I helped him with his studies because he was too busy

messing around to care about school. Eventually, we balanced out," Ethan added.

Mac tossed his beer bottle into the recycle bin. "You're still scarily smarter than me, dude. I chose premed and became an army medic. My brainiac friend here speaks four languages fluently and has a couple of advanced degrees. There's more to him than pretty packaging."

Ethan shook his head slowly. "You're like a brother, spilling all my secrets."

Mac glanced at her. "Thanks for the beer; my ride to the airport is waiting outside. Nice to meet you, Tia. I need my bag from your trunk, E."

She held out her hand. "Thank you for your help, Mac. I hope to see you again."

He took her hand in both of his and squeezed gently, looking deep into her eyes. "Likewise."

Tia lingered at the door, watching as Mac slid into the back seat of a dark Mercedes sedan. There was a whole lot more to that man than the self-effacing person she'd met. And there was something familiar about him, too, but she couldn't put her finger on it. He carried himself with the authority of someone in charge. Of what? She had no idea.

Ethan came back inside with his duffel bag and set it by the front door. "Considering the events of this afternoon, is it okay if I stay the night?"

She waved the question away. "Yeah, sure. I'd feel better with you here. Plus, I have questions for you. *Four* languages, Ethan?"

He faced her and bloomed crimson.

"Yeah, that. I wish he hadn't mentioned it." He pulled out his phone.

"A couple of advanced degrees? I'm surprised you're not teaching at a university or working for the federal government."

"Like I mentioned before, I'd wither on the vine at a desk job."

She bent down to pet Flynn. "Uh-huh. What else don't I know about you?"

His green eyes riveted on her. "A lot."

Oh my. "I'm curious. When did you install the front and back cameras?"

"I had other people do it in the evening."

She wheeled around. "What? Who were they?"

He held up a hand. "I had the Feds watching your house the night of your traffic stop. They put the cameras up. Easy enough to do."

Her mouth fell open. "You had the Feds watching my house? Like in the movies? Dark sedans and stale coffee?"

He pointed to his eye. "You can kick my ass again, if you want. But I'd like to have makeup sex after and, if you don't mind, no more shiners. This one's healing up."

Tia crossed her arms. "Are you really a local cop? You speak four languages, order a government agency to watch my house, and bring me doughnuts from Philadelphia at dawn. Who. Are. You? Is your name really Ethan Kelley?"

"Yes, that's my real name, and yes, I'm a local cop. Mac asked the Feds to watch your house when I said I wouldn't leave you unprotected."

Her eyes widened. "Who do you work for? Besides my uncle."

"I don't handle interrogation on an empty stomach very well. It's a nice evening. Let's go get a bite to eat. We'll sit outside somewhere, and Flynn can come with us." He strode to the fridge and opened it. "Or would you prefer uncooked tofu with horseradish and pineapple jam?"

"You're avoiding my questions."

"No, I'm not. I'm hungry, and it would probably do you good

to get out of here for a while, considering today's events. Plus, I need to drive by the precinct and drop off this fabric that Flynn found."

Tia drew in a resigned breath. "Okay, I could use a margarita."

34

They chose a cozy bayside bistro with renowned crab cakes, a reggae band, and a panoramic view of the upcoming sunset over the shimmering water. Tia took a sip of her salt-rimmed margarita. It fizzled, exploding tequila and lime on her taste buds. *Yum.* She leaned back and sighed with satisfaction.

This was the first time she'd been out socially without Mo in two years, and she wasn't even nervous. What exactly did that mean? Flynn lay down on the cool tile and rested his snout on his paws. Poor dog had to be exhausted after getting stuck for God knew how many hours. Ethan perused the menu across the booth while her foot tapped a Caribbean beat under the table.

She'd used to love this place before her life had turned into a series of horrors. Judging by the great music, the tiki bar, and the scent of savory seafood wafting from the kitchen, there was still a lot to love. Not to mention the very interesting man with stellar bedroom skills seated with her. What was the rest of his story?

Why had he decided to bring her here of all places? This resort town had dozens of fast-food options and quick-serve ethnic eateries vying to tickle their palates. But he'd chosen a restaurant with ambiance and music and a front-row seat to what promised to be a glorious sunset.

How odd. She'd stopped protesting his presence in her life and longed to run her hands up and down his massive chest.

The waitress sidled over to their table, batting her eyes at Ethan.

Nice try, honey.

Ethan glanced up from his menu, seemingly unaware of his effect on the present female company.

The server pulled out her pad and glanced at Tia. "You ready to order?"

Tia nodded. "The crab-cake platter, please, side salad in place of the fries, and a double cheeseburger for our dog."

Ethan flipped through the menu pages one last time. "I'll have the same but with a large side of fries." He handed the waitress their menus and leaned toward Tia. "You look delicious tonight, Miss O'Rourke."

The waitress offered the faintest mewl as she left.

Tia bit her lip to keep from laughing out loud. "I would've taken you for a soft-shell crab or raw oysters with hot sauce guy."

He snickered and waved an index finger. "No and no. I'm very discriminating about body parts that enter my mouth."

An image of him with her lady bits in his mouth flashed through her mind. She sat bolt upright and squirmed. It had to be the tequila—her face was hot. For goodness' sake, they were discussing seafood here.

Concern flitted across his expression. "You all right, T?"

She gave his hand a pat. "I'm fine; it's been a while since I had a mixed drink."

He gave her an appraising look and got up. "I'll be right back." He strode to the tiki bar, said something to the bartender, and returned with a basket of pretzels and peanuts. "Here, nibble on these. I don't want you going down on me."

Down on him? The sip she'd just taken caught in her throat. She gasped on the laughter trying to escape. After a few clearing coughs, she peered across the table and burst into laughter again. "Don't worry. I won't go down on you."

Understanding dawned in his eyes, and they morphed to playful and sparkling.

He raised an eyebrow. "A definite double meaning there. How Freudian of me—and you."

Their waitress walked by. "Would you like another round?"

"Yes, please." Ethan smiled. "No beer, just two margaritas."

Tia gulped. "I hope those margaritas aren't both for me."

"No, I want one of what you're drinking, and you need a refill." He gave her a teasing glance. "You mentioned having questions for me?"

Questions? Oh yeah. "What languages do you speak? Mac mentioned four."

He took the last draft of his beer and set it aside. "French, Italian, Russian, and Spanish. Next question?"

Tia sat back while the waitress placed their fresh drinks. "How did you learn so many languages?"

He shrugged a shoulder. "My parents both spoke Spanish and Italian, and I learned to join in on the conversation. They'd speak a different language when discussing something they didn't want me to know, but that didn't last long. Once they realized I understood them, they taught me more and hired tutors."

"Forgive me for bringing this up, but I'd like to know. How did you lose your parents? You don't talk about them."

"A boating accident when I was ten. I was spending the weekend at a friend's house, and my grandmother came to pick me up. It was a long time ago. I remember them, but my memories have faded a little."

Tia slid her hand on top of his. "I'm sorry. That's a tough loss to bear as a child."

He slipped his fingers through hers and sipped at his margarita. "My family lived in the Hampden area in Baltimore. After my folks passed, Nan raised me and started clearing out their house. But she'd already retired at the beach and wanted to live here. A year and a half later, she sold my parents' Baltimore home, and we moved back. After college, I became a police officer in Baltimore, but Nan is older now, and I wanted to be there for her during her later years. I'd no sooner moved back down here than she announced she was moving to assisted living, primarily for the social aspect, although she loves having meals cooked for her. She gave me the house in Fenwick Island near the Painted Ladies on the water." He stirred his margarita thoughtfully. "Losing my folks really defined me."

"How so?" Many questions had been whirling through her head.

"When I lost them, I knew I'd spend my life helping people, especially when it came to reuniting families. After the Mayday call, they located the sailboat but not my parents. It used to upset me terribly as a kid. But now, as an adult, I've made their loss one of my strengths and get a real kick out of helping people through sticky situations."

"And you get to do that as a detective?"

A muscle ticked at his jaw. "Sometimes."

"What do you actually *do* at your second job?"

"I work for a privately funded outfit named Sanctuary, Inc. They are separate from but work in conjunction with the government. We rescue people from human trafficking situations and return them to their families, if they have them and want to go home."

Stunned, she remained absolutely motionless for a second. "Rescuing people is risky business, Ethan."

"Tell me about it." His gaze was as soft as a caress.

"Does that mean I'll read about you and this Sanctuary organization in the news?"

"No. We operate under the radar. If we close down a trafficking ring, we let the Feds take credit for it."

"So you're vigilantes?"

"No, we're sanctioned by the powers that be. But we get in, do the rescue, and get out. We don't brag about it. Everyone in Sanctuary has a day job and a life in their community."

"But how do you do both demanding jobs?"

"My Sanctuary unit is on call eight days a month. It isn't full-time."

"Does my uncle . . . "

Ethan raised his palm. "He knows. So does Earl. And now, you know."

Awkwardly, Tia cleared her throat. "I won't say a word." She stroked Flynn's head. He must've felt the tension during their conversation and had placed his head in her lap. "Let's go back to those rescued people. What if they don't want to go home?"

"Then we help them resettle in another part of the country."

She considered him a moment. "I'm still bothered that the Feds watched my house and installed cameras on my property. How did that happen?"

"My Sanctuary team had an op that night, and I told Mac I couldn't go, because you needed protection. The Feds needed me as part of the op, so they sent a couple of agents over to watch the house while I was away. I asked them to install the cameras."

She pretended to scribble on a pad. "I should write you up for that." Although it hadn't escaped her that he would've skipped the op that night to protect her.

He cocked his head. "Well, you've already kicked my ass, and *something* happened that night, because your house was blazing with lights at three thirty a.m."

Ohhh. He knew about that? "I had a bad dream; that's all. Is that why you showed up with doughnuts so early?"

"Sort of. I'd planned on relieving the Feds anyway, and instead of waiting outside, I wanted to share my doughnuts with you. It was a last-minute thing, and I knew you were awake."

"So that's why you shaved your beard off . . . for the op?" She'd never forget the smooth feel of his freshly shaven face against her lips for the first time, and oddly enough, he hadn't let it grow back.

Ethan leaned back in his chair. "Exactly. I'm also very motivated these days to keep shaving." He punctuated the statement with a subtle wink.

Their waitress arrived with a tray and set their food in front of them. "I brought tartar sauce, cocktail sauce, extra Old Bay seasoning, and lemon wedges." She tucked the tray under one arm and set her free hand on Ethan's shoulder. "Can I bring you anything else?"

Ethan scanned the table and raised an eyebrow at Tia.

She shook her head.

He peered up at the waitress, glanced at her hand on his shoulder, and smiled. "My lady here says we're good, so we're all set. Thank you."

The waitress nodded and sauntered away.

Tia chuckled. "She's been gunning for you ever since we arrived."

"I know. This place can be a meat market, but I'm not on the prowl. I have exactly who I want sitting across the table from me."

Oh. Thank goodness she hadn't fixed him up with Susan at school. Her heartbeat ticked up with a giddy sense of pleasure as she broke Flynn's huge hamburger into pieces.

Ethan placed his hand over hers after she took a bite. "How's your crab cake?"

Her eyes lifted to his. "It's delicious. Thanks for choosing this place. I haven't gone out much in the past couple of years, and it's refreshing to be out—especially with you."

There was something warmly seductive in his look.

She quickly leaned over and set the burger plate in front of Flynn, then touched Ethan's hand. "What are you thinking?"

"I think I want you in my life. Are you willing to give *us* a try?"

She grabbed one of his french fries and traced it against his lips. "Yes." Elation filled her heart for the first time in months, or maybe years. "How long have you been thinking about this?"

He leaned closer. "Since the day you wore those cartoon pajamas and slippers to school."

Interesting. "For me, it was when you made those suggestive comments in the school office."

His eyebrows raised in surprise. "Really? So you weren't actually pissed at me?"

Tia waved a finger. "I was upset because the office staff heard you. But deep down, I liked you even though I didn't want to. But be forewarned—I still have a lot to work through."

Ethan waited for her to finish, then pushed their plates to the side. "Would you like to dance?"

"Yes, I'd love to. But we can't just leave Flynn here to take care of himself."

He jerked his head toward the bar. "Earl's sitting over there. He'll watch him for us."

Tia took a sip of her margarita and wrinkled her nose. "Did you plan this?"

He crossed his heart with two fingers. "No. Tina must have a meeting tonight. He's been known to eat out when she's working late."

"Let me go with you and say hi to Earl." She grasped Ethan's offered hand, and they sidestepped the crowd around the bar.

Tia placed a hand on Earl's forearm. "Sergeant?"

He spun around and grinned. "Hey, Tia. Give an old man a hug."

His embrace resembled a hard squeeze, and he still smelled like Old Spice. Aw, how she'd missed Earl the past couple of years. He'd always been a dear friend to her family and a trusted confidant to her uncle. Tia basked in the embrace and held it a few seconds longer.

Earl raised his eyebrows. "What are you kids doing here?"

"Crab cakes, margaritas, and a sunset," Ethan quipped. "I take it Tina's working late tonight?"

Earl nodded. "Figured I'd get a salad and watch the sunset. I guess great minds think alike."

Two guitar players on the stage broke into a country song while the drummer tapped his cymbals in a syncopated rhythm. Anticipation welled up in Tia's chest as her right foot moved to the beat. She hadn't danced since a friend's wedding a few years ago, and this band had a great reputation.

Earl smiled knowingly. "Give me the dog. You two go dance."

Ethan grinned. "You sure?"

"Of course. Where's your table? I'll sit over there with him." Earl grabbed his beer and took the leash from Ethan. "Have fun, Son. I looked at your upcoming schedule, and you're on duty a lot."

The words were barely out of Earl's mouth when Ethan tugged her forward, nudging them toward the outside deck where the band was playing. Most of the men she'd dated weren't into dancing unless they were smashed at a wedding. Nothing was further from the truth with Ethan. The smile on his face conveyed pure joy from the second their feet hit the dance floor.

He swung her into his arms and moved like a pro, spinning and gently dipping her as if testing how their bodies worked together. Or maybe he was seeing how agile she was on her feet. Whatever—at the exact moment she couldn't keep up with him, he'd tug her to his chest and sway so she could catch her breath.

It wasn't like her. The urge to close her eyes and let him catch her after too many spins was overwhelming. With his hands on her hips, he guided her from one move to the next. The few times they didn't sync on a move, they laughed. Thank goodness she'd worn low heels and not sneakers.

At the end of the second song, Tia pulled the scrunchie from her hair and let the strands fall, cascading free in the cool bay breeze. Something inside had begun to unfurl, and it had nothing to do with the margaritas.

The third song was an old hip-hop tune from her college years, and they danced apart, seeing which of them could perform the coolest moves. Laughing at their attempts, they fell into each other's arms when the song ended. The band announced a short break so the crowd could enjoy the sunset.

Ethan guided her to the railing with the best view of the bay. "Stay here." He headed for the tiki bar.

The evening's fireball hovered above the horizon as if daring the pink-and-lavender sky to become more stunning. Sunsets always took her breath away, but this one she'd remember forever as the night she broke free of an internal chain that had bound her to the past. The memories weren't worth the angst anymore. They were like tumbleweed bouncing away.

Something deep inside had been set free. Her therapist would have a good time with that one at her monthly check-in.

Ethan returned and slid in next to her, accompanied by two huge cups of ice water, and a tempting array of citrus fruit. They toasted and drank the cool and invigorating liquid like parched travelers.

Tia held up the cup. "Thank you, for this. And for the evening, too."

He slipped his free arm around her waist. "I hope you're having as much fun as I am. I haven't danced like this in a very long time."

Tia glanced up at him. His eyes sparkled with gentleness and humor and were the feature that enamored her the most. His physical demeanor virtually screamed sexy hot to the extreme, but his eyes held stories she couldn't wait to hear. She pulled the band from her wrist and started smoothing her hair back into a ponytail.

He touched her hand. "No, don't. Please. You have no idea how beautiful it is when your hair swings free."

"Really?" She plopped the scrunchie into his waiting palm, and he shoved it into his pocket.

The emcee grabbed the microphone. "Are you ready for more?"

"Hell, yeah," Ethan shouted. He bent down and spoke into her ear. "They're going to play a salsa set."

"How do you know?"

His eyes glinted in amusement. "Because I requested it."

"Ooh. Hmm," Tia murmured. She only knew the basic salsa steps and had never danced it except in front of her computer while trying to learn. This ought to be interesting.

Ethan grabbed her hand as the rhythmic music began. Two spins later, she was swiveling her hips and moving in unison with him as if they hadn't taken a break. She closed her eyes, threw her head back, and let him spin her over and again. Tossing her hands in the air, she let him catch her—never doubting that he would.

Reality might kick in tomorrow, but tonight was all she could count on. And tonight she was flawless and beautiful and desirable. Her face hurt from smiling as they swiveled to the music in perfect harmony for several songs in a row. She turned and looped her arms around his neck. "Can we go home?"

He planted a soft kiss on her temple. "If you want."

Ethan grabbed their dinner bill and found Earl while Tia visited the restroom. "Thank you for watching him. We really appreciate it."

Earl handed over the leash and stroked Flynn's bulky coat. "This dog wore himself out trying to keep up with you two on the dance floor. He never took his eyes off Tia. For that matter, neither did you."

Ethan ran a hand through his hair. "She's a beauty. That's for sure."

Earl leaned back in his chair. "I haven't seen her smile like that in years. And I've never seen you cut loose and have fun." The older man held up his hand. "Not my story to tell, Son, but after watching you two out there tonight, I think you may be writing a story you tell your grandbabies." One side of his mouth lifted into a rare grin. "Glad you had fun. I'm out of here. Tina should be home by now."

Ethan shook his friend's hand. "Thanks again."

"Happy to help." Earl spotted Tia on the way out and gave her a quick hug.

35

———

Ethan yanked the shirt over his head and made a beeline for the kitchen. He almost tripped over Flynn stretched out horizontally in the hallway right outside Tia's bedroom. The dog lifted his head and sniffed, then snorted in utter disgust. At least that was what it sounded like to Ethan.

He bent down to pet the dog. Flynn gave him the side-eye and turned away.

"Look dude," Ethan implored, "I'm sorry we made you sleep in the hallway last night. We excluded you, but there wasn't enough room in the bed, and sometimes dog parents need time alone."

Flynn closed his eyes and sneered, exposing his gums and eyeteeth.

"It'll probably happen again." *Oh, please, let it happen again.* Ethan rubbed behind Flynn's ears. "But that doesn't mean we don't love you anymore. You brought us together. You'll always be our special big boy."

Tia opened the hall-bath door in a cloud of steam. "Are you talking to Flynn?"

Ethan sighed. "Yup. He's very displeased with me right now."

"I know. He gave me the silent treatment, too."

"What do you think we should do?"

"Wait him out. See how long it takes for him to change his attitude."

Change his attitude? He stared at her, baffled. "And if that doesn't work?"

"Treat him special, spoil him. Maybe we'll tempt him with a big *b-o-n-e*. A real one."

"Do you have any, or do I need to run to the grocery store?"

"I'm fresh out of bones. You'll need to visit Tony's, bayside on Sixty-Seventh Street. They've got the best ones. Take Flynn with you. He needs to get out."

"T, he won't even look at me. How am I supposed to get him in the truck?"

She poked her head out of the bathroom again and gave him a big smile. "You'll think of something. I guess if you have to, you'll just pick him up and cart him outside. Our boy's smart. He knows exactly what's going to happen when you talk to the Italian guy in the stained white coat at Tony's. I guarantee you his tail will wag full blast."

"How many bones should I get?"

"Well"—she snickered—"if Flynn is going to be offended every time we're intimate, I'd say get a bunch."

Hmm. "A bunch. Is that like five?" Hopefully, Tony also sold a variety box of condoms.

"How do you feel this morning, Detective?"

He leaned back and smiled. "Freaking amazing. How about you?"

She cackled. "Like a brand-new person."

"That's good. So five bones or seven or eight?"

"I would buy as many bones as he'll sell you. We'll freeze them."

"Does that mean you're ready to make us permanent like we discussed last night?"

"Not yet. But it does indicate that you have first dibs on your side of the bed for the foreseeable future."

Maybe he was moving too fast. "You're going to make me work for it, huh?"

"Absolutely. I can't have you thinking I'm easy."

"Okay. Let me make coffee first. You want some?"

"I thought you'd never ask."

ETHAN OPENED the passenger window of his truck, hoping Flynn would enjoy the ride with his head in the wind and his tongue hanging out. Not this time. He tossed Ethan a disinterested glance and focused forward, ignoring the open window. It was baffling. Was Flynn really mad or simply having an off day?

"Did you do this to Margie and Guy Evans? Is that why they didn't get married?"

Flynn's head swiveled in his direction when he heard Margie's name. Of course the K9 remembered her name. Guilt welled up in Ethan's chest, and he kept his mouth shut the rest of the drive. Where was the happy canine he'd played fetch with yesterday?

He pulled into Tony's Market and urged Flynn through the front door. The place smelled delicious, like fresh baked goods and rotisserie chicken.

The meat department was in the back. If a bone would soothe the dog's hurt feelings, then so be it. He guessed it was kind of like buying flowers for a woman after a disagreement, although that sort of thing didn't make any sense to him. Wouldn't it be better to solve the disagreement first instead of trying to smooth it over with flowers and never discussing it? Yeah, whatever.

A salesperson offered to help him.

"I need to speak with your butcher about meat bones." He pointed at Flynn. "Is he in?"

The woman gave a firm nod and plunged through the swinging doors, yelling, "Tony, got a bone buyer. . . wants to talk to you."

Tony strolled behind the meat case, wiping his hands on a white towel. "You need goodies for a special dog? I got 'em."

Ethan smiled in relief. "Great. How many do you have?"

"Who's the dog?"

"This guy here. Flynn."

"For Flynn? I love that dog." Tony came out from behind the counter, got down on one knee, and held out his arms. "Who loves you, baby?"

Flynn's tail swished into overdrive, wagging and slapping the wood floor. Not only that, but he also licked Tony's face and barked, dancing in a circle. Ethan shook his head. Obviously, Tony the butcher wasn't on Flynn's shit list today.

Tony glanced at Ethan. "This is Tia's dog. Why do you have him? Oh, wait, are you the cop she shares him with?"

Ethan nodded. "That's me. Nice to meet you."

Tony rose from the floor. "I'm glad you stopped in. The strangest dude came in here about an hour ago. He had dead eyes; you know what I mean?"

Ethan switched into work mode. "Anything else strange about him?"

"Everything, man. His face . . . all busted up. The gauze fell off one side, and there were black stitches all over his nose and chin, across one cheek. Almost looked like he stitched himself up. Docs these days don't use black thread on the face. I told him about the medical clinic on Seventy-Fifth and how they'd fix him right up if he needed help, 'cause I don't know, he looked like he needed medical attention."

"What did he say?"

"He just looked at me with those deadpan eyes and told me to hurry up with his steaks." Tony shivered. "Those eyes, they really got me, man. The guy wasn't right. He didn't threaten anybody, just took the steaks, paid for them, and walked out."

Ethan squinted. "Which way did he go?"

"Turned left, hit the candy store, then drove off in his car. It looked brand-new. Temporary tags, but I didn't get the plate number."

Ethan pulled up the artist's rendering of Tia's traffic guy on his phone. He held it up. "Is this him?"

Tony leaned closer. "Maybe, there are similarities in the mouth and eyes. But my guy had dark-brown hair with a flattop."

"What color was his car?"

"White sedan."

Just like the local police cars. "Do you have security cameras?"

Tony nodded. "Wanna take a look at them? It was only an hour ago."

"That'd be great."

"Sure. How many bones you want?"

"As many as you've got. A dozen, maybe? Can I freeze them?"

"Twelve? No problem. I'll wrap them individually, and you can thaw as you need them. Come on back. You can review the security feed while I wrap bones. Okay to give the dog a treat to enjoy now? It'll keep him busy while you work."

"He'd love that. Thanks."

Ethan followed Tony back to the office and got busy scrolling footage.

A minute later, Tony reappeared with a bone, which he set down on a big towel. After he gave Flynn a second round of serious affection, the dog got right to work. "He can gnaw to his heart's content in here but not in the kitchen. Health department rules." Tony stripped off his butcher's coat and replaced it with a fresh one, then washed his hands in the corner sink. "Just stick your head in the kitchen if you need me."

Ethan wheeled around and caught the butcher before he closed the door. "Is this the guy you spoke of?"

Tony stepped around Flynn and peered at the monitor. "Yup, that's him. Strangest eyes I've ever seen. I don't know. Maybe I'm looking for trouble where there isn't any. What do you think?"

That this guy had a run-in with Flynn and the doggie door. "He does need medical attention; that's for sure." Ethan enlarged the face-forward picture from the checkout line. It was grainy, but a pro could analyze the bone structure and maybe get a positive ID on the man. "Do you mind if I forward this footage to the precinct?"

"Yeah, sure. Whatever it takes to get him the help he needs. That's one of the reasons we've got cameras, to protect ourselves and the public. Just make sure to black out our name on the feed so he doesn't get mad at us."

Ethan nodded. "Yes, of course. We've got the software to remove the background so the girl who checked him out won't be in the photos, either. We'll make sure of it." He forwarded the footage to his phone and Earl Thompson's. "Thanks, Tony."

"Sure thing. Let me get those bones ready for Flynn."

36

Harlan Brinker cursed as he got out of the pickup truck.

"Damn sciatica." Muttering a string of oaths, he hobbled to the entrance of the Sandpiper Diner. The bells jingled as he opened the door and stepped over a worn marble threshold.

"Happy Tuesday morning, Harlan," hailed Jake, the diner's owner. "Nice to see you in town. How's the farm these days?" He poured a glass of water and set it on the counter where Harlan usually sat.

"Fine, Jake, just fine. But this damn sciatica's put a hurtin' in my leg and back."

Harlan spared a glance at the blaring television hung high on the wall behind the counter. "Can you turn that contraption down a little bit, please? And would you cook me three sunnies with well-done sausage, no potatoes, and burned rye toast? Give me real butter and none of that margarine stuff."

"Sure, Harlan. It'll be about five minutes."

"Okay. I'm still mad at the cable company for raising my rates, Jake. How can a person afford to pay almost two hundred dollars a month for cable and cell-phone bills? It's nuts. Just crazy. I canceled the cable and internet a couple of months ago and go to the library now and use their computers when I need to order feed and seeds. Sure do miss the games on the internet though. There's nothing like playing backgammon with someone you don't know and can't see. It brings out the competitor in an old man." He gave a sardonic laugh.

"I'm sorry, Harlan. I know you enjoyed the old-time movies and game shows, too." Jake prepped the filter for another pot of coffee.

"I haven't seen the news in a couple of weeks. Can't say the sabbatical's done me any harm. All they do is talk about terrorists and politics anyway. I've read a slew of my favorite books instead."

Jake set the plate of breakfast in front of Harlan and reached under the counter to grab silverware rolled in a napkin. "You need anything else? Want some orange juice?"

Harlan shook pepper over his eggs. "Nah. I'll take a cup of that fresh coffee once it's done brewing. This looks great. You know how to burn food good and proper." He speared a blackened sausage link and poked a hole in an egg for dipping. Raising his eyes to the television, he watched a house fire burning somewhere in the world.

"Hey Jake, change the channel to the local news, would you, please? I may as well catch up on the town happenings. The international news will give me indigestion."

Jake aimed the remote, and the picture settled on a pretty blonde newswoman. He set the remote on the counter before pushing through the swinging doors to the kitchen.

Harlan stabbed a second sausage link and pierced another egg. He mopped the steaming yolks with burned toast and eyed the television again. The pretty blonde was replaced with Chief Carson speaking into a microphone on the left side of the screen and an artist's rendition of a suspect on the right. Harlan strained to hear what the chief was saying and squinted at the face in the drawing.

Something was familiar about that face.

I've seen that guy somewhere.

Where have I seen that face?

The screen changed, and a ticker ran across the bottom offering a twenty-thousand-dollar reward for information leading to the arrest of the person who'd killed Lieutenant Plante.

Harlan spat out a bite of sausage and dropped his fork. He swiveled his stool and ran for the remote at the end of the counter but crumpled against another seat and cursed, "Damn, damn sciatica." Reaching down the counter, he grappled for the remote, raised the volume, and froze the picture before hobbling back to his stool.

After dunking his spectacles into the glass of water, he dried them on his blue flannel shirt and perched them back on his nose. Harlan studied the picture on the screen again. "Well, I'll be a Christmas ham . . . hey, Jake! Come out here . . . I need you, Jake!"

Jake burst through the swinging doors, drying his hands on a towel. "What's the matter, Harlan? What's wrong?"

"Look at that face on the screen. I think that's my renter."

"What renter?"

"Remember I used to let Tilly rent out the apartment on top of the big garage? I had converted the second floor and told her if she could keep it rented, the money was all hers. We had renters living there off and on for twenty years. I cleaned it up about a year ago and started renting it again because I needed extra money to heat the greenhouse. I think that's my renter. Can that TV record?"

Jake grabbed the remote and pushed the red button. "There

you go." The broadcast resumed with the announcement of the reward. "You sure that's your renter?"

"I'm sure as chickens and shit go together." He studied the television screen.

"You can't go back home, Harlan. Call the police. Don't even think of going back to your house. They think that guy killed the retired policewoman."

"Gimme your phone, Jake. I gotta call the hotline. Wouldn't that be something if my renter was him? Geez, that reward would pay for a lot of internet backgammon. I sure hope my hounds are safe. I left them in the front yard."

EARL YANKED open the door to the diner, perused the clientele, and locked eyes on the table where Harlan was now sitting. He sauntered over, grabbed a chair, and straddled it backward.

"Harlan Brinker, how the hell are you? I haven't seen you in what . . . a week now?" He shook the older man's hand and motioned to Jake for a cup of coffee.

Harlan leaned back in his chair and shook his head. "Little Earl Thompson, I'll never forget the hot summer day I caught you skinny-dipping in my creek with EmmaMae." Harlan's eyes lit up as he motioned to Jake for a refill.

"By God, Harlan, that was decades ago. I thought for sure you'd forgotten it by now. My daddy made me muck stalls for a month after you brought me home in that old pickup and pulled me by my ear to tell him where you'd found me." Earl chuckled. "Did you get your fields planted last week?"

"Oh yeah, the tomatoes and cantaloupe, too. Gotta supply the farm stands in the summer. I hire seasonal help. They helped me get the planting done." Harlan took a sip of his fresh coffee.

"So what's this about somebody living on your property that looks like the suspect you saw on TV? Tell me about him." Earl set his pad of five-by-seven sticky notes on the table, pulled out a pen, and unfolded a composite drawing of the suspect.

Harlan tapped the picture. "This guy here sure looks like my renter, and he's an odd one, Earl. He showed up about three weeks ago in answer to my ad in the county news and wanted to look at the apartment over the garage. Said he was a little down on his luck, but he had a security deposit and the first two months' rent. Seemed like a nice enough young man.

"He said his name was Vince Jones and he was from up north. The guy has a New York accent so thick I gotta listen twice as hard to understand him. Anyway, I let him move in on a month-to-month basis, and I get to noticing that he's a little peculiar. Always real friendly to me, smiles and waves, but the minute I move on, he's talking to himself. Now, I know we all talk to ourselves once in a while, but mostly in our heads. Not him, he laughs and answers himself. Comes and goes all hours of the day or night, and he's constantly putting fancy lights on his car and then taking them off. He's just . . . unusual."

Earl rubbed his chin thoughtfully. "Well, Harlan, I could go over and have a little chat with him, but I can't say that talking to himself is enough probable cause to bring him in for questioning. Although the lights may be something we could look into."

Harlan pushed the spectacles higher on his nose. "I'd only tell *you* this, Earl, because I don't want anybody thinking I usually invade my renters' privacy, but he went away for a few days last week, mentioning he'd be back on Thursday. Once I was sure he was gone, I went up in the apartment. He keeps it real neat and everything, but the closet was empty. I started wondering if he'd left for good until I saw a big bag of laundry in the hallway. Everything in the bag was blue, right down to the socks and Jockeys. I just left it there, and true to his word, he came back on Thursday night."

Harlan took a gulp of coffee. "I haven't had TV and internet for a couple of months, so I haven't been watching the news lately unless I'm in a restaurant or doctor's office. And I don't have the newspaper delivered anymore 'cause there's a fox on the farm that steals it for his den. But this morning, I watched the television here at Jake's, and my renter really resembles this sketch." Harlan tapped the drawing with his finger again. "The eyes are spot-on, but the nose ain't right."

Earl leaned in closer. "Okay, Harlan, was he there when you left?"

"Yup, talking to himself per usual and tinkering with his new car, but there's a half acre between my house and the barn. I haven't gone over to actually talk with him since the weekend before last. I'm kinda concerned 'cause I left my hounds out in the yard. Guess I shouldn't worry, 'cause he's never hurt them before."

"What make of new car?"

"He used to have a dark-blue sedan, but now he's got a white one. It looks similar to the vehicle you drove into the parking lot today, but his looks brand-new." Harlan handed Earl a key to the garage apartment.

"All right, Harlan. Stay put, and have lunch on me. I'll call you here at Jake's once I've checked out your place. Don't be talking to people about this. Keep it quiet so I can do my job, all right?" He slapped some money on the table for lunch, picked up his notes, and left.

Via phone, Earl assembled a team for the raid before he left the parking lot. He'd much prefer to have Ethan with them when the search went down at Harlan's place, but the detective had taken a few comp days. *Shit.*

That was Ethan's code for being on standby for Sanctuary missions.

37

Two Suburbans loaded with officers met Earl at the end of Harlan's long, winding driveway. They strategized for a couple of minutes and finalized their plan. There'd been no mention on the police scanner just in case the suspect was listening to their frequency, and they drove in without lights and sirens.

Earl led the way up the lane while Harlan's hounds barked and chased them to the barn. Damn dogs could've woken a bear in hibernation with their racket.

The officers fanned out, surrounding the garage. The brand-new white car Harlan had referenced was not on-site. Earl nodded to the two detectives perched on the bottom of the stairs. They ran the stairs and slithered against the building at the top. One of them peered in. The open floorplan efficiency showed no signs of activity.

Earl slid the key in the lock and turned. The door banged open with a helpful nudge from one of the officers. They cleared each closet, the bathroom, and under the bed.

"Okay, fellas. We missed him, but we've still got a search

warrant. I want this place dusted for prints and picked over for any kind of evidence you can find about the person living here."

Earl scanned the apartment for the bag of dirty clothes Harlan had mentioned. To his annoyance, it wasn't there now. But he did locate a single military-issue dark-blue sock under the bed, and in a little crawl space storage area, he found a pair of size-nine ladies' Nikes. Earl bagged them for evidence. He'd bet his next paycheck they belonged to Margie Plante, but he'd been wrong before.

They searched the garage below for the lights Harlan had spoken about. No lights but they did find bits and pieces of cut automotive wires and cable ties in the driveway. They bagged it all.

Earl pulled out a fast-food bag with a dozen burgers in it. He gave a whistle for the hounds, who'd parked their hides on Harlan's front porch. The dogs bounded toward him with their tongues lolling.

"Aw, geez, Sergeant, you brought us lunch," joked one of the rookies.

"Dream on, Son . . . these are for the hounds." Earl unwrapped the warm burgers. "I can't let Harlan come back until we know who he's got living here. These burgers are a lure to get the dogs in the vehicle. We'll board them at Bayside Animal Hospital and put Harlan up at a hotel in town for a day or two."

Earl let the friendliest hound sniff his hand and then he tossed one burger into the back seat. It landed on Nelson's lap. The dog leaped in and snatched it. One by one, Earl got them all in the back of the Suburban with his rookie, who was getting tail slapped, licked, and crotch inspected by the dogs. Earl slammed the door shut and assumed his position in the driver's seat.

"Hey, Sergeant, why do I have to sit back here with these

dogs? We could've just called a K9 unit, and they would've picked them up for us," Nelson shouted.

"Because the closest K9 unit is an hour away and you and I are going to have a private chat, that's why. I have it on good authority that you closed down the Tidal Lounge last night *after* last call, rookie. You were soggy as a bartender's towel after mop-up. Then you got a cab home sometime around four in the morning. Am I right?"

"Yeah." Nelson elbowed the dog that was licking his face.

"You started work today at oh seven hundred. There is no way your system was clear of that liquor before your shift started. You put our team at risk because your head was still foggy when you arrived at work. You need to log it in your brain that when you man the early shift, you should be in bed by ten o'clock and have already poked your woman. Do I make myself clear, rookie?"

"My personal time is my own, thank you very much," Nelson retorted, protecting his face from the wagging tails.

Earl threw the vehicle in park and turned around. "Oh yeah? Well, I just claimed a little more of your personal time on Saturday to help you develop your work ethic during our work-out. You got a couple hundred burpees coming at you."

Nelson gave an exasperated sigh. "All right, Sergeant. You're right. I'm sorry."

Earl nailed him with a stare in the rearview mirror. He tossed the bag of burgers over his shoulder. "Good. I'm glad we're in agreement now. Please finish feeding the dogs."

Earl waited patiently for a flock of chickens to cross the driveway before he drove off. For all he knew, this raid might lead to another dead end. But eventually they would find the slippery bastard impersonating a cop, and Margie Plante's murderer. If that happened to be the same person . . . even better.

The hard part was getting it done before anyone else got hurt.

38

The salt water sprayed Ethan's face, sending chills through his body as his Sanctuary team cruised the mouth of the Chesapeake in total darkness. It was hard to believe that only a couple of hours ago, he'd woken with Tia's hair covering his chest and his burner phone buzzing incessantly that their newest mission was a go.

Mac relied on his instruments to locate and identify the yacht that held the captive teenage girl. Their source informed them that there would be three kidnappers and one child. At least the numbers were in their favor. As best they could tell, their intelligence from the Fed analyst was correct. Sanctuary preferred transfers that took place in port, closer to land, but the traffickers had moved farther out to sea and were harder to pinpoint but still in US waters.

The waves were choppy, and Ethan fought to maintain his footing on the deck. They'd need to swim the last fifty yards, board the yacht, and complete the rescue from there. Mac initiated the countdown, and everyone set their watches. On Mac's signal, they quietly slithered into the water and started swimming.

Five minutes later they were on board with weapons drawn and night vision in place, counting rooms as they moved stealthily from one deck to another. Sanctuary always provided the layout of a vessel before they boarded. That was part of what Mac brought to the team—his knowledge of ships and, of course, his uncanny ability as a sniper.

The armed lookout on the main deck dropped, compliments of Mac's rifle.

Gus's silenced weapon took down the brute in the galley. That left one more degenerate before they found the kid. Buzz cleared one stateroom as Ethan cleared the next. The third stateroom appeared empty, but when Ethan opened the closet, two young girls clung to each other with tears running down their faces. Relief washed over him to see the girls in good condition and not drugged.

There was only supposed to be one girl, but a second was a pleasant surprise. Maybe that was why the money transfer from the buyer had an extra ten thousand in it? He strapped life jackets on the girls while listening in his earpiece for information on the whereabouts of the third kidnapper.

Gus was quick to identify the new threat. "I smell accelerant, and the third perp is in the engine room. He might blow the boat. Evacuate now."

Ethan threw one girl over his shoulder and grabbed the second by her hand, then ran for the main deck. By the time he got them into the fresh air, Buzz had inflated the raft, and he seamlessly tossed the girls one at a time into it. He followed with a quick dive roll, started the small engine, and began to pull away.

Gus nodded for Ethan to join the raft, but that was when all hell broke loose. The third kidnapper sprayed bullets from the deck below. With one arm burning and useless, Ethan hoisted his weapon into his other hand while Gus took a barrage of gunfire and fell back against the rail of the main deck. Ethan raised his gun as the bastard landed on the top stair of the yacht with two automatic guns blazing. Ethan never got to fire. Mac ended the confrontation from his sniper perch in an ugly way.

Gus was in a heap on the deck. Ethan had no idea where he found the strength, but he hoisted Gus over the rail and dropped him like a rock into the waiting second raft. Winded and dizzy, Ethan rolled himself over the edge, landing with a thud just before the craft sped away. He was covered in blood, and he had no idea if it was his or Gus's.

The yacht exploded not a minute later, filling the predawn ocean sky with a massive fireworks display.

39

She'd just launched into a review of concrete nouns when Principal Decker showed up outside her classroom door wanting to speak with her. After directing her students to their worksheet, Tia stepped into the hallway.

"There's someone in the office needing to speak with you, T. Grab your things, and come with me."

"What? Who is it? My class . . . "

Yolanda nodded reassuringly. "It's okay, honey. Get your stuff. I've asked one of the student teachers to cover your class."

Who could possibly need to speak with her during the school day? She'd already gotten a late start this morning because the security company had come to fix the new alarm system at eight a.m. Tia dashed back into the classroom, swung her purse over one shoulder, and hoisted her work tote onto the other. She fell into stride beside Yolanda.

"Who is it?" Tia whispered.

"I left his business card on my desk, but he's got a government ID. He's a very nice man."

Tia's mind raced. She didn't know anyone in the government.

What the heck was going on? Her heart pounded. Had something happened to Carson or her mother?

Yolanda pulled the office door open, motioning for Tia to go ahead. The man waiting by the office window wheeled around.

Her heart leaped into her throat when she saw who it was. "Mac?"

"Hey, Tia, can we talk?" He nodded to the principal and took Tia's hand, guiding her to a more private corner, then raking a hand through his hair. "We had a mission go south on us this morning," he murmured. "Ethan's in pretty bad shape, and he's been asking for you every time he comes around. They've already removed four bullets from his chest. Can you come with me?"

And that was all she heard. Her ears rang, and the tote slipped from her shoulder to the floor. His mouth continued to move, but under oath she had absolutely no idea what he said. She turned to her principal and friend. "Yolanda, I have to go."

Mac grabbed her tote and ushered her out the door to a black sedan that drove them to a waiting helicopter. It was all too surreal.

They landed at the helipad on top of Mac's building in Baltimore. *Mac had a building?* Tia forced herself to speak, finally asking the question that had been crushing her brain. "How bad is he?"

Mac shook his head. "He took nine bullets, is in intensive care, and will undergo at least one more surgery today. We're talking Shock Trauma here. This place is the best at dealing with the bad and the ugly. My only consolation right now is that the animal who shot him is taking a dirt nap."

Tia laid her hand on Mac's and squeezed. "Thank you."

~

SHE RECOGNIZED the hallways of Shock Trauma, having spent weeks here herself after the car accident. But nothing prepared her to see him so still and ashen. Tia bit back the tears. The last thing Ethan needed was to wake up and find her falling apart at his bedside.

The first hour crawled by infinitely slow. Mac brought her a cup of coffee and a sandwich. She took one little bite, and as if on cue, Ethan opened one eye.

"Are you eating my lunch?"

Tia pushed the little tray to the side and leaned in close. "Hey, you, welcome back." She kissed his cheek.

He licked his lips. "I'm not staying long. Got another surgery. Get Mac."

She hustled to the waiting room. "Mac, he wants you." They hurried together back to the cubicle.

One corner of Ethan's mouth lifted into a pained grimace. "Mac, you're a witness here."

"You got it, man. What am I witnessing?"

"Tia, I made you the beneficiary of everything that's mine about a week ago. Just in case, Mac knows where everything is. He's my medical power of attorney. I would never burden you with that."

Her eyes widened in shock. "You're not going anywhere but home when you're better."

"You gotta take care of Nan if something happens to me. Promise."

"I promise," they said in unison just as a nurse came in and added something to his fluid drip.

"Tia, come close."

"I'm right here," she whispered, and kissed his nose.

"Tell Flynn I want my side of the bed back when I get home."

She chuckled through her tears. "Okay."

He licked his lips again. "And pick a day I can visit your classroom, okay?"

Tia nodded. "I will."

"And get some freaking food in the house besides tofu and horseradish."

She nodded as Mac snorted a laugh.

Ethan continued, "I'm all in, T. We're not done talking about it."

The orderly locked the screeching side rails in place, released the brake, and started pushing the gurney out of the room.

"Get Tia out of here, Mac. I don't want to see her until I'm up and moving."

And just that fast, Ethan was gone. When Mac put his arm around her, she folded into him and cried her eyes out.

40

Tia alternated between pacing the living room and sipping at the caramel macchiato she'd purchased on the way home from the airport. Flynn had given up on following her and lain down on his bed by the new back door, intently watching her.

The inside of her house resembled a humid inferno. The past two days had been swampish and in the high eighties, an unusual temperature for early May. Opening a few windows, she made sure the crosswind would cool the place down with the ocean breeze.

Had Ethan woken from the second surgery yet? She massaged her forehead with a couple of fingers. Mac had promised he'd call her when he had news. Glancing at the mantel clock, she plugged her phone into the charger. It might be a long night.

She was fried. Both physically and emotionally tired beyond her usual limits. But every time she considered the *what-ifs* of Ethan's injuries, the monitors, the fluid drips, and the lax expression on his bruised face while sedated, her body kick-started into overdrive again. And the exhaustion was fueling the vicious cycle.

What she really needed was to settle down and grab a few hours' sleep. She considered the huge iced coffee on the countertop. Surely it wasn't helping. If she had any sense, she'd pour it down the sink. But plain water or chamomile tea didn't appeal right now. Maybe accomplishing something would help her frazzled mind calm down enough to rest.

Her decision made, she whistled for Flynn and grabbed her phone and charger. The last thing she wanted was to miss Mac's call due to a dead battery. Flynn trotted up the stairs ahead of her and waited at the top. Halfway up—*the gun*—she jogged back down and retrieved the weapon from the hutch. *I promised Ethan.* It was a wonder she could remember where she'd stashed it from day to day at this point. Security was a practice she meant to keep, just so she could look him in the eye and say that seriously, she was watching her back.

Three stairs up, Tia sighed. *The alarm system.* She backtracked and reset it, allowing for open windows and the cross breeze upstairs. Taking the stairs two at a time, she joined Flynn at the top, plugged in her phone, and placed the Glock on her dresser.

A blessed coolness blew across her face as she opened the bathroom window. The gusty ocean wind she often cursed in the winter was a welcome friend today. After lifting a sash in each of the bedrooms, Tia got to work switching out her closet from winter to summer. As usual, it was exciting to see the vibrant summer clothes again and hide the subdued winter colors in the cedar closet she'd customized by herself.

May as well purge as I go. She made a discard-and-donate pile on a chair and held up a seafoam-color gauze midi dress with a plunging neckline. *Love, love.* What she wouldn't give to wear it again. Well, that meant she'd have to make a decision soon between skin grafting or a tattoo to cover her elongated scar.

Ethan's velvet bass voice whispered in her memory, *That scar brought you back to me.* Inhaling a quick breath, she stepped back from the closet. He wasn't a flowers-and-candy kind of guy. She liked to pick out her own flowers anyway. He was a new red coffeepot, Thai food, and salsa dancing sexy-as-hell man who made her heart race and was perfect for her.

After spending almost an hour hustling clothes from one closet to another, she changed the sheets on the bed she and Ethan had tumbled into several times. She opened the closet door and tossed the soiled linens down the laundry chute. On reflection, she dropped the pink-rosebud winter comforter down the big funnel, too. A thump echoed as the dirty laundry landed on top of the washer.

Every time she used the chute, Flynn would still combat crawl to the huge opening, peer over the edge, whine, and back away. Tonight was no different. His apprehension was healthy as far as she was concerned. After the ordeal of extricating him from the old doggie door, she couldn't imagine trying to get him out of the laundry chute. That thought was so not funny.

A minute later, a noisy blast of wind slammed the bathroom door shut. Huffing, she propped it open again with a painted brick one of her students had gifted her.

Tia yelped when her phone rang, because the volume was high enough to wake the comatose. Jumping over Flynn, she grabbed the phone.

"Mac?"

"Yeah, hi. He's out of surgery. They said it went well, but he's in for a hell of a recovery with the repaired tendons and ligaments in his arm. The good news is . . . they fixed everything."

"Is he awake?"

"Not now. He's out for the night."

"What's his prognosis?"

"They're cautiously optimistic about a full recovery, but it will take time. The orthopedic doctor said she doesn't expect him to be back at work until at least the fall."

Tia's heart sank. "Oh, wow. That was really hard on him last time."

Mac's voice perked up. "He told you about that, huh?"

"Yes, it was difficult for him."

"Well, his marriage to that narcissist was rocky back then. He'll be okay this time, and they don't prescribe painkillers as freely nowadays. He's got a lot to live for, you know?"

"He'd better. I'm counting on him."

Mac chuckled. "I'll tell him you said that."

"Did you call his grandmother?"

"Yes. Right before I called you. She knows everything."

"Okay. I'll stop by and check on her tomorrow. When can I see him again?"

"If Ethan said when he was up and moving around, then he meant it. I'll send the chopper back for you, because he'll stay in Baltimore until he's able to fend for himself with most things."

Tia pulled the scrunchie from her ponytail and set her hair free, the way Ethan liked it. "Okay, I'll text you for updates?"

"That's fine. I'm planning on catching a few winks, so wait until the morning if you can."

"Thanks, Mac. I appreciate you keeping me in the loop."

"No problem, you're family, T." He disconnected the call.

Tia sank down onto the freshly made bed, smiling with relief. *He's gonna be okay.* She'd help him if he let her. The previous exhaustion rolled over her tired mind and body once again. It would feel so good to crash right here. Closing her eyes, she stretched out her fingers and pulled a clean pillow under her head. *He's all right. I can rest now.*

But the house alarm wailed as a rush of refreshing cool air skimmed over her shoulder. *Damn security system.* It was the same problem she'd had after they'd installed it. The system was so sensitive, especially during windy weather. Groaning, she forced herself to move and padded down the hallway.

Once she caught a few hours' sleep, she'd explore the security app on her phone and get comfortable with it. After installation two days ago, she hadn't had any time to familiarize herself with the usage options. As of right now, she wasn't sure she could even reset the thing remotely. And Ethan's yard cameras were gone in favor of the bells-and-whistles system they'd just put in.

Halfway down the stairs, her bedroom door slammed shut. *Oh, to hell with it.* After resetting the security system, she'd close the windows and turn on the air-conditioning. The fresh breeze wasn't worth the trouble it was causing. Sure, it was windy outside, but most seaside towns experienced stiff winds. Why couldn't they make a security system that knew the difference between wind and a break-in? *Ridiculous.* And yeah, she was grumpy.

Overtired.

Freaking exhausted.

She'd damn near lost the man she loved and hadn't slept.

Her fingers skimmed across the keypad, resetting the system.

When a rope cinched tightly around her neck.

Tia's hands flew to her airway. He walked backward, choking her and dragging her with him. As she struggled to get her feet situated for a strike, she pulled at the rope, hoping for a quick breath.

He laughed. "Thanks for resetting the alarm. Now we won't be disturbed by the cops or a nosy neighbor."

Where was Flynn? Her heart plummeted when she remembered. He was trapped upstairs in her bedroom, along with the gun and her phone. Terror sprinted through her veins. She held onto a bookcase, hoping to slow the guy down, and pulled it over on the way to the kitchen. Books cascaded across the floor, and the crack of splintering wood reverberated as the unit crashed to the tile.

"You like it noisy, huh? I can do noise. But I really like mess. You saw what I did to old Margie, didn't you? I messed her up real good."

Tia forced one finger under the rope and dragged in a shaky half breath. The man stopped in the kitchen, and she collapsed against the countertop, eyeing the knife block. Lightheaded as she was, she still recognized that if she pulled a knife, he'd likely use it on her. But if he faced her straight on, she could take him down.

Pulling in as much air as possible, Tia wheeled around to face him. *Omigosh.* Covered in infected, oozing black stitches, his face resembled a patchwork quilt. He must've performed a self-stitch job after Flynn had bitten him in the video she'd seen. *Ugh, gross.* His stench permeated the air around them.

He swung a fist at her, and turning aside, Tia brought the flat of her hand up and nailed him from his chin to his forehead, ripping out stitches as she moved. He cried out in pain and yanked the rope around her neck tighter than before. "You bitch. You'll pay for that."

The growling upstairs morphed into the same other-worldly werewolf seething she'd heard during the traffic stop. But there was nothing Flynn could do for her now. Her survival was up to her. All of her preparation had been to fight a person, not a rope. She clawed at her neck, desperate for another fingerhold.

The man laughed and twisted the cord tighter. "You're a little panicked, huh?" He took a quick look around. "Where's your fucking dog? He's somewhere close by, because I can hear him."

Empowered now, he called out, "Oh, Flynn, where are you? I'm here to do your lady friend. Wanna watch?"

Tia's thoughts faded as black spots invaded her vision and her knees buckled. The air all used up, she crumpled to the floor.

~

ON A SHARP INHALE, her eyes fluttered open. She remembered passing out as a wave of panic slammed her heart into overdrive.

The alarm system blared in the background, and the end of the rope lay next to her. With stiff fingers, she pulled it close and frantically worked it loose, dragging in massive drafts of air as she slid the noose over her head.

Adrenaline pumped like gasoline through her body, and nausea threatened to kick in. Turning on her side, she caught the intruder facing the keypad and cursing. "You fucker, all I did was open the door so I could get something from the car." He slammed his fist into the picture frame next to the pad while the silver glint of a gun sticking out of his pocket danced in the flashing emergency lights.

Tia crawled behind the cabinets and hauled herself to a shaky standing position. If she could disarm him, it would be an equal fight. Whatever Flynn was doing upstairs resounded through the walls. Poor dog must be beside himself locked in that room. Tia squinted at the distance. She'd never make it past the guy to run the stairs two at a time to unleash Flynn.

This was her battle to win or lose on her own.

She took a few seconds to strategize. Judging by the sounds coming from upstairs, Flynn had to be body-slamming her bedroom door in his effort to get free. On her third deep breath, Tia rushed the guy, grabbed his gun, and kicked his knees out from under him. The tall man hit the floor with a groan. Considering the size and weight of the gun, it had to be a standard police-issue firearm. Could this have been stolen from Margie Plante's home?

She spun around and ran toward the kitchen. Seconds later, his big hand latched around her ankle and yanked her down. Rolling over, Tia kicked his face.

His nose spurted blood. He let go of her ankle and staggered to his feet as she leaped up and ran.

Roaring like a wounded beast, he seized her hair with one hand and held her wrist with the gun in his other hand. Tia squeezed the trigger, firing a shot into his foot.

Enraged, he forced the gun toward her head. "You're gonna get messed up, girl."

Tia sent two more upward shots into the living-room ceiling in an effort to empty the gun of bullets. She headbutted him, but his strength and body weight pulled her toward him. Sucking in a huge breath, Tia launched into a crotch shot meant to disable, but he let go of her hair and jumped out of the way.

He laughed and sneered. "You think you're the only one who knows self-defense?" He grappled for her hand holding the gun and shoved it at her face.

She ducked and pulled the trigger, blasting a bullet into a kitchen cabinet. The tinkle of shattering glassware echoed from inside. It didn't matter. As long as she controlled the gun, she had an honest chance at survival. Four bullets spent. Two more to go.

But the man gripped her wrist and shoved it toward her head again, clawing at her fingers to release the firearm. Her back was to his front as they fought for control. Tia squeezed the trigger and sent a bullet through the kitchen window. Only one more.

He tore at her hair again. She jumped as high as she could, nailing him in the chin and knocking him off-balance. She ran like hell. Her reprieve was temporary. The perp lifted a butcher knife from the block, smiled, and strode toward her.

Flynn didn't sound as far away anymore. Had he escaped? She trained the gun at the guy's heart and screamed, "*Fass, Flynn, fass.*" There had to be one more bullet in the gun. She couldn't remember. Tia took a step backward.

There was an eerie screech of groaning metal close by as the man raised the knife and barreled toward her. But in a flurry of white percale, Flynn flew out of the laundry chute like a snarling avenging angel wearing a pink-rosebud sheet. With momentum behind him, he sprang from the washer, caught the perp by the throat with his jaw, and in one smooth strike knocked the intruder to the kitchen floor.

Stunned, Tia gawked at the heap of dog and man. A puddle of scarlet spread under them.

No, no, no. Still holding the gun, she rushed over and felt for a pulse on the man—nothing. Flynn was growling underneath the guy's body. She grabbed hold of the man's shirt and rolled him over. He'd fallen on the knife intended for her.

Flynn had his jaw firmly affixed to the man's neck, as if he were waiting for the command to let go. He gave Tia an eye, and his tail started to wag.

Bursting into euphoric tears, Tia got down on her knees. "*Aus*, let go, *Aus*." He growled once but obeyed, releasing the man. She held out her hands, coaxing her canine protector away from the invader with gentle praises. Flynn shimmied closer and whined.

"I know, buddy, I know. You're so brave. You overcame your biggest fear and went down the laundry chute. I love you, Flynn. I'm so grateful."

With Flynn's left side covered in blood, he scrambled upright, licked her face, and barked.

An older neighbor whose name she didn't even know rushed

through the front door with a baseball bat in his hand. "I heard gunshots and called 911," he panted. After taking one look at the carnage, he stepped back. "Are you all right, Miss?"

Tia nodded and ruffled Flynn's fur. "Thanks to this guy. Do you have a phone I could borrow?"

He reached in his pocket and held up a phone. "That's a big dog you've got there," he commented with a hint of trepidation. He bent down and slid the phone across the floor to her. "It's unlocked."

"Thank you." With a trembling, grateful smile, she tapped in a number.

"Carson."

"Uncle, there's been a break-in at my house. I need you. And bring Mom." She disconnected the call and slid the phone back to the neighbor.

Tia wrapped her arms around Flynn, holding on to him for dear life, as the cacophony of sirens in the distance grew closer.

41

3 *days later*
Ethan drummed his fingers against his breakfast tray, considering if he should eat it or not. The congealed oatmeal and fruit in a plastic cup did nothing to appeal. Maybe Mac would have mercy and raid the cafeteria for him when it opened?

He took three deep breaths and decided to count his blessings. He was alive. They'd finally removed the catheter and adjusted his bed so he could sit up this morning. Yesterday, he'd had to lay flat and count the teeny holes in the dropped-ceiling tiles. It was maddening.

He'd already skimmed the scant television channels searching for news about Margie Plante's murder and Tia's attacker. But he was in the Baltimore metro area now, and coverage about the Eastern Shore happenings wasn't as thorough. All he really knew was that Tia was supposedly okay and her attacker was dead.

Mac had been kind enough to get his girl on the phone yesterday, so Ethan had heard her voice. She'd sent a smiling picture of her and Flynn, but Tia wore a floral scarf in the picture, and her face looked drawn and tired. He wasn't stupid. His woman had taken a beatdown and was hiding it behind the neckerchief.

The docs wouldn't allow him to have his cell phone. They said it had something to do with the sensitive machines in his room. *Nah.* He knew better. He'd seen the distress on the nurse's face when he'd found out about Tia. The machines had started beeping, and a couple of alarms had gone off. It had taken them almost an hour to get him resettled.

He stabbed a spoon into the oatmeal. *Ugh.* It was cold now.

Earl Thompson leaned against the doorjamb. "Are you going to eat that shit? Because I brought you something way better here." He held up a bag. "It's fresh from the deli, and the nurse said you could eat it as long as you don't try to get out of bed by yourself again."

Ethan leaned back against the pillow and felt his eyes mist up. "I'm so freaking glad to see you, Earl. How'd you get here?"

The older man glanced into the hallway. "Your friend, Mac, had a chopper pick me up at the ass crack of dawn. It was beautiful watching the sun rise over the Chesapeake Bay." He moved the unappetizing breakfast tray to the windowsill and unwrapped the sandwich.

After setting the food in front of Ethan, he pulled a chair close to the bed and sat down. "You look pretty good for someone who stared the grim reaper in the face and told him to fuck off."

Ethan barked a laugh and bit into the sandwich.

"Take your time eating, Son, and I'll give you an update on the case."

Earl crossed an ankle over his knee and leaned back in the chair. "You really helped me change my mind about Sergeant Guy Evans when you told me about his and Margie's piano playing. Breakup or not, they were having a good time that day."

"Our perp was a guy named Vincent Michael Manheim, which explains the initials we found on the lock pick set under Margie's stove." He shook his head. "Vincent had a score to settle with Margie because she didn't clear him for the cadet program. The kid couldn't seem to pass the mental screening, and he tried a half dozen times or so. It wasn't Margie's fault. Vincent just never qualified. Sadly, the kid had a long history of mental illness. But the shocker in all this is that Vincent was Sergeant Guy Evans's nephew, and he worshipped Guy. When Vincent found out from his sister that Guy and Margie had broken up, that's when he killed Margie. I guess there was nothing holding him back at that point."

Earl sighed and changed positions, crossing his arms. "I'm figuring Vincent went after Tia because she had Flynn, which makes no sense to me, but we're uncovering more details every day. I'll stop by and give you updates as we learn more. I owe you about a dozen of those sandwiches, by the way."

Ethan sipped at his water cup. "I wonder what Flynn had to do with Vincent's reasoning."

"Don't know, but the crew found a notebook with his musings, and they'll be going over it with a fine-tooth comb. I'll keep you up-to-date. You know, we were only a step behind him at the end. Had an APB out and everything." Earl stood. "I don't want to see you back at work before Labor Day."

Ethan rolled his eyes. "C'mon now, I'll be able to do office things."

"We'll see, Son. They gave me a rookie to field train, name's Nelson. So I've got someone to bark at while you recover." He moved closer. "I'm just so damn thankful you're going to be all right. You're the closest thing I've got to a son." Earl bent and planted a peck on top of Ethan's head. "If you tell anyone I did that, I'll deny it and call you a pussy."

Ethan burst into laughter. "Thanks, Earl. The feeling's mutual."

Mac leaned his head into the room. "Your twenty minutes are up, Sergeant. You ready to go?"

Earl faced Mac. "Yup. Is the chopper ready?"

"Yes, and the car's waiting for you downstairs."

"Hey, Mac," Ethan called out. "How's Gus today?"

"He's much better. His prognosis improved dramatically overnight. And I think I already told you that Buzz was treated and released at the scene."

"Yeah, you did. Thanks." Ethan thought a minute. Maybe an orderly would wheel him down to Gus's room tomorrow so he could cuss at him in Russian.

42

---

3 *weeks later*
 Tia fidgeted with her watch as she waited in the school office for Ethan's official visit to her classroom. In a few minutes, her students would leave math class for a fun period of *My Life as a Policeman* with Ethan. They'd chattered all morning and asked her questions at recess. A frenzied energy had surrounded her classroom for the past two days in anticipation of this event.

It had not escaped her that many of the classroom doors were decorated with pictures of beach weddings and honeymoon escapes, especially the all-inclusive resorts in Mexico and Belize. She doubted Ethan would even notice the antics of her fun-loving coworkers.

Her heart leaped as he entered the office to sign the visitors' log. His recovery was remarkable, and even though they'd struggled this morning to get him into his police uniform, minus the thirty-pound duty belt, he wouldn't have it any other way for the kids' sakes. Tia bit her lip, keeping her distance when she really wanted to throw her arms around his neck and kiss him. But first things first.

"Afternoon, Miss O'Rourke, you're looking well today."

Ethan winked and set his walking cane behind a chair. He nodded at Doris and Principal Decker. "Nice to see you ladies."

Principal Decker piped up. "Thank you, Detective Kelley. Not using the cane today?"

"I'm sure I'll be fine without it. See you in a bit."

Tia held the door for him, a reversal of roles she was getting used to. He lagged behind her as they walked the long corridor to her classroom. "Detective, your legs are a foot longer than mine, and yet you are walking behind me?"

"The view is mesmerizing from my vantage point," he quipped. "Have you ever given the kids your report on the ride along?"

"No, of course not! What would I say?" she whispered as she swiveled a graceful hundred and eighty degrees on her heels. "The ride along was fun? First, I saw a murder victim, got blood on my hands and shoes, hurled on one of our finest, and peed myself? Oh, wait . . . that was before I took a ride in an ambulance, was fingerprinted, DNA swabbed, examined by a doctor in the emergency room, and driven home in a squad car? Thank goodness they haven't asked about it."

She introduced Detective Kelley to the boys and girls, and the class erupted into a round of applause and cheers. He stuck to the script she'd asked of him, covering stranger danger and how to safely use the pedestrian walks crossing the highway in the resort during the summer.

Next, Ethan told them about the computer in the police cars and how he could access information on a person's driving record during a traffic stop. He followed with pictures of the Little League team he'd helped coach last summer with one of his friends and explained how it was nice to give back and help the community.

The man was perfect—for her, for the kids. He distributed coloring books and crayons, explaining how to use 911 properly, and showed them his cell phone with its emergency call button. They hung on his every word.

As he passed around multiple-choice worksheets for them to fill out that reinforced the information he'd just taught, Ethan promised a surprise after they'd completed the review sheet.

While a surprise was news to her, she had given him some freedom with his presentation.

Ethan gave the children five minutes, set the stopwatch on his phone, and walked the aisles peeking at each child's work and handing out sheets of stickers.

One of the kids asked, "Detective Kelley, what's our surprise?"

Ethan leaned against Tia's desk and stretched his legs. "Miss O'Rourke tells me that she hasn't given you a report on her ride along. I thought you'd like to hear it today." The children cheered and clapped enthusiastically.

Tia gasped and almost fell on the floor scrambling to extricate herself from the tiny desk in the back of the room. What was he doing? Her mind raced on how to proceed with this devious and sudden addition to the schedule. And then he began . . .

"Miss O'Rourke rode in the police car with me that day, and she saw the computer we use and learned all about the lights and sirens. Our first call was for a minor traffic accident, and everyone was okay. Then, we were called to help an injured dog, but he's all better now. As a matter of fact, that dog is a retired police dog who now lives with Miss O'Rourke. Maybe she'll bring him to school for show-and-tell one of these days."

The children leaned forward in their desks.

"She also met one of our crime-scene investigators, and he showed her how to do fingerprinting and take a DNA sample. It was fascinating. Do you know that no one has the exact same fingerprints as another person?

"Miss O'Rourke spent the better part of an hour with a couple of our emergency medical technicians, and they showed her the inside of an ambulance, where they have beds, medicine, and oxygen in case a person gets sick and needs their help.

"That's when you got to hear the sirens again, isn't it Miss O'Rourke?" He kept a perfectly straight face and peered at Tia as she nodded and some of the kids turned around to look at her.

"I believe Miss O'Rourke also met one of the policewomen in town, who is also a nurse. Her name is Officer Odessa Wright."

One of the children called out, "Then what happened?"

"Well Miss O'Rourke had to go . . . " He took a few steps toward the front of the room and picked up a stack of kid-friendly DNA kits they could take home.

Tia froze in the back with both hands clasped over her mouth, fearing the worst.

Ethan gave her an ornery smile. "It was the end of the day, and Miss O'Rourke needed to go home. But she had a very educational adventure."

Tia damn near swooned with relief against the bulletin board when he didn't tell the whole story.

43

———

Tia slid into the waiting black sedan in the school parking lot. She set her work tote on the floor and laid her head against Ethan's arm. "I could get used to being chauffeured around all the time."

He chuckled. "Well, Mac insisted I have transportation until I'm fully recovered, so we are blessed to have Gerard for the duration of the summer." He slipped his fingers through hers. "Did you know that Gerard is Mac's personal assistant when he travels? He'd been hoping for some time at a beach instead of jetting around the world. Right, Gerard?"

"*Oui*, Detective. I'm so happy to be in one place for a while, and the beach here is *magnifique*."

Tia smiled. Gerard's French was lovely.

Ethan leaned closer to her and kissed the barely visible bruise on her neck. He still seethed inside every time he saw it. "Do you have time for a little field trip tonight? It's close by."

She gazed into the emerald-green eyes she'd grown to love. "Sure. Will it include a bite to eat? I forgot my lunch today."

He nodded. "Of course. Hey, Gerard, would you please drop us off at Fifteenth Street and the boardwalk?"

"*Oui*, Detective." He turned left on Route 50 East.

Tia squeezed his hand. "Fifteenth Street, huh? I seem to remember being at that location with you a long time ago."

Gerard pulled up alongside an old landmark hotel and opened Ethan's door. "Here you go, good people. Don't forget this, Detective." He tucked a blanket under Ethan's good arm. "You text me when you're ready to go home, okay?"

Ethan pulled Tia close to his good side, headed up the boardwalk ramp, and immediately turned into an Italian restaurant. It had one table already set up outside with wine and flowers and colorful balloons. He kissed the top of her head. "Will this do?"

Aw. And she'd thought he didn't have hearts and flowers in his repertoire. "It's lovely, thank you."

He sat down and poured the wine. "I already ordered for us. The salad will be here shortly, and I asked for lemon-chicken entrées. I didn't want us to be disturbed."

"Okay, that sounds wonderful." What in the world did he have up his sleeve? Her insides danced with anticipation as she sipped the wine. He'd already popped the question three different times. But she wasn't ready—yet. And she wasn't very materialistic, so a diamond wouldn't sweeten the deal.

He drew little circles on her palm. "Have you decided between a tattoo or surgery yet?"

Tia rolled her shoulders and breathed deeply. "I'm pretty sure I'm going for the tattoo."

His eyes lit up. "Really? Maybe we could get them together, then. I'm getting a new one."

"Oh? Where?"

He slapped a hand across his heart. "Right here, it'll cover the new scar from the bullets. I've already picked out a teacup design. It'll be colorful and have little flowers on the saucer and cup. It'll look just like one of Nan's good china cups."

She scrunched up her face. "Why a teacup? You're a huge guy with a broad chest. Why would you ever tattoo a teacup there?"

His gaze held hers. "Because you're my T and in my heart to stay."

What? Her lower lip trembled, and tears slipped down her cheek. "You can't do that."

He lifted his eyebrows. "I almost died three weeks ago. I can do any freaking thing I want. You could've died three weeks ago, but you refused to give up. Life is tenuous, Tia. I'm getting a teacup so you're always right here."

The salad and chicken arrived, and all she could do was stare at it. She could've said no to a diamond, but not to his teacup.

He held a forkful of salad to her lips. "You'll love the dressing. It's fresh. How's your living arrangement working out for you?"

Wait—she was still thinking about the teacup. She took the bite of salad and chewed. It was phenomenal. "I've really enjoyed living with my mother and Carson these past few weeks, especially the catch-up with my mom, but I'm about done, and they need their privacy, too. I've decided to sell the house. I can't live there anymore. It pains me to let go of all the sweat equity I've poured into the place, but that guy died on my kitchen floor. He tried to kill me in the living room. And Flynn can't relax at all when I go over to retrieve things. I need a fresh start somewhere new."

He nodded reassuringly. "Have you decided on a place to live?"

She set her hand on his forearm and stroked the hair. His bruises and puncture wounds were almost gone. "I don't know yet. I'll keep looking. I've spent a lot of time at your place since you got home, but I don't want to live together unless we decide to get married. Maybe that sounds really strange considering how often I stay with you."

Ethan tore a hunk of Italian bread from the loaf and offered it to her. "Have you ever been in the guesthouse behind Nan's place?"

She lifted the bread from his hand and dipped it in the herbed olive oil. "That little yellow house in the back?"

He nodded. "Yeah, that's the one."

"I had no idea it belonged to you. When I watered your plants while you were gone, I figured it must be someone's summer rental because no one ever came or went."

"It's ours. Nan purchased it years ago so no one would obstruct her view of the water. It could use a facelift and is a two bedroom with an outdoor shower for the summer and a jetted soaking tub in the main bathroom."

She leaned into him, tilting her face toward his. "Really? Would you rent it to me?"

He ran his thumb gently across her bottom lip. "I'd like to give it to you, but I understand that you want your independence. What if you fix it up inside and do the gardening? You love that stuff, and I don't. I won't be much help this summer, but I can find people to lend a hand when you need or want it. You'd be doing me a favor. I can't get the main-house and guest-cottage gardening done for the nice weather."

Her insides tingled with excitement. She could already picture the window boxes with petunias tumbling out of them. "Okay, I'm in. I love that idea."

His eyes lit up. "Good. You know, Nan's house is one of the larger grandes dames from a bygone era. I intend to rehab the whole place and keep it." He cleared his throat. "If you ever decide to move into the big house, the smaller place can be your she shed."

She laughed. "Yeah, well, you've gotta love the view of the water and the dock."

He nodded. "I do. Someday I'm going to fish with my kids from that dock."

Tia set her fork down and sighed. "Oh, Ethan, I'm just not ready. Not after what happened last time, and I've spent so much energy gearing my life toward staying single that I need time to transition."

Ethan lifted her chin with a finger, peering into her eyes tenderly. "I know, T. I get it."

She leaned over and kissed him long and deep. "I love you, Detective."

He lifted her hand and kissed the palm. "I love you, too. Let's walk. They'll store our leftovers for us."

He unfurled the faded blanket with the American-flag pattern.

She stood back in admiration. "Oh my goodness, that *is* our blanket. You really did keep it."

"Of course I did." With the ocean breeze picking up, he wrapped the blanket around both their shoulders and tugged her close while they strolled the boardwalk.

"Could we make out under this blanket again?"

He groaned. "I thought you'd never ask."

"This is our beach," she noted, pointing.

"Yes, it is. Good memories. But according to the decorated doors at your school, this beach is nothing in comparison to the ones in Belize and Mexico."

Tia laughed out loud. "You caught that, huh?"

His chest rumbled with mirth. "Discreet, they're not."

She glanced up at him. "They mean well. But perhaps they had us pegged from the start, because I've always been partial to beach weddings. They're so romantic."

He kissed the top of her head. "If that's what you want, then I agree. I hear Belize is beautiful this time of year."

"Maybe we'll go there when you're healed up, Detective."

And as they'd longed for, they walked arm in arm, laughing and kissing as the wind whipped at the blanket that had brought them together so long ago.

ABOUT THE AUTHOR

Nonna Henry hid under the covers as a kid and devoured every mystery she could get her hands on. A lifetime reader of everything, she especially enjoys the Bible (what an adventure), romance stories and happy endings. Her first book, *The Rough Ride,* won The Holt Medallion and the Golden Leaf award for Best First Book.

She writes romantic suspense and contemporary romance. Her favorite place is on a beach with her hero and their family. A Jersey girl at heart, she currently lives in Maryland.

Find out more by visiting Nonna's website:

www.nonnahenry.com

Want to stay up-to-date with new releases, sneak peeks, discounts and more? Sign up for Nonna's Newsletter!

NEWSLETTER

Nonna also loves hearing from readers. Contact her through her Facebook page or email her at: authornonnahenry@gmail.com

ALSO BY NONNA HENRY

SANCTUARY, INC. SERIES

Hostile Witness

Under the Radar

The Rough Ride

* 9 7 8 1 7 3 7 0 3 4 6 4 3 *